THE CASTLE OF WIND AND WHISPERS

BRIARWOOD WITCHES, BOOK 4

STEFFANIE HOLMES

THE CASTLE OF WIND AND WHISPERS

My mom returns from the dead to give me the down-low on how she defeated the fae twenty-one years ago. But there's a catch.

Fuck my life, there's *always* a catch.

Briarwood is no longer safe. The castle walls have been breached. The fae give us their terms – we surrender, or we die.

I don't do ultimatums.

Not when I have five powerful men, an ancient witch, a prostitute with a heart of gold, a faithful sister, and the ghost of my dead mother on my side. Plus, my ancient castle still has a few tricks left.

If the fae want Briarwood Castle, they'll have to get through us first.

The Castle of Wind and Whispers is book 4 in this spicy fantasy romance series by USA Today bestselling author Steffanie Holmes. This full-length book glitters with love, heartache, hope, grief, dark magic, fairy trickery, steamy scenes, British slang, meat pies, second chances, and the healing powers of a good cup of tea.

JOIN THE NEWSLETTER FOR UPDATES

Can't get enough of Maeve and her boys? Find out what Flynn got up to when he came to her school in Arizona in *The Summer Court*. This Briarwood short story is free in *Cabinet of Curiosities*, a Steffanie Holmes compendium of short stories and bonus scenes, which you can get when you sign up for updates with the Steffanie Holmes newsletter.

www.steffanieholmes.com/newsletter

Every week in my newsletter I talk about the true-life hauntings, strange happenings, crumbling ruins, and creepy facts that inspire my stories. You'll also get newsletter-exclusive bonus scenes and updates. I love to talk to my readers, so come join us for some spooky fun :)

To Andy,
For teasing me about not being able to say 'penis'
and doing all the crazy things
I only write about.

Sisters in Metal, forever

ONE: MAEVE

"Hello, Maeve," the figure croaked, her voice dry and hoarse. She outstretched her arms, lurching forward as if she intended to embrace me. "We meet at last, my daughter."

My daughter.

The world froze. The apparition's words hung in the air, fuzzy and devoid of meaning.

It's saying I'm its daughter, but that's not possible, because my mother is dead.

And yet ... the ice-blue eyes that looked at me with such haunting vengeance were the same eyes that stared out of my mother's portrait. The delicate hands that had once been folded in her lap extended toward me. The bow-shaped lips that had once turned a mysterious smile out at me now trembled with anticipation. The only thing that was different from the portrait was the long, thin cuts across its face.

It's impossible, but...

The citrine stone at my throat dragged on its chain, heavy and warm against my skin. The diadem around my forehead pushed my head toward the ground. My legs gave way beneath me. I sank into the soft grass, touching my hands to the green blades as if they might give me some answer. "You... but... how?"

The apparition sank down beside me, her white skirts fanning out around her long legs like a ballet dancer. Behind her head the pillar of fire sank back, becoming a small blaze – like the campfires Andrew and I used to roast marshmallows over during our overnight astronomy trips. I could just make out the dark figures of my coven as silhouettes against the glowing flames.

The apparition reached out her hand to touch mine. The ring around my finger flared with heat as her hand approached. I jerked away. No way did I want the spectre touching me.

That would make it real. And no way was this real. *No way.*

"I've been trapped inside that canvas for twenty-one years," the figure grinned, that beautiful smile like a knife through my heart. "You freed me, Maeve. I always knew one day you would. I just *knew* you would be the most powerful witch the world has ever known."

"We were only trying to release the magic trapped inside the painting," I said woodenly. "I didn't know about you."

Another figure dropped down beside me.

Corbin's tattooed arm slid around my waist, and he pressed his lips against my cheek. "Maeve, I think this *is* the magic trapped inside. She might be a ghost or a wraith or just an imprint of her former life."

"Corbin?" Its eyes widened as it swept across his features. "Is that really you, all grown up? When I last saw you, you were a tiny toddler ordering everyone around. You have your mother's kind eyes." It turned back to me. "Does he look after you, my daughter? Does he protect you? His parents always protected me."

Corbin stiffened.

The figure swung around, its eyes leaping between the guys. "Arthur, that must be you with those huge muscles. You were such a big baby you nearly killed your mother during birth. I'd recognise that golden hair of hers anywhere. Flynn, you were always running after Corbin and getting into mischief. And Rowan, beautiful Rowan... you were only a babe when the fae came for us. You were the most peaceful baby, hardly ever crying or making a peep. Your parents loved you more than the moon and the stars."

Rowan made a strangled sound in his throat and staggered back. I felt a surge of anger toward the ghost...apparition...hallucination...whatever it was. It upset Rowan by talking about his parents, like it knew them, like they were friends.

It stretched long fingers out toward Blake, curling the ends as if beckoning him forward. Blake just stared with his smirk frozen on his face. "Blake Beckett... you were the sweetest boy. You used to bring flowers from the garden for your mother to make garlands for the rituals. You must have come into possession of your spirit magic by now – I hope it hasn't been a burden to you."

Blake said nothing, just kept staring and grinning.

Tears glistened in its eyes. "It wasn't supposed to turn out like this. We wanted to raise you all together – one big happy family. We wanted to teach you all about your powers and what miracles you are capable of. Instead, we abandoned you to fight our battle for us. I'm so glad you all found each other again... my heart just flutters with happiness." It clutched its hands over its chest like a melodramatic actress in the throes of passion. I might've laughed if its very presence hadn't robbed me of the ability to form sounds.

Corbin blinked. "Is she a ghost?"

"If she's a ghost, why isn't she falling through the earth?" Flynn asked.

His question stirred something in me, the innate need of mine to puzzle out strange phenomena, to subject even this terrifying vision to the scrutiny of science. I opened my mouth and found my voice.

"Ghosts don't exist," I said. "There's a logical explanation for what we're seeing. We've been breathing in who knows what chemicals from the burning paint, and it's caused this hallucination."

"If we're hallucinating, then why do we all see the same thing?" Arthur said from somewhere on my left.

"We're in a highly suggestible state – it could be possible—"

"I'm not a ghost, Maeve. If you touched me, you would know." The apparition raised its hand to its cheek, palm toward me, begging me to try it. "I felt the heat of those flames against my skin. Right now, I'm wiggling my toes in the grass. The wind's blowing through my hair. I'm real, and all I've wanted to do these last years is hold my daughter in my arms."

I touched my finger to the Briarwood ring. The stone glowed with warmth. The metal seemed to have grown tighter around my finger. "I'm not touching you until I know for a fact this isn't some fae trick."

It smiled.

"So logical. So questioning. Such amazing hair." It tilted its long, slim neck, sweeping around to take in the five guys. "And commanding a coven of beautiful men? You are *definitely* my daughter."

"We'll let the DNA test confirm that," I growled. "Unless ghosts can't take DNA tests."

"I'll happily take any test you ask of me, my darling Maeve. I'll walk over coals if it means I could hold you in my arms—"

Horror clawed at my belly as the apparition's words cut off with a hacking rasp. It's eyes rolled back in its head. It toppled forward, the body (that appeared solid now) crumpling as its forehead slammed against the dirt. I screamed and darted back, my heart pounding against my chest.

"Aline?" Corbin cried, rocking forward to reach for it. I grabbed his arm.

"Stay back. Don't touch her!"

Her.

My mother.

But it's impossible.

I stared at her crumpled form, half expecting her skin to melt into a puddle, or ugly black spiders to crawl out of her white robes like they did in horror films. But she just lay still with her head and her arms draped at awkward angles.

She didn't move.

My heart leapt into my throat. *Why isn't she moving?*

TWO: MAEVE

As I watched the not-ghost's lifeless body, Rowan crept forward and picked up the corner of her sleeve between his fingers. "Don't touch her!" I cried, terrified she might place some spell on him.

Rowan leaned close to her face, his dreadlocks spilling over the ground. 'She's breathing, so that's good. Do ghosts breathe?"

"Um, I'm not sure." Corbin brushed the curtain of hair off her cheek. I braced myself for something horrible to happen to him, but nothing did. "Aline, are you okay?"

"Is she…" I choked out.

Is she dead? I wanted to ask. But the words were ridiculous because we were talking about my mother, who was already dead. My eyes drew to the cuts on her face, drawn in lines down her forehead and cheeks like…

…like *claw* marks.

"Aline?" Corbin rolled her over onto her back, cradling her face in his lap. Her body flopped like a ragdoll. He held up her wrist. "I can feel a pulse, but it's faint."

How the hell can she have a pulse? She's dead.

Rowan touched her face, murmuring under his breath. "She's in some kind of catatonic state," he said. "I think it's a side effect of the spell's reversal."

"What do we do?"

"We take her back to Briarwood," Corbin said.

I shook my head. "Not happening. We don't know what she is or why she's here. It's not safe."

"It's the safest thing we can do. You want to know if she's a fae? Well, trying to take her through the wards is as good a test as any. We can't just leave her in this field for the local farmers to discover. It wasn't that long ago that she was the mistress of Briarwood. People will recognise her. They'll ask questions, like why she hasn't aged in twenty-one years."

I glanced down at the serene face of the woman who looked just like my mother. "She needs a hospital."

Rowan bent down and touched her cheek. "This isn't something a hospital can fix. I think I can help her, but I need my herbs."

I glanced between the two of them – Rowan's wide, frightened eyes, and Corbin's steady, intelligent gaze. I marvelled at how they'd managed to steamroll right through my protests. The two of them together are trouble. "You definitely think this is the right thing to do?"

"I think it's the *only* thing." Corbin squeezed her wrist. "We'd better hurry. Her pulse is getting fainter."

I nodded and stepped back. Arthur rushed forward and reached under her body, draping her arm over his shoulders. My heart lurched as her head flopped against his chest. Her skin was so pale, it looked translucent, the veins standing out like dark webs. Corbin moved in to help, but Arthur shrugged him away. "I've got her. She's as light as a feather. Pity that artist lover of hers didn't think to paint her a nice sandwich."

The fire sizzled as Flynn doused it in water. Corbin picked

up the grimoire and slammed it shut, and Rowan and Blake collected the rest of the equipment. We traipsed across the field and stepped over the stone wall that marked the boundary of Briarwood Castle, moving back into the protection of our wards. The figure of my mother flopped lifelessly in Arthur's arms.

Corbin and Blake flanked me as we ascended the slope and cut through the orchard, wrapping their arms around my waist. With every step, the jewels of the High Priestess of Briarwood weighed heavier against my skin. Lights glowed through the Great Hall windows, and I could see the TV blaring on the wall and Connor bouncing in his swing. *Good, Kelly and Jane are occupied.*

We rushed through the wooden gate leading to the high-walled kitchen garden. Flynn held the kitchen door open for Arthur. Rowan rushed around, grabbing bottles and jars from the shelves. "Lay her down on the island," he said.

Arthur laid the ghost/spectre/wraith/zombie/figment of our imagination out across the table, knocking the pepper shaker on the floor. Under the LED lights, her skin glowed with ethereal translucency. Her lips moved slightly, and I caught the faintest whisper. I leaned in close without touching her, trying to catch what she was saying, but it was too quiet.

Rowan dumped herbs and oils into his mortar and crushed them into a paste. "Open her mouth," he said, his voice taking on the quiet authority I only ever heard when he was treating someone who'd been hurt. Corbin tipped her head back, holding her jaw open. Rowan dumped a spoonful of paste on her tongue.

"We need water," he said.

Flynn rushed to the sink and returned with a glass of water. Rowan dribbled some into her mouth so the paste would slide down her throat.

"Incline her head, so she doesn't choke," he said. After another dribble of water, she'd swallowed all the paste.

"What happens now?" Arthur glanced at me and then back at the sleeping figure. My stomach flipped and churned like mad. I didn't know whether I was excited or hopeful or terrified or all of the above.

"We wait," Rowan said. "We've no idea what she's been through. Her body will take a while to deal with the trauma. We should take her somewhere more comfortable, get her blankets and—"

"Maeve?"

I whirled around at the sound of the voice. Kelly stood in the doorway, dressed in jeans and Arthur's Blood Lust sweatshirt, her hands disappearing inside the enormous sleeves. She folded her arms across her chest and peered around me at the kitchen island. "Why is Rowan forcing herbs into a strange woman in a white dress? What happened to her face? What's *really* going on?"

THREE: MAEVE

*S*hit, shit, shit.

"Um, it's kind of a long story."

Kelly glared at me. "I've got time."

"Right." *So here it is; I'm really a witch, and my coven of hot guys – all of whom I'm sleeping with – have just completed a releasing ritual that seems to have brought my mother back from the dead. We're hoping if Rowan can revive her then she'll be able to tell us exactly how to stop the fae who are threatening to raise the souls of the restless dead to lay waste to the earth.*

Yeah, that's not going to fly. It sounded like the plot of some stupid teen witch TV show. The trouble was, I was frantically trying to think of another explanation that Kelly would believe, and I had nothing. I was never good at creative writing at school.

"Maeve?" Kelly prompted me.

"Yes. Right. So..." I glanced at Arthur with his hair wild around his face and his sword still hanging at his side, and a lie fumbled its way to my lips. "This woman is a friend of Arthur's from... from his medieval reenactment club. They were going to have a training weekend here but Arthur cancelled it because we were travelling, only she didn't get the message. She's a bit eccentric and old school, and doesn't have a mobile, you see. So... yeah. She came and the castle was all locked up and she didn't have any money and it looks like she was just sleeping in the woods and she must've stumbled into the briar and cut herself. We just found her and she's a bit messed up so Rowan's giving her medicine..." I trailed off.

Kelly isn't going to believe this absurd story. Maybe you should just tell her the truth, or at least part of it. It would be easier than lying, especially if this woman wakes up—

"Is that true?" Kelly narrowed her eyes.

I opened my mouth, but I couldn't push the words out. Kelly tapped her nails against the cuff of Arthur's hoodie.

"Kelly, I—"

CRASH.

Startled out of my stupor, I whirled around to see Aline sitting up, clutching her chest as she wheezed and spluttered. Her eyes bulged out of her head like a demented frog. Rowan's pestle lay in pieces on the tile.

"Don't let her roll off," Rowan cried. Arthur and Corbin grabbed Aline's arms, bracing her as they helped her sit up. She coughed and sputtered, her tiny body convulsing as she fought for breath.

"Omigod, is she on drugs?" Kelly stepped closer, her expression horrified.

"Get away from her!" I shoved Kelly away, terrified that she'd touch Aline and end up with some horrible hex and how the hell would I explain that?

I shoved harder than I intended. Kelly stumbled back and slammed into the kitchen cabinets. Rowan's jars rattled on the shelves. She clutched her side, glaring at me as tears rolled down her cheeks.

"I can't believe you did that," she whispered.

Tears sprung in my eyes. "Kelly, I'm so sorry. I didn't mean—"

"Yes you did!" Kelly yelled through her own tears. "You've been pushing me away ever since I got here. You're piling lies on top of lies just to avoid telling me what's really going on. I knew you were selfish, but I never, ever thought you'd..." she hiccuped, her body dissolving into sobs.

I reached out to embrace her, but she shied away. "I swear, Kelly, I didn't mean to hurt you. She might be dangerous and I—"

"Why, is she a *witch?*" Kelly sneered. She got to her feet, fumbling for a hold on the edge of the bench. "Like you, right, Maeve? You're a witch."

The room disappeared. The only things I was aware of was Kelly's cold glare and my heart pounding in my ears.

"I'm not a witch," I said, but the words were weak, full of resignation.

Kelly snorted. "Jeez. I didn't even really believe it, but if Maeve Crawford can't even muster up the strength to deny the existence of witches, then I guess I'm convinced."

"Moore." Someone behind me rasped.

Kelly whipped around. "What?"

"Moore," the woman who might've been my mother spoke, her voice like dirt being shovelled into a hole. "Her name is Maeve Moore."

"Maeve," Kelly said through gritted teeth. "Who is this person *really*, and why does she know your birth name?"

My shoulders sagged. At least giving her this one truth might distract her from the witch thing for a while. "We're not a hundred percent sure, but we think she might be my mother."

"No." Kelly slid down the cabinet and sank to the floor, hugging her arms to her knees. "This is *not* happening."

"Like I said, it's not confirmed yet, but... I gestured at the coughing woman. "There's a certain family resemblance. It's kind of a long story and I... I don't want you to hate me."

"Why would I hate you?"

"Don't you hate me already?"

Kelly laughed. "Only because you've been lying to me and sneaking around and cheating on Arthur and that's really gross and sinful, and I don't understand why you'd want to hurt someone you care about."

"I don't want to hurt anyone, and I'm not cheating on Arthur."

"You know I saw you with Flynn, and you're still denying it!" Her voice rose an octave. "It's disgusting, Maeve. Adultery is a sin. How can anyone trust you when you're not faithful—"

Like a switch flicking in my brain, the mention of the word *sin* turned my distress into anger. "Just because your stupid religion doesn't allow for girls and guys to have platonic friendships, or for girls and girls and guys and guys to hook up, doesn't mean you get to lecture me on my relationships—"

"My *stupid* religion is the only reason you have a fucking family in the first place!" Kelly screamed. "Do you think if Mum and Dad had been atheists like you, they'd have taken pity on some unholy daughter born in sin? And now you're trying to tell me your mother is some random druggie in your kitchen. Look at her, Maeve! She can't be a year or two older than you are. That's not your mother. You're lying again."

"Christians don't have a monopoly on kindness or love. I've learned more about morality in the last few weeks than I have in my entire *life* living in that backwards, judgemental hellhole of a town."

"You mean you learned about morality while you were cheating on Arthur?"

"Um, Kelly, it's fine," Arthur said, but I held up a hand to stop him.

"I'm dealing with my grief in the best way I can," I hissed. "You can ask the guys. I haven't hurt anyone."

"Except Uncle Bob." Kelly shot back.

"That was different," I flinched. "I did that for *you*. Because you were hurting in a hospital bed and I had to help you. It seems you're fine to take the help of a sinner when it gets you a plane ticket to England and a bank account full of money, but as soon as it shits on your puritanical sensibilities you get all holier-than-thou."

"This is so typical of you!" Kelly yelled. "Twisting everything around so I'm the one who looks like the bad guy. Nothing's changed for you – your life is still perfect. You have an inheritance and a hot guy and a whole future. You could have sold this castle and gone to MIT and lived your life just the way you always wanted it. Instead, you chose to shit all over Mum and Dad's memories. The sand isn't even cold on their grave and you've already thrown everything they taught you out the window."

"Get out," I growled.

Kelly's face froze. "Wait, Maeve, I didn't—"

"No. We're done." I turned away. Behind me, Kelly let out a strangled sob. A moment later, I heard her feet running down the hall. *Good. Let her go. Let her take her stupid glitter Barbie backpack and her seven deadly sins bullshit and fuck off to Germany, if that's what she wants to do.*

The woman coughed, her eyes meeting mine. Once again, I was struck by how exactly she resembled my mother's image from the painting.

"She's hurting," The woman – I still couldn't bear to think of her as Aline, my mother, not yet – gasped out. "Don't judge her by the things she says in desperation."

"I don't take relationship advice from ghosts."

"You have to ask yourself what hurts more..." Her eyes

rolled back again, and she collapsed against Corbin's chest. A moment later, she emitted a loud snore.

What hurts more? I rubbed my tear stained cheek. *What does she mean by that?*

"Take her to the library," Rowan said. "Light the fire and make her comfortable with lots of blankets. I'll make her some food for when she wakes up."

"She's really going to wake up?" The woman looked halfway to the grave. *She's supposed to be all the way in the grave.*

Rowan nodded. "She's fine, just exhausted. Being three-dimensional for the first time in twenty-one years is hard on the body. We'll take care of it, you should go talk to—"

"Don't finish that sentence. Why the library? What about one of the guest rooms?"

"Kelly and Jane are using the last two rooms on our floor, so that only leaves the rooms on the tours, and they're filled with creepy wax figurines. I think she should be next to a fire, and I'm sure she'll like waking up in the library with all the books. After all, didn't it used to be hers?"

"She's not my mother, Rowan."

"If you say so, Princess." Blake winked, as he helped Arthur lift her off the counter. "Excuse us while we settle your not-mother back into her castle."

I followed the guys upstairs to the library. They settled the woman on the couch and piled her up with blankets and pillows. Corbin went behind his desk. "We should take turns to stay with her, so she's not alone when she wakes up. I'll take first shift—" he glanced at me, and gave a shy smile. "That is, if it seems like a good idea to you, Maeve?"

Oh Corbin. He still struggled to let go of his sense of responsibility for the coven. I was supposed to be admonishing him every time he issued commands and tried to take over.

But since the idea of being alone in a room with the woman

who claimed to be my mother freaked me the hell out, this time he could have his overprotectiveness. "It's a good idea, and I'm fine if you go first. I'm tired as hell, anyway."

"I'd say we should sit down and figure out what to do next, but I don't think we'll know anything until we can talk to her again." Corbin's eyes met mine with a warmth that melted my heart. "Maeve, you need to talk to Kelly."

Forget that. My heart turned to ice again. I shook my head. "I'm going to bed."

"But don't you think—"

"No." I glared at him. "And don't you talk to her, either. She's my responsibility. I don't have to tolerate being spoken to like that in *my* castle. Wake me up when it's my shift. And don't any of you—" I glared at the rest of the guys. "—even *think* about coming up to visit me. I am *not* in the mood."

I brushed my teeth in my bathroom (more furiously than my dentist would have recommended, but he hadn't just met his zombie mother and had a horrible fight with his sister, so he could go to hell), climbed the stairs to my tower, and collapsed into bed, worn out by the emotional trauma of the day.

As soon as I turned out the light, part of me wished I hadn't told the guys to stay away tonight. I could have done with Rowan's cuddles or Flynn's tickles or Corbin's soft whispers in my ear. I debated going down and climbing into bed with one of them, but I fell asleep as soon as my head hit the pillow.

My dreams gave me no respite from terror. The vision of burned and blackened earth and a maze of towering briar woke me several times. I lost count of the number of times I stumbled through that briar and found the six stakes pointing toward the sky, the charred remains of my beloved guys clinging to their forms. I struggled against the invisible barrier that prevented me reaching the sixth stake, but I couldn't get close enough to see the face of the wretched figure that hung there. This time there was a crowd of people in black cloaks crowded around, jeering and pointing and tossing sharp objects that slammed against my skin.

"Burn the witches," they chanted. "Burn the Devil's children."

The one in front lifted its hood, revealing a cascade of shimmering blonde hair. Kelly's accusing eyes stared back at me. "Burn the witches. Burn them all!"

FOUR: MAEVE

A hand shook me from my nightmares.

"Maeve," Rowan's gentle voice soothed me into the real world – the world where my men weren't pierced on wooden stakes. "Your mother is awake."

Your mother is awake. Four totally normal words that made absolutely no sense. And yet, here they were being uttered. I guess nothing was really normal at Briarwood Castle.

I dragged my tired body into some jeans and my new Blood Lust t shirt, and followed Rowan downstairs to the library. My mother's ghost lay across the sofa, her dainty feet resting on top of the arm, and her body wrapped in layers of blankets. A tray of scones with jam and cream and a pot of tea sat on the coffee table next to her. Corbin sat behind his desk, poring through a thick volume. Flynn, Blake, and Arthur stood or sat around the room, watching her with various expressions – from curiosity to reverence to blatant distrust.

"Where are Jane and Kelly?" I asked.

"In the Great Hall, watching reality TV and demolishing a pile of Rowan's scones," Corbin grinned. "I figure that's going to buy us at least an hour."

"You talked to them?" I asked, a warning creeping into my voice.

"Not really. We grunted good morning to each other." He shot me a meaningful look, which I chose to ignore.

"These scones *are* delicious," the woman on the couch said, smacking her lips together. "It's been twenty-one years since I last tasted food. I used to dream about roast potatoes."

I eyed the scone in her hand, then touched the one left on the plate. It was real. "So you're *definitely* not a ghost?"

She smiled. "I seem pretty corporeal. Truthfully, I don't know what I am. The magic that held me inside the painting is not something I've ever seen before."

"Are you up to this?" Rowan asked, pouring out tea. "Maeve and Corbin are going to have a million questions."

"I'm fine, Rowan." She took another big bite of scone. "The power of English baking sustains me. I'm not surprised you're a whiz in the kitchen. Your father was the most incredible cook."

"Don't talk about our parents," Arthur growled.

Rowan bowed his head, staring at the floor. I wanted to wrap my arms around him, but Corbin beat me to it.

The woman's eyes widened. "But why not? Don't you want to know what they were like when they were young and foolish?"

Cold silence answered her question. She shrugged, and took another bite of her scone.

I leaned forward. "Rowan's right about the questions. I'll start. What should we call you?"

"Aline. Or Mum. You could call me Num." Tears glistened in the corners of her eye.

"That's not happening." I rubbed my tired eyes. I wished I'd thought to have some coffee before we did this. "*Aline*, presumably if you were declared dead, then there must've been a body. That body is still buried somewhere in the ground, turning back into stardust. So how are you here now with a body that looks perfectly fine and not at all like a zombie?"

Aline looked down at the baggy black t-shirt Arthur had given her clinging to her shapely body. "I can't answer that one."

"I can." Corbin met my gaze and gave me an apologetic smile. "I was going to show you one day, but I didn't think you needed it right when you were mourning the Crawfords. Aline's body was never recovered, but there was a lot of blood and a charred patch of earth in the circle, along with a lock of her hair. The witches assumed the fae destroyed her body as a final insult, since she had stopped them from raising the Slaugh. My parents placed a memorial stone for her in a corner of the orchard."

Shit.

I don't know what my mother's lack of remains meant, but I knew it was important.

Aline patted her breast, grinning. "Phew, that explains that, then. This body is all mine, baby."

Baby? I watched her face. Was she trying to... *flirt* with Corbin?

This whole thing is way too fucking weird.

I was still trying to wrap my head around the physics of her presence. "So you've been trapped in that painting ever since the ritual twenty-one years ago? Where was your body? That frame was big, but not big enough to hide a corpse."

"It's hard to explain. I don't understand it myself. It's only recently I've had self-awareness. Prior to that I existed in darkness, awake but devoid of my senses, trapped in a nightmare from which I could never wake. Some months ago, I began to hear again, and to register the language and the meaning of the words I heard. I didn't realise how many years it's been until Flynn mentioned Maeve's birthday. I've been listening to the conversations in the castle ever since." She turned to Corbin. "Your voice kept me company the most. I don't think anyone else ever heard the doubts you have when you pace the hallway at night. Except me."

Then she turned to Rowan. "You barely spoke, but you used to pace around in front of me at night. I worried you might wear a hole right through the floor."

Corbin looked uncomfortable. Rowan stared at the floor. I wrung my hands, not sure what to make of these intimate moments she'd shared with my guys, when they didn't know she was there.

"And you," she glared at Flynn. "You made me want to laugh all the time. But I had no stomach to rumble, no larynx to vibrate, no mouth through which to issue forth my mirth. It was like trying to hold in a giggle during a Eulogy. You, good sir, are *cruel*."

Flynn took a deep bow. "Finally, someone appreciates my genius."

Aline smiled at me, but she must've seen something in my expression, because her smile fell away. She hurried on with her story. "After hearing came scent. Delicious smells wafting from the kitchen, the distinctive scents of each of you as you went about your business." Her eyes met each guy in turn. I'd noticed it too, how each of them had their own distinct scent. Rowan was sweet herbs and flour. Arthur was smoke and ash. "Every day you spoke about Maeve. She was ever present in your thoughts, and I knew that my good friends Andrew and Bree had kept their promise to me and sent you four to watch over her. As you grew closer to coming into your powers, Maeve, my own magic started to wake up again. That first day you arrived at the castle, when you gazed up at the portrait, that was the first time I'd ever been able to see out into the world again. And the first thing I saw was *you*, my daughter."

I nodded, not trusting myself to speak.

"I've been following you ever since, although how I cannot explain. My conscience seems to sense what goes on with you even when you weren't directly in front of the portrait. I've watched you come to terms with your magic, and piece together the details of what happened at the ritual. And sometimes, if I tried really, really hard, I could channel my own magic through you and change things in your world."

Arthur's eyes widened. "You did it, didn't you? You brought my sword to me in the fae realm."

Aline smiled. "I heard you cry out. You needed it."

Realisation dawned on me. "You changed the canvas so we'd notice you. And you... you spoke inside my head." Aline nodded again. Another thought occurred. "Was it you who baptised the guys during the fight at the church? They all heard a female voice praying inside their heads and water splashed on their faces and the fae couldn't take them."

"Yes, also me. That bit of magic made me blind for three days, but it worked. I'm so pleased it worked."

Flynn threw his arms around her. "You may be a ghostie, but I'm not afraid to hug the woman who saved my bacon. Speaking of which," he drew away in horror. "You haven't tasted bacon in twenty-one years? Rowan, why aren't you rectifying the gross injustice right this minute!"

"Er—"

"Don't you dare," Aline clamped her hand around Rowan's arm, and shot him that dazzling smile of hers. "The scones are amazing. They're more than enough."

My head spun. I just didn't know what to make of this. So many times I'd thought about who my mother might have been if she lived beyond my birth day, what it would have been like to go to her with my fears and my triumphs. But Aline was nothing like I'd pictured. She was practically my age, and seemed like she'd give Kelly a run for her money in the flirting game. She didn't seem to know *anything*.

I wanted to feel an instant overwhelming love for her – some deep cosmic bond that had connected us across twenty-one years – but all I felt was confused and freaked out and sad.

"Go on," she waved at me. "I be that's not the last of your questions."

I sighed. *Not even close.* "What do you know about how you got inside the painting?"

Aline's eyes darkened. "Ever since I gained conscious thought i've been trying to figure it out, but the ritual is a complete blur. I'll tell you what I do remember – I'd figured out that Robert was being compelled by Daigh, so I knew that if I wanted a chance at catching the fae off-guard, I'd need to keep the ritual secret. You were squirming around in my belly, poking your tiny limbs into my bladder. I was determined that no one would hurt a hair on your head. I also knew that the ritual would take me from you, leaving you without either of your parents." She reached out to me.

This time, I let her take my hand. Her skin felt warm and soft, her fingers long and delicate. Across her palm was a raised bump – a strange imperfection on her perfect porcelain skin. A lump rose in my throat, and my body trembled as though I was cold. But it wasn't cold. Is this the visceral reaction I was hoping for? Because now that I had it, it totally freaked me out.

This doesn't make any sense. Even if this woman is my mother, she's a stranger to me. A weird stranger who flirts with my guys. Why does her touch give me this shiver?

All the emotions swirling around in my head were reflected back at me in Aline's eyes. Tears flowed down her cheeks as she rubbed a finger over my knuckles. "Oh, Maeve. I'm so sorry I never got to be there when you grew up. I missed so much, but I don't want to miss any more. Please, tell me about your life. I want to know everything. Have you been happy? Have you been loved?"

I glanced around at my guys – from Rowan's kind, open face to Blake's dark smirk. The Crawfords' faces flashed in my mind, but I pushed them aside. If I thought of them now, I'd completely break down. "Yes, I have been loved. But we can't get distracted by sentiment now. We need to stop the fae, and having you here may be the biggest advantage we have. Tell us about the ritual – everything you remember."

Aline's smile froze for a moment. I drew my hand back. The ghost of her touch lingered on my skin. More tears toppled down her cheeks.

"You're protecting your coven. It just...it's so beautiful to see you all together. I remember you all as children and I...I loved your parents very much."

"Most of our parents are dead," Flynn blurted out.

Aline buried her face in her hands. "No."

I glared at Flynn. "Aline, the ritual."

"You have to excuse Maeve," Flynn said. "She likes every-thing to be logical."

She shook her head. "Yes, sorry. It's hard to be logical after what I've been through. I'll try to remember everything that might be useful. Back then, I had this idea that maybe the belief in magic would be just as powerful as actually *performing* magic. Belief, after all, is one of the most powerful forces on earth. Belief makes Gods of men. It topples nations. It changes hearts. I wondered if drawing on belief instead of our elemental magic in a ritual would enable us to collect belief from the people around us and weaponize it. The fae have fallen out of knowledge – so belief is not a force they can wield – but thanks to Christian dogma and modern pop culture, witches are still very much part of the human psyche, and very much tied to Crookshollow's mythology in particular. I didn't think it would be too hard to stoke the fires of belief in the village."

That's an intriguing idea.

"I couldn't find much in the books about the power of belief, but I did a little experiment. I used Daigh's belief that he had pulled his deception over on me to capture some of his magic." She reached over and touched the pendant on my throat. It flared with heat under her fingers. "I stored it in there, because I knew I'd need it during the ritual to perform a glamour that even Daigh would believe. I tested it first, giving myself the appearance of my friend Bree and eating a meal with the coven. They were completely fooled. Even Andrew chatted away to me without realising I wasn't his wife."

"You're very scientific about your magic," I said. Rowan took my hand and squeezed it, his wide eyes signalling he understand what I was thinking. Aline's experiment was exactly what I'd have done, testing a theory before jumping in.

Needles stabbed at my heart, and I had to gulp down another lump in my throat.

Forget coffee. I needed a glass of Arthur's strongest mead.

"Magic and science were one and the same for many centuries," Aline said, in a haughty voice I wondered might sound similar to what Flynn referred to as Corbin's 'Boring Professor' voice. "Alchemists made many scientific breakthroughs while searching for their philosopher's stone."

"We could have done with your help when we first told Maeve about her powers," Flynn said. "This stubborn wench took ages to believe what we all knew was true."

"How I wish I could have been there," Aline said. "I wish you'd been able to grow up knowing what you would be capable of. You could have prepared for it."

I yanked my hand out of Rowan's and folded my arms across my chest.

Aline straightened up. "As I was saying, once I knew that my glamour would work, and it would work on Daigh, I knew what I had to do. I made plans with Andrew and Bree, and prepared myself to die."

"How would you know you would die?" Corbin asked. I glared at him, knowing what Aline was going to say. *I'm not dealing with the predestination issue today on top of everything else.*

"Because I saw it. I see the future in visions that leave my mind open and my body bleeding. The last vision I saw was my own death. I knew I would die to protect Maeve, so I made sure that I stopped the fae on the way out." She lifted her hands, indicating the room and all of us. "It turns out, even Fate can play tricks on her most ardent servants."

That's because fate doesn't exist, and premonitions are completely impossible, I thought, but didn't say. Flynn looked at me like he expected me to bite at the Fate comment.

"The ritual," Corbin took her back to the story.

"Yes, yes. Witches started arriving at Briarwood from miles around – the new age hippies from Avebury and Glastonbury, the German coven in their black goth gear, the eastern Europeans with their folk magic and dark auras. The presence of so many strange people converging on Briarwood fueled the town's simmering distrust of us. Belief in witchcraft soared. I could feel the power pulsing in the streets, exuding from the church steeple. If this worked we would have more than enough.

"We had to wait for your birth before we could perform the ritual. It was dangerous to wait, because Daigh was assembling a fae army. He'd killed many Seelie and taken their power for himself. His warriors moved up and down the countryside, stealing unbaptised children to grow his power still further. The night you came, the wind howled outside, but the castle was warm and filled with love. Robert was by my side the entire time, but I was too far gone to know when it was him or Daigh whose hand I crushed with my grip. You were born in the early hours of the evening, a slithering alien of a thing, covered in blood and mucus – and yet, you were the most beautiful thing I'd ever seen. Monet's water lilies didn't come close to the sublime wonder of holding my child in my arms. I cradled you to my breast and wept. All I wanted to do was curl up with you and sleep. But instead I called the witches for the ritual, and wrote you the letter. Did you get my letter?"

I nodded, digging my shaking fingers into the pocket of my jeans. I drew the letter out and handed it to Aline. She brushed her hand over the broken seal, inhaling sharply.

"I remember every word I wrote," she whispered. "I'm so so sorry."

"The ritual," I whispered, struggling to hold back tears of my own.

"Yes. You must know the truth of it." Aline gripped the edge of the letter, where her tears from all those years ago had thinned the paper. "We gathered in two circles in the field – an inner circle of the High Priestesses, and an outer circle of the other witches. They called up their powers, and I drew that power into myself, becoming the conduit for their belief in me. I'd made sure to spread gossip in the village that something interesting would be going on at the castle that night, so a bunch of local kids were hiding in the bushes. One ran back to report of women dancing and chanting under the moonlight at the pub, creating a chain of belief that funnelled into our ritual, extending me more power than I'd ever known possible.

"It was time. I touched my fingers to the amulet, and I was able to use Daigh's power to cast a glamour. I picked up the knife. I held it above your head. Twelve High Priestesses and Bree and Andrew and Robert and Daigh inside Robert's head saw me plunge that knife into your heart."

She held up her hand, and I noticed a long scar across her palm, the tiny imperfection I'd felt on her skin. "Instead, I plunged the knife into my hand. I knew I could not hold the glamour for long, and for it to be believed Daigh would expect to see blood. Unfortunately, I cut too deep. Weakened by the birth, my body shuddered under this new trauma as Daigh tried to rip your body from me. The witches – knowing that I had committed this horrific act to save the world form the Slaugh – held him back, and Andrew bundled you away. Robert escaped from their grasp and fell on me, clawing at me, torn between the twin minds sharing the same body, both wallowing in the horror of what I'd done to them." She rubbed the cuts on her cheeks. "I think that's where I got these cuts."

"I had a balm for them," Rowan said.

"Thank you, beautiful." That flirtatious tone was back. "Fae poured out of the sidhe, answering Daigh's anguished call. They rushed the circle, breaking the outer ring. But they were too late. Daigh's belief in my breaking his pact with the underworld by killing his daughter had, in fact, broken his pact with the underworld and robbed him of all his power. And he thought I'd killed his child. Robert thought I'd killed *his* child." Darkness passed over her face. "It was twice the amount of pain one soul was able to hold. The grief on his eyes, in *their* eyes – it broke me to see it. I could feel myself losing my grip on life.

"Robert wrapped his hands around my throat, tightening, loosening, as the great internal struggle tore apart his mind. Which one of them wanted me to live and which wanted me to die, I did not know. I have no clue into whose eyes I stared as my life drained from my body. I was too weak to fight back, even if I'd wanted to. But I had to die. I had to go to the underworld, it was the only way to be sure we'd won.

"The cut in my hand bled profusely, and soon my vision swam and the carnage of the ritual fell silent. The world went dark. I thought he'd choked the life from me, and that I'd awake in the underworld. But instead, I slumbered in the nightmare of darkness inside that painting until you lot woke me again."

"Robert was the one who placed you inside the painting," I explained to her what we learned from our visit to Robert Smithers, how we believed he'd traded his mind with Daigh in exchange for the fae king's artistic talent, and how he said they were both in love with her. Aline looked distressed as I described the institution he lived in and the precarious state of his mind. "We couldn't get it out of him when we visited him – he's not exactly coherent. But the painting bore traces of water magic, not fae magic, and we recently found out that witches can store energy inside objects." I touched the pendant on my throat. "The same way you stored that piece of Daigh's magic inside here."

Aline's eyes lit up. "I'm impressed, Maeve."

"Don't be. Just help us figure out how to stop the fae a second time."

And tell me who my father is.

I didn't say it. I wasn't ready to hear the answer, not from her. I had a feeling I wasn't going to like what she said.

"What's happened with the fae now?" Aline leaned forward.

"They have moved into the underworld and taken a sacrifice of 22 unbaptised humans and 22 high-ranking fae," Corbin said. A collective shudder passed through the group at the memory of those lives burned away.

"How many days until the full moon?" Aline asked.

"Eight days."

Aline tipped her head to the side. To me, it didn't look as though she was considering the problem nearly hard enough. "Daigh must know I tricked him all those years ago, because you are alive, and he found you. I do not think we can fool him again."

"Then what can we do?"

"Even if we destroy Daigh and strip his power, we're still screwed," Blake said. "The Slaugh will still ride, and Liah will simply rise up to become queen in his place. And if you ask me, we should be more afraid of meeting her in battle than Daigh."

"Who's Liah?" Aline frowned. "And while we're on the subject, what happened to you, Blake Beckett? I heard in the painting that you came from the fae realm, but you were born a human and fae—"

"—can't be inside the castle walls. I know." Blake smirked. "I'm just amazing," Blake explained what happened to his parents and how Daigh adopted him and he'd escaped the fae realm to join us. At the mention of his parents' grisly death and the tortures he'd endured under Daigh's control, Aline winced. I wondered if she was thinking what might've happened to me if Daigh had known I was still alive.

"Thank you, Blake, and you're right. Destroying Daigh won't stop the Slaugh riding. We'd literally have to overthrow the demons of hell in order to call this off now. There's only one other solution that I can see."

"We retire to a desert island and rejoice in the fact we now have a lifetime supply of free Irish whiskey?" Flynn asked hopefully.

Aline shook her head. "We have to get the fae to change their mind and call off the deal they've made. Which means I have to speak with Daigh."

FIVE: MAEVE

he wants to what?

"No." I shook my head, my pink fringe flapping against my temples. "No way."

"It's our only choice. Even if we had every witch in the world lending their power to us, we could not reach into the underworld. But Daigh can call off the deal – he could stop the Slaugh, if I gave him a compelling reason."

"He's never going to do that."

"Agreed," Blake folded his arms. "Daigh's been building up to the Slaugh his entire life. He won't give it up for anything, especially not the woman who stopped him last time."

"He will if we give him what he really wants – his family restored."

I snorted. "Daigh doesn't care about us. He hates you, and I'm not even really his daughter. He has to know that."

"You didn't see what I saw that night," she insisted. "When he thought I had killed you, his face...I've never seen anything more terrifying. He loved me, and he loved you, and for all his talk of reclaiming the earth for the fae, he wants us to be together. When he thought I'd destroyed that, it broke him completely. That was what really robbed him of his power – a broken heart."

"You said you didn't even know which face was Daigh and which was Robert?"

"I did, didn't I?" Aline flipped her hair over her shoulder. "But I'm *positive* this was Daigh in anguish over losing you."

"Why, though? I'm not Daigh's daughter. He may have been inside Robert's head when I was conceived, but that doesn't mean he contributed any genetic material. That's not how biology *works*."

Aline shook her head. "It's more complicated than that. There's a type of fae magic—"

"The binding." Blake picked up the last scone from the plate and took an enormous bite "Compelling a human during sex causes some kind of magical bond. It's forbidden for a reason, and I'm guessing you know something about it we don't."

Aline nodded. "The day I found out I was pregnant, the coven had a huge celebration. We all went down to the sidhe and danced and ate and drank and howled at the moon. I believe you boys were there with your parents – although you'd all be too young to remember. Robert was in one of his savage moods that night, and he'd had a lot to drink, and he told this story about a fae woman who fathered a child through a binding. Everyone thought he was just repeating some fae legend he'd heard, but something about the tale unsettled me. It was a couple of months later I figured out he was really Daigh, and I realised the significance of the story."

"What was the story, then?" Corbin leaned forward. This was his area of interest.

"Many centuries ago, a fae princess was gathering food in the forest on a cold winter's day when she came upon a young woman huddled inside a hollow tree. The woman was travelling to visit her betrothed, who lived on the other side of the forest. She strayed from the path and become lost, and not knowing what to do, she'd taken shelter in the tree.

"As soon as the fae laid eyes upon this woman, she fell into madness, which is how Robert always described love. She desired to possess the woman. 'I will lead you back to the safety of the path,' the fae told the woman. 'But in exchange, you must grant me a kiss.' This particular fae princess was famed for her sensual beauty, and she knew the woman wouldn't be able to resist her as soon as their lips touched.

"The girl was frightened. Night was falling, and carnivorous creatures stalked her scent. She agreed to the fae's bargain. The fae princess took her hand and led her back to the safety of the path.

"'I've kept my part of the bargain. I shall have my kiss,' the fae demanded. Out of the corner of her eye, the girl saw her lover in the distance, running along the path and calling out to her. She became terrified he would stumble upon her just as she kissed the fae princess, and know that she had betrayed him.

"Knowing fae folk have the ability to slip unnoticed into a person's mind, she begged the fae to become one with her lover and so have her kiss as they reunited. 'You will feel his lips against mine as though they were your own, and I will not lose him. Please?'

"Overcome with lust, the fae complied. She hid her body behind an ancient oak, and slipped herself inside the mind of the woman's lover as he came around the corner and saw her standing on the path. He swept her up into his arms, and devoured her lips with his.

"Their kiss turned deeper as they explored their bodies in joyous reunion," Aline grinned. "I believe at this point Robert gave a descriptive account of their wild copulating. He even had two of the coven members act out the scene. Oh yes, I remember! It was Andrew and Bree."

"Bloody hell," Corbin covered his ears. "Warn a person before you say stuff like that about his parents."

I couldn't help but laugh. "Please, keep going. I think we can use our imaginations for that bit."

"I can't," Flynn piped up. "I have no imagination. Tell us more about Corbin's parents' wild copulating."

"La la la, I'm not listening," Corbin sang, his hands still plastered over his ears.

"It's okay, Corbin, I won't speak of it any more." Aline grinned again. "Instead, I can tell Flynn about the time I found his Dad in the spa pool with three Californian yoga instructors."

"Argh!" Flynn clamped his own hands over his ears.

"I think we should get back on track here," Arthur said, although he was smiling. "Before we all find out stuff about our parents we'd rather not know."

"Yes, of course. So the fae remained inside the man's head while they made love, and she shared every sensual moment along with him, enjoying the woman's body as though she herself were the lover. Inside the man's head, she learned something else – the man and woman had powers of their own. He could manipulate water, so he had held off the snowstorm while he searched the forest for her, and she was an earth user, which is why she'd sought the comfort of the tree when she was lost.

"The magic of the two lovers sizzled under their skin. The fae felt the power rising and swirling within her as though it were her own magic – but that wasn't possible, because her magic was back with her body, wasn't it?

"As the man and woman basked in the afterglow of their lovemaking, the fae returned to her true from and slipped away into the forest. She returned to her people, but as her days passed in the forest, she noticed that her magic had diminished. She could no longer cast glamour or compell the minds of others. She was convinced the woman had tricked her some-how, so she travelled to the village where the woman and man now lived as husband and wife to get her power back.

"She discovered the woman had given birth to a child – a son – who carried power that had never been seen before. He commanded the magic of water, of earth, and of the fae world. The fae fell to her knees in reverence before the babe. Her heart opened, for she knew that he was her son.

"The husband saw her standing over his son, and he chased the fae princess back into the forest. She returned many times to try and see the son, but every time the husband chased her away, fearing she was an evil changeling come to steal him. She could not get close to the house again. As the son grew up, his father's fear of the fae imprinted itself on him. He used his powers to become the most powerful witch in the land, and he led the covens together to build a new realm for the fae. There was a bloody battle, and he pushed all the fae into that realm, and shut the portal behind it. That was the last time the fae were allowed to roam the vast forests of earth, and the last time the fae princess laid eyes upon her son born of the binding. Separated from the source of her magic, she withered and died."

"Well isn't that a story of sunshine and rainbows?" Blake licked cream off his fingers.

"That's why the fae forbid the binding," Corbin nodded. "Because it gives a human power over them."

"So that's it, then. I'm a freak child of a binding." I'd guessed as much back when we'd met Robert at the institution. But to hear it like this – told in a fairy tale instead of from a scientist at a genetics lab – well, that was just rubbing salt in the wound.

"You're so special." Aline reached for me. I tore myself away, and fell into Arthur's arms. I relaxed into his embrace, seeking comfort in the familiarity of his touch.

And then I remembered the cuts on his wrist. Not even

Arthur was strong enough for what we had to endure right now.

This is all too much.

I squeezed my eyes shut, wanting just a few moments respite from this woman who had birthed me. But we needed to know everything we could. "Robert and Daigh are both my father?"

"Yes. And if the story is to be believed, when you were conceived you took some of Diagh's power. Perhaps enough that when the time of the ritual came he wasn't strong enough to stop me from crippling his powers. He didn't know you were alive until recently. Now that he knows, he believes it's vital you're by his side. Because if you remain out here…" she trailed off.

I alone have the power to stop the fae. I've got it. I just don't want it to be true.

"We've talked about this before," I said. "I've never done anything that could remotely be considered fae magic."

"That doesn't mean it's not possible," Corbin said.

Someone touched my shoulder. I opened my eyes to see Blake's emerald gaze. "I think she's right, Princess."

I glared at Blake, but he kept on talking. "All of this, everything that's been going on, has escalated since Daigh discovered you were alive. I thought it had just taken him this long to build up his power again, and that's probably true. But what if he's desperate?"

In the corner, Corbin was nodding. "All this time we've thought this was about the fae reclaiming their territory and Daigh having his revenge on our coven for stopping him last time. But maybe it's not. Maybe it's more personal than that."

"And what if none of the other fae knew about the binding?" Aline said, her eyes shining.

"Liah knows," Blake said. "That's how she's blackmailing

him. She knows that Daigh was in love, and that his choice compromised the fae. If they find out, they'll overthrow him for sure."

"Good," I growled.

"We could expose him," Arthur suggested, tightening his grip around my shoulders. "Blake could go to this Liah with what we know. We could lend her the power and muscle she needed to take the throne if she agreed to break the Slaugh."

"Liah won't touch us. Apparently you humans polluted the world or some shit." Blake frowned. 'Honestly, I think she's more of a concern than Daigh. But that doesn't mean we can't make him think we're going to help her overthrow him. If we—"

"No," I said.

"We have to try," Aline's eyes blazed.

"I don't see what we going to achieve with this chat. Daigh isn't the problem – the Slaugh are, and this won't stop them. Aren't we just giving away our one advantage by revealing that we have Aline?"

"We're looking for weaknesses," Aline said. "Daigh has all the power right now, and he knows it. All he has to do is wait. His weakness is his arrogance. He believes he will win."

"Right now, he's right."

"If I go to him, begging him to reconsider and humbling myself before him, it will put him into that power position again. I'll beg him to spare the human race. He'll eat it up."

"I don't like this." I folded my arms. "It's not precise. There's no reason he'll tell us anything."

"Remember, we're witches. We might see something that he does not want us to see."

I looked around at the faces of all my guys, waiting for an answer. I thought of Jane and Kelly and Connor, and everything that was at stake here. Finally, my eyes met my mother's and I forced myself to push aside the swirling emotions inside me and consider her suggestion from a logical, scientific perspective.

"No," I said. "We're not doing it."

"But—"

"I'm High Priestess here," I said. "I'm not placing any of you in danger unless I can see a valid reason. I'm sure as hell not endangering anyone to invite Daigh to tea."

"Then what are we going to do?"

"Corbin will look for more information about this magic of belief," I said. "Flynn, you're going to teach me how you imbue objects with your magic. The rest of us are going to find out everything we can about making protective charms against shades. We know the Slaugh are going to come out of the cracks, like the fae in the church. Maybe there's a way we can use the belief magic to spread some kind of protection over a large area... prevent them from raising local spirits and building their ranks."

"Like a fire – starve it of oxygen." Arthur grinned.

"Exactly." I glared at everyone in the room. "And I don't want anyone trying anything on their own any more. No more sneaking off to the underworld by yourself." I glowered at Blake and Flynn, "No more keeping secrets because you want to save people's feelings." That one was for Arthur and Corbin. "We're in this together."

We finished up the meeting and the others wandered off. Corbin gave me a look like he was hoping for his library back, but a quick flick of my head in my mother's direction and he left with stack of books under his arms. I settled myself in the wing-back chair behind the desk, buoyed up by Corbin's scent ingrained in the plush leather.

My mother ate her way through another plate of scones. Crumbs bounced across the blankets and cream smeared across her chin, but she didn't seem to notice or care.

"You must have so many questions," she said between bites.

"Actually, no." I tapped Corbin's montblanc pen against the corner of the grimoire. "You're yet another thing on a very long list of shit I don't have time to deal with until we've sorted out how to stop the Slaugh."

"You're the same sign as me, you know. Cancer. We're sensitive. We have to wait for our feelings to lead the way. My birthday is ten days before yours. I always thought that was a good omen."

"You believe in astrology?" I asked, barely managing to suppress a groan.

"Oh yes, don't you?"

"The stars are burning spheres of gas millions of light years away. They have no bearing on our love lives or career decisions. If you argue for astrology than you're arguing for predestiny, which is completely opposed to quantum physics unless you subscribe to retrocausation. And even if the stars in the sky when you were born *did* somehow impact your personality and future, then astrology would *still* be wrong, because of precession and the earth's wobble. I'm not actually a Cancer, I'm a Gemini, which doesn't matter because it's complete bullshit."

She laughed, that tinkling, singsong sound that made my chest ache. "Oh, you are wonderful. You have Robert's intensity."

"You mean Daigh?"

She shook her head. "Robert, I think. He was so *serious* about his art. Daigh infused him with talent, but he already had the visual eye. He excelled at figurework because he liked the preciseness of the classical proportions. The problem was, he was *too* scientific. His paintings didn't breathe, not the way Daigh's did. Did he keep painting after Daigh left his body?"

"He made some weird pictures of the fae." I debated telling her about the triptych hanging in the National Gallery that mirrored my own dreams, but decided against it. "And one final painting – a portrait, I think. It's in some private collection now, but apparently it was terrible. The critics were quite mean."

Aline shook her head, a tiny laugh escaping from her lips. "He wouldn't have liked that. He couldn't handle criticism. Neither of them could. They were alike in so many ways, it was a clever ruse – they fooled me for many months."

I did have a question. "Did you love Daigh?"

"I don't know," she answered. "I suppose I did. When I fell in love, I thought Daigh and Robert were one person. I thought the person I loved was broken, intense, passionate. Even when I discovered the truth I couldn't separate the two of them in my mind or heart."

"I get that, in a weird way." I thought of the guys. They were each a part of me now, a part of the whole. I couldn't separate my love for them as individuals from my love of the whole. If I lost one of them, it would be like losing them all.

"Enough about me. I want to know everything about *you*, my daughter. You came out of me and you were whisked off from the ritual to that dodgy orphanage, and by your accent I presume you ended up in the States. Please, indulge your mother. What happened between then and you tossing my painting on a fire?"

I told her about the Crawfords finding me on their mission trip and how they'd arranged an illegal adoption and raised me in a tiny, evangelical town in rural Arizona.

"They were good people?"

"A little too willing to believe creationism is a science, but yeah." My throat closed. "They were the best people."

"I love that the same religion that reviled me and my kin was the one that saved my daughter," she smiled. "That feels like the hands of fate."

The idea that my aversion to Christianity might have been an inherited trait, and that I had this thing in common with the woman who'd birthed me – even though she believed in astrology – made a shiver run down my spine. My spirit magic prickled against my skin, teased to life by the connections Aline and I were making.

I kept talking, telling her about I'd always felt out of place in Coopersville, that I'd looked to the stars for answers, but not in the way she did. I explained how the Crawfords indulged my fascination with science, how they brought me all the books they didn't believe in and scrimped and saved to send me to space camp, how they drove me out into the mountains for scientific surveys and helped me fill in my scholarship application for MIT. My throat caught as I talked about Kelly, who despite her popularity always ignored her friends' attempts to exclude me. She always tried to make me feel like a normal teenager, even though I wasn't.

And now she hates me. And I hate her.

Tears streamed down Aline's cheeks as I spoke. I kept stopping to ask if she was okay, but she'd shake her head and beg me to keep going. I talked until my throat closed up and my own tears rolled down my cheeks.

"My heart hurts to see you upset. To me, it's as if you were still that tiny little babe in my arms. The feeling of your soft skin, that amazing baby smell." Aline sniffed. "And now you're all grown up and I missed it all. Is it me? Is me being here upsetting you?"

"No." I shook my head. "I mean, yes, but it's fine. My whole world is upside down. My parents who've looked after me my whole life are dead. You're supposed to be dead but here you are. And Kelly—"

A shadow moved along the bookshelf behind the door. I whipped my head up. "Who's there?"

"If that's you, Rowan sweetie, I could do with another plate of those fabulous scone," Aline held out the empty plate.

A figure lurched from behind the door, grabbed the plate from Aline, and smashed it on the floor. Aline yelped. Sherds of crockery scattered across the room.

I jumped out of the seat, heart pounding. "Kelly?"

Kelly's blonde hair hung over her face as she stared at the broken plate, her chest heaving. She stabbed her arm out, pointing a shaking finger at Aline. "That's your mother."

Kelly heard everything. She knows about Aline being trapped in the painting and about my powers and who my father was. There was no lying my way out of this now.

I nodded.

"That's your mother. And she's a witch. And you're a witch, and your father was... a fae. And also some guy named Robert."

I nodded again.

Kelly's eyes blazed into mine. "And you didn't think I deserved to hear any of this before I came to live with you? You didn't think I should know that when I got on that plane I was stepping into the middle of some kind of supernatural war? Or that I'd end up sharing the house with the ghost of your dead mother?"

"Not a ghost." Aline piped up. I glared at her.

"To be fair, I didn't know about Aline when I invited you here."

"But the witchcraft and the... the *fae*, you knew about that. You said you were going to look after me, and you just let walk into this, you let me believe you —"

"I am still your sister. I wanted to tell you, but I was afraid you'd react like this. I knew you wouldn't be able to accept it. Your Bible has all sorts of choice things to say about witches, and I didn't think you could handle the truth about me."

"And you could?" she yelled. "You're the one who's railed against any kind of belief your whole life. You're the one who acted like I was a fool for believing in God and Jesus, and here you are throwing spells around and talking about fairies and rituals."

"Kelly, I didn't mean to—"

But Kelly had already disappeared.

SIX: FLYNN

"You fecking bastard," I grunted, drawing the screw out of the hole. *Wrong size.* Of course my boxes of screws were on the other side of the workshop, where I couldn't get to them because I was currently holding two halves of a giant scrap-metal statue that would crash to the ground without my hand or the elusive screw holding them in place.

I inched my feet across the room, dragging the two halves of the statue after me. The flimsy skeleton groaned in protest as its corrugated iron feet scraped across the concrete. "Look, if I don't get that screw, you're going to lose an arm, which is going to really mess with your artistic integrity. It's your choice," I groaned as I dragged it forward another foot.

I wished I'd thought to ask Blake to come out and help, but he'd gone straight to his room after we finished talking with Aline. I had a feeling he wasn't happy with Maeve's decision not to speak with Daigh, or maybe he was thinking about his friend Liah, or maybe he was just weirded out by Maeve's mother coming back from the dead like that. I had to admit, it creeped me out a bit, too.

Maeve had barely left her mother's side since she woke up

this morning. Her eyes leaked with tears. I couldn't even imagine what she was going through. What if it had been my Ma? What would that even be like?

I wanted to make her feel better, but I knew she didn't need my irreverent humour or sexy body right now. She had the other guys – Corbin loved this emotional stuff, and Rowan just wanted to hold her and never let go. I trusted them to look after her. There was something I *had* to do.

I needed to *create*.

Aline's ideas about belief and magic nagged at me. Memories from our return to Crookshollow swirled around in my noggin – of the villagers crossing the street to avoid us, yelling weak insults and saying we weren't welcome.

Belief in witchcraft was growing, spreading through the village like a potato famine. Belief that we were somehow responsible for what happened in the church. Belief that we would do something terrible to all the godfaring people of Crookshollow.

I could do something to fan the flames of that belief, and maybe help us to collect it and store it for later use, like a giant metal belief tupperware container.

I'd already bent and welded lengths of rebar together to make a skeletal frame. Now, I was using bits of the body off an old car, corrugated roofing iron, and some old boiler to give the body shape and form. I'd curled the ends of the feet up like pointed shoes, and used motorcycle chain for dangling sleeves. If I can just get this hat to stay in place while I...

I dragged the frame another inch while I stretched out my fingers toward the tool chest. *Nearly there—*

"Can I help?"

I turned my head. Maeve stood in the doorway, hands shoved in her jean pockets, shoulders hunched. A shaft of sunlight shone behind her, highlighting her face like a halo.

"Yes, actually." I jabbed my nose at the tool chest. "Can you grab a box of screws for me? They're in the third drawer down on the left."

Maeve grabbed the box and held it open in front of me. I pulled out a screw and inserted it and the washer into the hole, tightening it with my drill. I followed it with another three, and stood back to admire the completed skeleton, now with the hat perched on top. "What do you think?"

"I think... er, it's a mound of junk?"

"Can't you see it?" I pointed to the bicycle handle sticking out, "That's the hooked nose." I kicked one of the corrugated iron feet. "There's the pointy shoes. " I grinned at the old gramophone horn I'd just flipped upside down on top. "And that's the pointy hat. I'm just going to finish off her clothes and hair, and I've even nicked a bunch of fencing wire from the groundskeepers cottage I'm going to use to make a broomstick. I think I'm going to put her right down by the gate so anyone driving past will see."

"It's a sculpture of a witch." Maeve frowned. "Flynn, are you sure that's a good idea?"

"It's a *brilliant* idea. One of my *most* brilliant, in fact. The whole village believes we're witches. After what they saw at the church, that belief is leaping around like wildfire. It's probably even stronger than when your mum was messing around with it."

Maeve sighed. "But this isn't like last time. They're not just mildly amused by the commune of hippies up at the old castle. They *hate* us, and they've got that mob mentality. We've already seen them attack Jane for her career choice, and they were willing to hurt Connor. But after all those people died at the church... we don't want to incur their wrath."

"I think that's exactly what we should do." I patted the statue. "We feed the beast and then collect all that belief and store it in my sculptures. That way, we can collect even more power than you and Aline and Blake can hold yourselves."

Maeve's eyes blazed. I thought she was going to scold me, which was kind of hot, especially when the little vein popped out in her neck.

"And I know you said no going off and doing things by yourself," I finished hurriedly. "But I wanted to make a statue anyway. Even if we don't use it for collecting magic, it will at least make a fun addition to the courtyard."

Maeve's mouth twisted up into a grin. She reached up and kissed me, her lips fire on my skin. "You're right, Flynnmeister. You *are* a genius."

"Told you." I grabbed a mangled exhaust pipe from Arthur's last car and tossed it at her. "Now hold that for me. Our witch is going to need a wee familiar."

SEVEN: CORBIN

*A*t least I got my library back.

I'd come running as soon as I heard Maeve and Kelly screaming at each other. Kelly pushed past me on the way down the hall and disappeared into Jane's room. Maeve collapsed into my arms, but left a few minutes later, as if all she needed was a moment with me to steady herself before she went off to tackle her next foe. Aline followed behind her, and I'd got to work hunting for information on belief magic.

The grimoire of the Georgian-era Briarwood coven contained some references to belief, so that was the first book I pulled out to study. The author of this text was the magister at the time, and he also happened to be the Bishop of the local Anglican diocese. He believed the magic the coven wielded and the power of the Holy Spirit were one and the same thing.

We speak of the powers of good and evil, of angels and demons. Godly men believe that the Lord's grace channels through them — they have no choice but to perform His will. Because witches wield magic of their own will and volition, they are believed corrupted by demons. They are in violation of Scripture, for all miracles must come from God. In truth, there is only one kind of magic – the power of belief. Can not we—

Noises outside pulled me from the text. I leaned back in my wingback chair, staring out the window at the gardens below. Flynn's workshop door was open, and judging by the bangs, crashes, and curses coming from within, he was working on some new project. Maeve headed out the kitchen door and stopped to speak to Rowan, before heading along the path toward Flynn's workshop. Aline and Rowan moved between the vegetable and herb gardens in the walled courtyard behind the kitchen, talking and laughing with each other as they filled up wooden trugs with produce and sprigs. Rowan raised his gaze to the library window. I almost leapt back, feeling guilty for looking, but then I remembered that we were a thing now. I waved at him. His whole face broke into a smile.

Fuck, he has a gorgeous smile.

Rowan and me – I didn't know what to make of it. I'd never considered that I might want to be involved with a guy. Of course, there was the group thing we all had with Maeve, but that was all about her – pleasing her, worshipping her, loving her the way she deserved to be loved.

Maeve's presence at Briarwood had thrown so much into chaos. From that chaos had risen this uncertainty about *everything*. This battle with the fae could go to a dark place. We could all die any day now. The future was a big black hole. Every time I looked into the black hole and tried to figure out what would happen, I got scared.

I don't do uncertainty.

There were only two things that made that fear seem worthwhile.

There was Maeve, and there was Rowan.

Rowan deserved happiness and love and a future. Of all of us, he'd had the worst start in life. From the moment I found him in that shitty squat, I'd wanted to give him everything. If that meant my heart too, than I was glad to do it.

Rowan turned back to the garden, and I went to return to my book, but something in the corner of my eye caught my attention. A figure in a bright blue dress walked quickly across the grass. Maeve? I'd seen her head out toward Flynn's workshops a few minutes ago. The figure was heading the wrong way.

Kelly.

Maeve still hadn't explained everything, and I guessed from Kelly's yelling before that she'd been hiding in the library while we spoke to Aline. I wondered why she was still here – if I'd been Kelly I would've left for Jane's house, but then I remembered how Dora had threatened Jane at her cottage. With the villagers on the warpath, Jane probably didn't want to go back there with Connor. At least here, they had Briarwood to protect them.

Sighing, I turned away and pulled our own grimoire across the desk, spreading it open on top of the other book and flicking to the page about pouring magic into objects. I'd always interpreted the spell as using magic to manipulate objects, which was not something we'd ever needed to do. But now that Maeve and Flynn had figured out the truth, I could see how I needed to rethink my translation.

I picked up my pen to start work on the text, but all I could think about was Maeve's sister running across the lawn. Maeve wasn't the best at dealing with Kelly's religious beliefs. Maybe it someone a bit less *scientific* should speak to Kelly first.

I dropped my pen and raced downstairs via the secret staircase. I went out the kitchen door, waving to Rowan as I cut across the kitchen garden. I followed Kelly's path down toward the rear of the property. The gate to the orchard was slightly ajar. I swung it open, scanning the trees for any sign of Kelly.

"Hey, Kelly, it's Corbin. Are you in here?"

No answer except the twittering of birds in the trees.

My heart pounded against my chest. I didn't like going in the orchard. This was where I'd found Keegan hanging from a bent old oak on the lower boundary, just beyond the gate where the orchard met the woods. Dad cut the oak down before they left Briarwood, but the ghost of that tree still loomed over the orchard.

An image flashed in front of my eyes – a figure hanging from a gnarled branch, her face all blotchy, her eyes glass. Blonde hair trailing over the rope. Kelly following where Keegan had led.

I shook the image away as I ducked down the next row, calling Kelly's name. *You're just scaring yourself. Surely Kelly wouldn't...*

But she'd attempted suicide only a week ago. There were no coincidences in magic, and Briarwood was the most magical place there was. I picked up my pace, crossing into the next row and peering between the towering plum and citrus trees.

"Kelly!"

"Over here."

The voice was so faint I wasn't sure I'd heard it or it was just my imagination. But at least it was a voice. I jogged down the next row of apple trees. Kelly came into view, starfished on the ground in front of an enormous plum tree, her mouth stained red from the fruit. A trail of pips led across the grass. She pulled herself up and rubbed her eyes.

"Hey," I slid in beside her. "What you doing out here?"

"It's pretty," Kelly said. She pulled a wide-brimmed yellow hat lower across her face, and sighed.

I waited. I knew that if you waited long enough, usually a person would start talking. That's how I always smoked Rowan out.

It didn't take Kelly long. One thing I knew about her was that she loved to talk. "Maeve hates me."

I wanted to say she didn't, but Maeve had said those exact words to me, and I wasn't going to lie. "You may not realise it now, but her hating you is actually a good thing."

"How could it possibly be a good thing?" Kelly sniffed.

"Hate is just the other side of love. If Maeve didn't love you, she'd be indifferent. Instead, everything you said cut her deep because it came from you. And so she said some things that cut you, because they came from her."

"Gee, you're soooo good at this cheering up thing." Kelly stared at the sky – a brilliant blue cloudless day, one of those rare English Summer days that we should've been spending at the beach or on the footy field, not solving existential crises in the middle of a pile of ripened plums. "I guess I messed up real bad, huh?"

"Nothing that can't be fixed."

"I never should have said what I said. But she was lying to me again. I wanted her to see that she could trust me with her secrets. That's why I snuck into the library when I heard you all moving around this morning. I just wanted her to see that I could deal with all the witchcraft stuff."

"So you know everything now."

She laughed. "I already knew, Corbin. I saw that cult ritual thing you guys were all involved in at Avebury. And there's the little fact that last night you carried in a woman who looked an awful lot like Maeve, which makes no sense since Maeve's an orphan with no family."

"She does have family. She has you."

"It's not the same to her," Kelly sniffed again. "Maeve never belonged with us. She never *tried* to belong."

"You can't force a person to believe in something. Better for her to be the way she is than for her to pretend to be a Christian when in her heart she doesn't believe."

"She took everything for granted that our parents gave her." Kelly picked up a plum and tossed it hard, so it splattered open against the grass. "And they just kept on giving and giving and giving. She got everything, and because I was the real child and the good Christian, I got nothing."

Right then. We'd hit on the crux of the issue – good old fashioned sibling rivalry. To Maeve, Kelly would always be the treasured one because she shared something with her parents Maeve never could – their blood, and their faith. But to Kelly, Maeve was the special one because she was the miracle baby with the super smarts. She was the one who was going to escape their small town and have an amazing life. And now, she was the one with the magical powers and the castle in her name, and the parent who'd come back from the dead.

I understood. Bloody hell how I understood. Keegan got all my parents' attention, between the doctors and the specialists and one fancy tutors. And then, when he died, all his sins were forgotten. He became the perfect son because he was the one who lost his chance to redeem himself. It was just this belief thing again – They believed he'd turn into the perfect son, and so he became the perfect son. I missed Keegan, and I loved him, and I hated him all at once.

I thought about saying all that, but this wasn't about me. It was about Kelly.

"You're eighteen soon," I tried, instead. "You're practically adult. You don't have to define yourself by your parents' standards, or Maeve's standards. You get to decide what you believe and how you want your life to turn out. I think you know that already – that's why you came here with the world's most insane rucksack."

Kelly laughed.

"I know what the Bible says about witchcraft. Revelations was pretty specific with the cowardly, the unbelieving, the vile, the murderers, the sexually immoral, those who practice magic arts, the idolaters, and all people who talk at the cinema will be consigned to the fiery lake of burning sulfur. But I figured if you're still here after everything you heard today, you're choosing to make a more liberal interpretation."

Kelly tossed another plum. "I'm freaked out. I mean, *witches*. The bible is full of people like Saul who died because he consulted mediums instead of trusting the Lord. Messing with the occult is a bad idea. Demons are real, you know."

"Oh, I know." I picked up a plum and tossed it, loving the satisfying splat as it exploded across the grass. "I'm a witch, too."

"But you're a guy."

"Magic isn't a gendered trait. All of us at Briarwood are witches. Does that make you feel any different about us?"

Kelly's eyes widened. "Even Arthur?"

I nodded. "He's a fire witch. You should see him toast marshmallows."

Kelly snorted.

"What are you thinking right now?"

She didn't look at me. "I'm thinking that this is scary as hell. I'm thinking that God has sent me here to test me. I just wish I knew what the test was. I'm thinking that if Arthur's a fire witch, then he might have had something to do with my Uncle's house burning down. And I guess I'm thinking...that Maeve's my sister, and I'm supposed to love her no matter what, even if she is cavorting with the devil."

"You're an amazing woman, Kelly Crawford." I patted her shoulder. She looked up at me then, and her lopsided smile told me she still wasn't sure. "I think if your parents were alive, they'd say exactly the same thing. Maeve says they fought about religion a lot, but they always supported her. She's not perfect. She should have given you more credit and she should've respected your beliefs more. But she's Maeve and she doesn't think like that." I laughed. "You should've seen how skeptical she was when she first saw us wield magic and we told her what she was. I think it would be easier to convince her the earth was flat."

"That's saying something. You should hear her rant about flat earthers." Kelly laughed. "You love her, don't you?"

Her question came as a shock. I knew what Maeve would want me to say. But as Kelly's eyes bore into mine I knew that she'd see through the lie anyway. I sighed. "I love her very much."

"But she's with Arthur, and he's your friend."

I nodded. Both of those statements were technically true. "Love doesn't always obey the rules. That's why so many people believe the rules are bullshit."

"Flynn said something weird to me once, back in London at that tower." Kelly chewed on her lower lip. "He was making up these silly history facts, and he said the monarchy of England practiced polyamory. He was asking me all about it, as if he really cared about my answer."

My pulse sped up. "Don't pay any attention to Flynn. He loves stirring up shite."

"I said that being with more than one person was an abhorrence against God."

"Do you believe that?"

She laughed. "My parents are dead. My science nerd sister is practicing satanic witchcraft, and her mother's come back from the dead. I don't know what I believe anymore."

"It's okay to not know. It doesn't make you a bad Christian, or a bad person."

Kelly glanced up at the tower. "Seeing Maeve here with all of you guys…she belongs here. I know that, even though all this witchcraft stuff is scary and I don't understand what's going on. I don't want to deprive her of it. I guess I just wish she felt she belonged with me."

"I'm sure she does."

Kelly shook her head. "I always tried to include her. I invited her to hang out with my friends, even though no one liked her. She'd come to parties with me and then hide in the corner with a book. I'd drag her to Bible Study class so she'd have something to do, but she'd just get into arguments with the Pastor about evolution."

I laughed. "I can imagine."

"She was always going to leave." Kelly stared down at the plum she clasped in her hands. "Ever since I could remember she's been talking about MIT and what her life would be like when she finally escaped Coopersville. It's hard being a sister to someone like her, knowing she'd choose the stars over you."

Kelly squeezed her fingers. Plum juice dribbled between them, staining the front of her dress. I thought about our recent visit to Oxford, how Maeve's eyes had lit up as she'd explored those learned halls. How at home she'd looked there, because a fancy university like that was her destiny. I understood what Kelly meant, and after talking to her I thought I understood something about Kelly that might never have occurred to Maeve before—

"What are you two doing out here?"

I jumped. Maeve stood at the end of the row, her hands folded over her dress – a summery one Flynn had brought her in Avebury, covered with a pattern of twisting vines. It looked like an old woodcut, and I half expected to see the faces of fae peeking out from between the vines.

"Talking," Kelly snarled, her voice instantly turning hostile. "Or am I not allowed to talk to anyone else now?"

Maeve sighed. "I didn't say that. I came to find you, because I wanted to explain all the things you heard this morning. There's stuff you need to know so you can stay safe...unless Corbin's already answered all your questions."

Her gaze flicked to mine. I could see she'd been crying. I wanted to run to her and wrap her in my arms, but I knew it was more important she and Kelly talk and figure this out. I shook my head.

"Unlike everyone else around here, I can actually have a conversation with someone that doesn't revolve around you," Kelly shot back. "What do you *want*, Maeve?"

"I thought *we* could talk, like we used to..." Maeve trailed off.

"That's rich. You've barely talked to me since I got to England, but now that I know your secret you want to pretend to be the perfect big sister. Fuck off."

Maeve winced at Kelly's words. In all the time she'd been with us in England, I'd never once heard Kelly swear. The words sounded strange on her lips, like she wasn't sure how to form the syllables. "I didn't mean to hurt you. You weren't talking to me, either, if you recall."

No Maeve, no no. That's not how you make things better.

Kelly stood. "I'll be gone soon, so you won't have to worry about keeping up the lies."

"Kelly," Maeve stepped forward. "Don't do this. There's fae out there who are preparing something truly evil. They might come after Jane because of Connor. They might come after you because you're my sister. You'll be safer if you're here and we can protect you—"

Kelly bent her arm back, her face twisting into an ugly snarl. Before I realised what she was doing, she'd hurled the plum at Maeve. "I don't want to be protected by you. God will protect me from demons and magic. Go back to your witchcraft and your sinful adulterous relationships. There's no place for me here anymore. As soon as Connor wakes up, I'm leaving with Jane."

"Kelly—" Maeve rushed forward, plum juice dribbling down her cheek. But Kelly had already disappeared between the trees.

I opened my arms. Maeve dropped to her knees and toppled into them. Sticky plum juice trickled down her cheek, mingling with her tears so it had this weird sweet and salty taste by the time it rolled over my lips.

I rubbed circles on her back. "It's gonna be okay," I whispered.

She nuzzled into my neck, the tears drying on her cheeks. I could practically feel the wheels in her head turning, wondering what I might've said to Kelly, if I'd told her something that made things worse. My suspicions were confirmed when she sat back, her eyes focused and a little bit pissed. "What did she say to you?"

"We were just talking, Maeve."

"About me."

I gave her a nervous smile, and held out a plum to her. "No, about the plum harvest."

"You heard what she said to me. She hates me." Maeve waved a hand, rejecting my fruity offering. It made sense, given the sticky red juice now drying on her chin. "I don't want to talk about her anymore."

"Okay." I grinned, waiting.

Maeve lasted a full three-and-a-half seconds before she blurted out, "What did she say about me?"

Maeve and Kelly, not that much different.

This time, I wasn't playing the game. Maeve needed to see what was going on with Kelly, and I thought I might know a way to get her there. "What do you think's going to happen after we stop the fae?" I asked.

"Don't change the subject."

"I thought you said you didn't want to talk about her anymore?"

Maeve gave an exasperated sigh. "Corbin, just tell me what she said about me."

"Answer the question and I'll explain."

She shrugged. "I don't know about the future. I've been busy trying to stop everything falling apart to think about it. I guess we'll carry on with our lives here."

"So we're going to stay at Briarwood and do what?"

"I don't know! Read books, eat scones, drink tea, watch Arthur beat Flynn to a pulp."

I smiled at that. Arthur beating Flynn was definitely a thing that would happen. "So you don't still have your acceptance letter for MIT sitting on your desk upstairs?"

She looked away. "I'm not thinking about that now."

"Really? Because it feels like something we *should* think about." I touched my finger to her chin, pushing lightly to turn her back to face me. Her hazel eyes swam with liquid sadness. "They won't keep that position open for you forever. It's your dream, Maeve. You have to go."

"And what about Oxford?" she shot back. "I saw the way you looked when we were there, how much you loved the history of the place and debating all those esoteric facts with your dad. You know you could get in, easily. You're wasting your talents re-reading all the books in the Briarwood library."

My face grew hot. *Bloody hell, why'd she have to bring that up?* "Oxford's not in my future. I can't leave Briarwood, Maeve. I can't *ever* do that. I made a mistake many years ago, and that mistake binds me to this castle. As long as these walls still stand, I have to be here – a last defence against the fae. The castle needs me, and Flynn and Arthur and Blake and Rowan need me... especially Rowan. I won't abandon my post the way my parents did. But you... you're different. You're going to *space*. You're going to have a amazing life."

Maeve's mouth set in a line, her eyes flashing with determination. "Not without you, I'm not. We're bound together, the six of us. Briarwood is my home now, and you guys are my family. I'm not running off as soon as the immediate threat is gone."

"That's not what I want," I sighed. "I love you, Maeve. I don't want you to be stuck here just because I'm stuck here."

"You're not stuck here, but I don't know how to make you see that. If you don't leave, then I can't leave." Fresh tears sprung in her eyes. "I'm the High Priestess. I'm responsible."

Was she crying because she was sad for me, or crying because she'd just realised what her oath meant she would give up?

I shook my head. "You can be the High Priestess and an astronaut. I mean, it's never been done before, but I bet we can make it work. You've been waiting for MIT your whole life. I don't want to trap you here beside me. Kelly doesn't want that either, even though it might not seem like it."

"Corbin, where's this come from? What's MIT got to do with Kelly?"

"Come on, Maeve. You *know*."

She threw up her hands. "I don't know."

"Kelly is jealous of you."

Maeve narrowed her eyes. "She's not."

"She is."

Her laugh raked bitterly against her lips. "Not likely. Kelly's the bubbly, popular, social one. She's the pretty one who always says the right thing. There's no way she'd be jealous of nerdy, dorky, friendless me."

"High school doesn't last forever. All her life Kelly's been counting down the years and months and days until that MIT letter came in the mail, until you got your ticket out of Coopersville. All this time she's been listening to how you couldn't wait to leave so you could start your life for real."

"Yeah. So?"

"So, did you ever think that maybe she felt like she was living in the shadow of your future? That your life with her was just your way of passing time until your real life began? What were Kelly's plans for post-high school before your parents died? Did she even plan to leave Coopersville?"

"She..." Maeve looked uncertain. "Of course she could leave. She can do anything she wants. She did leave!"

"Did she really? Or did she just come here to live in your shadow again?"

Maeve's lips pursed. "You're saying all this is *my* fault. Kelly can go around saying horrible things about me and that's fine because she's jealous of me since apparently my life has been sunshine and rainbows and not a fucking disaster where everyone I love dies or just randomly turns up inside paintings!"

"I'm saying that Kelly feels as though she's been living in your shadow, and as long as she's here at Briarwood, she's going to feel that way. And you keeping secrets from her – however well-intentioned – isn't helping."

Maeve stood up, shoving my hands off her. "I'm *trying* to keep her safe. I took her on a trip all around England. Hell, I *extorted money* off her uncle and burned his house down just so she could have a new life. Everything I've done has been for her. Well, I'm not doing it any more. I'm done with her. I know you want to solve everyone's problems and make us kiss and make up, Corbin, but this is one fight that you should stay way the hell away from."

"Maeve, that's not what I'm saying at all—"

Too late. She'd stormed off, taking my heart with her.

NINE: MAEVE

I slammed the kitchen door so hard it split the wooden lintel. Rowan jumped so high he knocked the chopping board off the counter, spraying perfectly-square-cut salad ingredients across the flagstone floor.

"Maeve." He dropped to the ground, not looking at me as he scrambled after a rolling tomato. "You scared me."

"I'm looking for Kelly," I growled.

Rowan's bottom lip trembled. Corbin burst through the door behind me. "I think you should calm down first—"

"So Flynn can practically punch a guy on the street and we buy him a pint, but if I'm upset, it must be because I'm hysterical?" I stormed toward the hall. "Kelly came in a few minutes ago. Where did she go?"

"In the-the-the Great Hall," Rowan stuttered. "But Maeve, I wouldn't go in there—"

"Why not? It's where we keep the fainting couch!" I shoved open the heavy wooden door. "Kelly, I want to talk to you—"

I stopped in my tracks.

Connor sat in his bouncer on the rug, squealing as he

sucked on a rattling giraffe. But it wasn't the giraffe that had me transfixed. Kelly and Jane sat on the couch, their bodies turned toward each other, their hands raised as they caressed each other's faces.

Their lips were locked in a passionate kiss.

CHAPTER NINE

TEN: MAEVE

I stood, frozen, unable to turn away as I watched my kid sister swap saliva with my only female friend in England.

But...I don't...how?

Have I fallen into an alternative universe? Have the fae somehow penetrated the castle and cast a glamour to disorient me?

Is this...how can this be real?

Neither of them noticed me. It was no surprise – what they were doing looked pretty intense, the kind of kiss that stole your breath and left you panting and wet. A kiss that said a hundred things you couldn't say yourself.

Do I say something? Do I back away quietly and let them have their moment?

This is insane. It's not happening. No way is my pentecostal sister swapping saliva with another women. It's just not possible.

I rubbed my eyes, but the sight in front of me didn't change. It was no hallucination.

They *still* hadn't noticed me. *Okay, maybe if I just leave and pretend I never saw anything.* I backed toward the door, still unable to tear my eyes away. *That's it. I'll back out and let them finish and I'll have it out with Kelly later—*

My leg brushed the side of the coffee table, knocking off one of the game controllers. I winced as it clattered across the flagstones.

Jane's eyelids fluttered open. They met mine across the room. She jerked back.

"Ow," Kelly complained, pressing her hand against her mouth. "Yah bit mah lip. Wha—"

Her gaze followed Jane's across the room until she fixed on me. I expected her to give me that disgusted look she'd had on her face every time she saw some new part of my life she didn't approve of, but instead, her eyes widened and her cheeks paled.

"Maeve, it's...It's not what it looks like," she blurted out.

"It looks like the two of you were kissing," I said. "Is that not what happened?"

Kelly glanced at Jane. Neither of them replied.

"Did you trip and fall into each other's lips? Did Jane get stung by some kind of poisonous airborne jellyfish and you had to suck the poison out before she went into anaphylactic shock? Did a fae possess you and force you to act against you will?" I tried to smirk to cover up the fact that was a very real fear right now.

How else could I explain this insane behaviour?

Jane looked at Kelly, as if to say, "you're handling this one like we agreed, right?"

As if they had a plan.

Of course they have a plan, my rational mind screamed. *They've been sneaking around in a relationship behind your back all this time, and they've been talking about you, about how they would handle you, like you're some wild beast who has to be tamed.*

"Maeve, don't be angry," Kelly said, her voice wavering.

"A bit late for that. How long has this been going on?" I said tersely.

"A few days, ever since..." Kelly's eyes blazed, her body

language changing from pleading to recalcitrant. "Since I saw you doing *witchcraft*. Since I realised I didn't know my sister any more."

I glared at Jane. "You swore you wouldn't say anything to her."

"She figured most of it out on her own, Maeve," Jane said. "She was upset. I was angry at you. You asked me to keep her occupied. One thing led to another. I didn't tell her anything. I kissed her instead."

She reached across to Kelly, clasping her hand in a familiar gesture that made red spots appear in front of my eyes.

"So all those shopping trips and private lunches, you two were sneaking around behind my back?" I demanded.

"Like you've been sneaking around with Flynn? With Corbin?" Kelly shot back. "That's called hypocrisy, Maeve. I learned all about it from you, remember? From all those lectures you used to give about the evils of organised religion. 'You don't need religion to be a moral person' you said. I guess Stephen Dawkins didn't have anything that matched Corinthians 6:18 – Flee from sexual immorality. You're the biggest hypocrite of all!"

"That's not true. I—"

But Kelly wasn't listening. "You don't own Jane's affections or feelings. At least she listens to me. At least she hasn't been lying and sneaking around and hurting the people she supposedly loves."

"I was trying to protect you!" I yelled, balling my hands into fists. Fresh, angry tears rolled down my cheeks, mixing with the sticky plum juice. "I was trying to save your precious Christian fucking Corinthians 6:18 sensibilities from finding out that I can do magic and that I'm fucking all five guys!"

Oh shit.

Did I say that?

Jane gasped.

Yup. I said that.

I squeezed my eyes shut so I didn't have to see Kelly's face. I couldn't bear to see what my love looked like when it was turned into disgust.

I spun on my heel, opened my eyes a crack, and fled the room.

Corbin caught me in the hallway. "What happened in there? You were yelling."

Rowan and Arthur stood behind him, looking at me in concern.

"Kelly and Jane is what happened. They were kissing."

Corbin smiled. "Like, sexy kissing? Wow."

Behind him, Arthur grinned.

"You can wipe those stupid looks off your faces. Yes, they were kissing, okay? Like it meant something."

"So your sister has feelings for someone of the same sex? Why is it that a problem for you?" Corbin's eyes looked dangerous.

I gripped his shoulders, digging my fingers in to accentuate my point. "It isn't that. You *know* it isn't that. It's the fact that she didn't tell me. This is a paradigm shift for Kelly. She grew up believing that homosexuality was a sin. And now she's kissing a girl and she didn't even come to me to talk about what that means."

"You mean, the same way you couldn't go to her about us?" Corbin said gently.

I opened my mouth to yell, but all the fight whooshed out of me like a deflating balloon.

Shit. He's right. The way I feel now is exactly how Kelly's been feeling ever since she arrived. And if I add that to what Corbin was saying before, about her being jealous...maybe I get it.

I've been a total bitch, and a hypocrite.

I have to make this right.

I tore myself from Corbin's grasp and raced back to the Great Hall. "Kelly, wait, I'm sorry—"

But there was no one there. Jane and Kelly and Connor were gone.

The front door slammed.

I ran into the entrance hall and threw it open, just in time to see the two of them struggling to drag Kelly's large backpack across the courtyard toward Jane's beaten up old Fiat.

They must have already been packed and ready to leave.

"Kelly, please stop. I didn't mean—"

"I hate you, Maeve!" she yelled after me as they raced under the portcullis. "I never want to see you again."

ELEVEN: ARTHUR

"Woah, *easy!*"

Sweat streaked Maeve's face, plastering her long pink fringe against her skin. She stepped back and swung the sword again, winding the heavy blade through her hands like it was made of cardboard. Metal clashed against metal, and it was all I could do to hold the cross while she forced her weight against my blade.

"Are you sure you don't need a break?" I gritted my teeth as her superior position forced my weapon aside. The tip of her practice sword slid dangerously close to my face.

We disengaged, stepping back and preparing to go again.

"Nope." Maeve raised the blade, her eyes blazing. "Again."

We've been drilling and fighting for two hours. Unlike our other sessions, Maeve had hardly spoken. I knew she was upset about Kelly leaving, but unlike Corbin I didn't have the conversation skills required to get her to open up. She knew that, which is why she'd come to me demanding a sword fighting lesson using metal reenactment swords (with blunted edges).

After all, I was the expert at fighting my way through my pain.

Our swords clashed. This time Maeve's arm spasmed, and my blade slid down hers, hitting her on the shoulder.

"Ow!" She dropped her sword and clutched her collarbone.

"Shit, Maeve. I'm so sorry." I tossed my weapon aside and ran to her. "Let me look."

"It hurts," she moaned. I prised her fingers away from the spot. Her pale skin was already starting to bruise. She winced when I pressed the spot, but it didn't look like anything was broken.

"I really am sorry. Come sit down." I scooped her into my arms and laid down against our favourite apple tree, wrapping my arms around her. She fought me for a few moments, but then she settled against me, resting her head against my chest. My heart beat beneath her, my chest inflating like a balloon.

"It's not your fault," she grumbled.

"Do you want to talk about—"

"Nope." Maeve grabbed my arm. Before I could stop her she'd torn up my sleeve, revealing my cuts. "Tell me about these," she said.

"Don't change the subject," I croaked out, my heart hammering. I didn't want to talk about myself.

"You sound like Corbin. He's already made me talk the Kelly subject to death. I want to think about something else. Namely, why my favourite medieval knight is hurting himself."

"I told you, I cut myself sharpening my sword."

"Bullshit, Arthur."

I shrugged, shuffling away from her so she couldn't feel my heart pounding against my chest. "It's not a big deal."

"As your High Priestess, and your girlfriend who loves you, I'll be the judge of that. Spill it."

"You love me?" Slipped so casually into her scolding, the words threw me. *Your girlfriend who loves you.*

I never had one of those before. Never in my whole life did I imagine that someone like Maeve could feel that way about me.

"Of course I do, you fool. Which is why I want to know what's going on with you."

"You're going to make a big deal out of it, like Corbin does. He thinks it means I'm thinking like Keegan, but it's not that at all."

"What is it, then?" Maeve traced the cut across my skin, running her fingers over the layers of parallel scars.

She loves me. She loves me.

Maybe if she loves me she'll understand.

My chest fluttered with hope.

No, this is stupid. I stared down at my arm. The scars dominated my vision, moving in and out of focus. Looking at them in the light made my stomach squirm. I wanted to turn away, but I didn't want Maeve to think I was weak, that I was ashamed.

Maybe she'll understand. This is who I am. I'm not ashamed. This is a completely normal thing lots of people do.

"Sometimes when I get upset or angry, I'll make a little cut on my skin," I mumble. "The blood reminds me that I'm in control over myself and my body."

Maeve's fingers squeezed my skin. "Oh, Arthur."

"It's not a big deal. It's not a suicide attempt. They're just surface cuts. It's a little nick to remind me that I'm real."

It sounded so stupid when I said it out loud.

Maeve shook her head. "You sound like you're trying to convince yourself."

"Why did you come out here today to swing your sword around? You don't feel in control of the situation with Kelly. So you came out here to assert some control. It's the same thing."

Maeve rubbed her neck. "Yeah, but when I got hurt, it wasn't fun anymore."

I looked up then, into her eyes. They widened into shimmering pools of mottled blue-green, shining with hope and desperation and love…A lump rose in my throat.

She's looking at me, *right inside me. She sees* me.

"Most of your scars are old." Her words came out in a whisper as she brushed her hand over my cuts again. "You haven't cut yourself in a long time. But those two cuts are recent. Why?"

"I did one when I found out about you and the other guys. I wanted to join in, but I couldn't. I did the other one after the church."

"Why?"

"Because all those people died, and I couldn't save them." I slid my arm out of her grip and rested my hand on the hilt of my sword. "I failed, and that failure was impacting my ability to protect you, to be what you needed. One small cut, and that feeling went away."

"So this is me?" Maeve's eyes swam with sadness. Her gaze make my stomach queasy. "I'm making you feel like this?"

"No." I clamped a hand around her arm. "That's not it at all. It's just a thing I do. It's *really* not a big deal. I've never hurt myself."

"Yet." Tears sprung in the corners of her eyes, all that emotion spilling down her cheeks.

I knew what was going on here. I'd been with her in Arizona when she had to sit with Kelly in the hospital after her suicide attempt. She was thinking exactly like Corbin did, that this was me crying out for help. She thought she needed to save me, when really it was the other way around.

"Hey, hey." I wiped the pink streak of hair off her forehead. My chest felt heavy, like some bastard was standing on it in heavy Docs. "Don't be upset. I'm not going to leave you. I'd never dream of leaving you. I just need this sometimes."

Maeve sniffed. "I don't like it, Arthur."

"It's okay. You don't have to. Maybe when this fae thing is over with, I'll go talk to a doctor about it." Unlikely, but if it made her feel better... "Now come on, let's go back to our drills and forget this whole conversation, aye?"

Maeve glanced over at her wooden sword lying in the grass. She shuddered. "I don't think I want to practice any more." She scrambled to her feet. "I think I'll just go back inside, see if Corbin's found anything in his books. Bye Arthur."

"Do you want—"

But she was already running back toward the castle.

I slumped down beneath the tree, staring at the cuts on my wrist, hating myself for telling Maeve about the scars.

I scare her. The woman I love is afraid of me.

The rage inside me flared, the heat against my skin rising to an unbearable temperature. The worst kind of hatred – the kind that turned inward, at myself. *I hurt Maeve.*

My pulse pounded in my ears. I balled my hands into fists, fighting to contain the fire.

"Oh no, you don't," I growled, shoving my hand into my pocket and pulling out my pocket knife. I flipped open the blade. A fleck of sunlight peeking through the apple tree caught the stainless steel.

They don't understand. Warriors bleed. My blood makes me strong.

I placed the knife against my skin, slashing a deep cut over the scars. Red welts flashed into front of my eyes as my bloody trickled down my arm. The stinging pain hit the wall of heat inside me, and the fire fizzled out as my attention focused on the blood.

See? I'm stronger already.

CHAPTER ELEVEN

TWELVE: MAEVE

"Kelly, it's me, again. I know you're not picking up because you don't want to talk to me, and I get it. I'm just wanted to say I'm sorry. I've been thinking a lot about what you said and you're right. I've been treating you like crap, and I want to fix it. I want to fix us. I'm going to give you some space but I really want you to call me back so we can talk. Please. I love you."

I hung up. In my lap, Obelix yawned leisurely, and rolled over, presenting his fat belly for rubbing. I obliged him with shaking fingers while I dialed Jane's number. She answered after two rings.

"Jane, I—"

"Fuck off, Maeve." The dial tone buzzed in my ear.

I clicked off the phone and tossed it at the bookshelf. It hit the spine of a tarot-reading guide and bounced on the rug, sliding into a square of moonlight pouring in from the window behind Corbin's desk. Obelix shot me a filthy look and stood up, jumping down and going over to bat the phone with an inquisitive paw.

I glanced up at the moon, noting how only one thin edge

was cut off by the dark of space. Only eight days left until it was full, until the Slaugh could begin their ride across the earth. My skin *itched* to do something, to grab Daigh around the neck and shake him until he called off the attack, or break down the door to Jane's cottage and force Kelly to listen to me.

But there was nothing *to* do but wait, and think, and hope Kelly forgave me.

I slumped down in Corbin's wingback chair, frustration welling up inside me. Corbin had gone to the Great Hall for supper, leaving behind a stack of magic books with post-its sticking out of every second page. He'd been working all day while I'd been arguing with Kelly and interrupting lesbian action and finding out the horrible truth about Arthur's cuts.

Arthur. Oh God. What is going on in that thick skull of his?

When I told him I loved him, he looked shocked, completely flummoxed. Not like Flynn – not scared of his feelings – but completely unable to believe the someone was capable of loving him. And he was hurting himself...

My beautiful warrior was slashing at his own skin so he'd be strong for all of us. That was messed up.

I needed to find a way to help him, to make him see how much he was loved, how he was enough just as he was, and that it wasn't his responsibility to save the world on his own.

Aline moved across the room, the hems of the jeans she'd borrowed from Rowan dragging along the rug. She picked up the phone from under Obelix's feet and turned it over in her hands. "Remarkable thing. What does this button do?"

"That opens up the browser."

"Browser? Like the internet? You have the internet on your *phone?*"

"Yeah." I took the phone off her and scrolled through the apps so she could see. "This little baby does all sorts of amazing things. This one lets me make text messages and share photos with my friends. This is the NASA app that sends me pretty pictures from space. This is an interactive star chart. It's *not* for astrology," I confirmed as I saw her face light up. "This one claims to turn my phone into a geiger counter but it's not accurate enough to be useful. And this one lets me make video calls."

"Just like Star Trek?" Aline's eyes widened.

"Um...yeah. I guess so."

"If you have this phone, then why can't you just video call your sister – by Astarte, it's really weird to think of you as having a sister – and let her see how sorry you are."

"I tried that, but she won't pick up. You just swore by Astarte?"

"She's an ancient goddess of sensual pleasure, fertility, war, and destruction. Love and hatred, violence and sex were her *forte*. She was worshipped in the Eastern Mediterranean before the Greeks co-opted her, took away her warlike attributes, and transformed her into Aphrodite. She's my patron goddess."

Interesting. I thought of my own cursing, which I must've learned from the Crawfords. "I never thought about it before, but I always say 'Oh god' or 'What the hell?' or 'God help me.' The guys say 'bloody hell' or 'you wanker!' and I like those much better."

Aline grinned. "Why choose a patriarchal god as your own, when our faith has a matriarchy that extends back to the earliest human civilisations?"

Because he means a lot to my parents, I thought about saying. I didn't have any more attachment to a female goddess than I did their god. I didn't consider magic a faith. It was science...sort of. Basic Newtonian laws applied – every action having an equal and opposite reaction, etc.

Gods and goddesses meddling in the lives of humans were just make-believe. But I was too fascinated by the discussion to argue with Aline. It was a welcome distraction from worrying about Kelly. "What goddess would be good for me?"

Aline thought for a moment. "Athena."

"Who's she?"

"An ancient Greek goddess – she protects the city of Athens, which is named after her. She's also the goddess of philosophy, which is as close as I can get to a science goddess because the two things were one and the same until very recently in history. She helps many heroes to complete their quests," Aline raised her eyebrow toward the door, indicating the guys. "And she also presides over war strategy, but she much prefers to use wisdom to settle disputes."

I nodded. "Okay, I like that. Athena it is."

"You can pray to her for guidance on what to do about your sister," Aline moved toward the desk. "I'll show you a spell you can use—"

"No thanks. I don't pray."

"Our gods are not the same as the Christian—"

"Yes they are." I jabbed my finger at the ceiling. "Magic I can believe in, but there ain't no one up there answering prayers."

"Maybe you just never asked the right question."

Jeez. I rolled my eyes. *This subject is now closed forever.* "What about you, then? No motherly advice for me about dealing with Kelly?"

"You're kidding, right? I'm only a few years older than you, and I was your mother for exactly three-and-a-half hours before I pretended to stab you and sent you off to an orphanage. I'm not exactly a fountain of maternal wisdom."

"Good point." I leaned back in the chair and crossed my legs on top of the desk, shoving off the top volume with my toes. Obelix yowled as a corner landed on his tail. He streaked from the room, padding off down the hall to find his favourite people – Arthur or Rowan. "I just wish I could do something. Between this and waiting for the Slaugh to strike, my stomach's a big bag of knots."

"We *can* do something," she said.

"If you're suggesting we speak to Daigh, the answer's still no."

"You've had a day of hunting through the books. Do you have a better idea?"

"Not yet. But we don't know that we can't use the belief power to stop the Slaugh."

"I guess we don't," she said brightly. But her voice said it all. "You could ask Daigh about his DNA."

"What?"

"You want to know if the binding is real, if you really have inherited power from Daigh. If you throw your DNA science in his face, maybe threaten to tell this Liah fairy about it, he'll *beg* you to let him take the test."

I opened my mouth to tell her that was a stupid idea, but I couldn't make the words come. I imagined Daigh's face when I told him he couldn't possibly be my father. How his entire plan centred around my ruling beside him. I saw what Aline saw – the chance to crush his ego and open up the weakness we needed.

Plus, if he gave me DNA, I could actually get it tested. I'd know once and for all what scientifically tied me to him.

"Fine." I sighed. "We'll try it. I'll do anything at this point."

Aline's eyes danced. "You mean it?"

"I do." I slid my legs off the desk, knocking several heavy books onto the floor, and called out into the hall. "Guys, could you come to the library?"

From the room at the end of the hall, Arthur let out a loud moan. "I was trying to sleep."

"Well, wake up. I've got to talk to you all about something important."

Footsteps clattered from every corner of the house, and one by one the guys filtered in – Corbin and Rowan carried plates of savoury scones (half-eaten, I couldn't help but notice), and Arthur, wearing boxer shorts with pictures of Asterisk characters on them and his bloodlust hoodie.

"Where are Flynn and Blake?" I asked.

Rowan offered Aline the plate. She swiped three scones, looked thoughtful for a moment, and then grabbed a forth. "They went to the village about an hour ago, with that trailer."

"What trailer?"

"Flynn came inside at dinner and there was a car with a covered trailer in outside his studio, like a horse float. I saw it from the salad garden." Rowan shrugged. "I assumed you knew."

I groaned. Only this morning we'd discussed *not* going off with hairbrained schemes on our own, and now Flynn and Blake had disappeared with a mystery trailer. Those two together was guaranteed to equal trouble. What the hell had they got themselves into now?

CHAPTER TWELVE

THIRTEEN: FLYNN

"Shift it over there!" I snapped as a large metal spike bore down on my foot.

"Where?" Blake lifted the other end of the statue, digging the corrugated iron into my toes.

"Not there. Pull it left!"

"That *is* left!"

"The other left, you eejit."

We managed to wobble our way out of the trailer and drag the statue across the darkened town green. In the center was a low concrete plinth that had once housed a statue of Winston Churchill. Two years back, some local gobshites lobbed one of the arms off and the Council had taken the statue away while they argued over how much it would cost to repair. Along with other local artists, I submitted a proposal that we should replace the arm with a steampunk-style machine-gun. My proposal went unacknowledged. Wankers.

This Irishman's getting the last laugh.

It took us three tries to heft my statue on top of the plinth. I checked the feet. *Perfect.* I'd lined the bolts up exactly.

I went back to the rental car for my concrete drill. Blake held the statue while I drilled in the bolts. The sound shook the night and my heart pounded. Any moment I expected someone to run over and stop us.

One. Two. Three. Four. I tossed down the drill and reached under the balaclava to wipe away a sheen of sweat from my forehead. The greene was surrounded by shops, none of which were open after 9PM except the pub. And tonight was the monthly folk night, so the place would be busier than a confessional after Saint Paddy's Day. If anyone heard the drilling, they'd be too legless to investigate.

Maybe we really will get away with this.

I fitted and tightened the bolts, then stood back to admire the statue.

"She looks wicked fierce," Blake grinned.

She did indeed. I'd made the witch a flowing dress out of sheets of corrugated iron. Hair made from wire brushes stuck out from all angles from beneath her pointed gramophone hat. She held her broom in one hand, the other raised – a garden fork with the tines bent and curled into a claw. On the end of the broom sat a tiny, long-necked cat, with its paw raised in a similar menacing gesture.

Some of my finest work, and it wasn't even the half of what I had planned. "Now for the *pièce de résistance*," I slapped my hand on the witch's shoulder and retreated into my feelings, the way Candice taught me to do. I forced myself to think of all the times people had looked at me weird, told me I didn't belong, all the times my uncle belted me around the head for being too much of a gas, all the times I'd wished I could be normal...and I poured that into the metal.

You want to believe we're witches. You want to believe we're the ones who are going to marmalise you. Have at it!

I poured more magic into the statue, focusing on the bolts,

on holding them true, making them impenetrable by any human tool that might try to remove them.

The metal heated up as Blake's spirit magic shot through mine, mingling together to create a vacuum for belief. When it was so powerful it tugged at my power, pulling more into itself than I'd been willing to give, I stepped back. Blake sealed it with the spell we'd memorised from the grimoire, so that the statue would collect the belief rising from the village and store it like a giant belief grain silo.

I might have let go of a tiny piece of my own magic, but as the village woke up in the morning and saw this statue on the greene – having appeared from nowhere in the dark of night and held down with bolts that couldn't be broken – we'd have all the magic we could possibly need.

I tugged my balaclava down over my face. My heart raced. I was just like Banksy, sneaking around in the dead of night, planting controversial art in a public space like a subversive curator. Only, unlike Banksy, the village would be interacting with this piece in a way they'd never believed possible.

We stood back to admire our work. The edges of the statue shimmered with magic. The air hummed with anticipation as our spell called belief to itself. I grinned back. "And to think, I was just going to stick it beside the letterbox."

"I'm impressed," Blake whistled. "This is a plan so tricksy it's worthy of the fae—"

"Hey, what you think you're doing?"

Footsteps thudded on the grass behind us. I didn't even turn around, just ran like mad toward the car. No time to shut the doors on the trailer or pick up my concrete drill. Luckily, I'd left the engine running. I dived into the driver's seat and shoved my foot on the pedal. Blake grabbed the back of the seat and yanked his legs inside the car just as I swung away from the curb.

Something thudded against the bonnet as we skidded around the corner. "Satanic scum!" a deep voice roared after me.

"Eat my bollocks!" I yelled back as I sped toward Briarwood, leaving a trail of sizzling belief in my wake.

FOURTEEN: BLAKE

"You did *what?*" Maeve screeched.

She raced out from under the portcullis and battered my window before Flynn had even stopped the car. Behind her, the other guys crowded around, inspecting the trailer with a mixture of bemusement (Corbin), worry (Rowan), blankness (Aline) and mistrust (Arthur).

Maeve however, was *furious*. The vein above her eyes stuck out like a Seelie at a metal-detecting convention.

"Hi Princess," I waved at her through the window.

"Get out of that damn car and tell me *what you did.*"

She was beautiful when she was mad, all slanted eyes and flushed skin and that fearsome *glower*...when she looked like that, all fury and sex, I could see the resemblance between to Daigh.

Not that I'd ever tell her that.

I grinned to myself. *Or maybe I should...*

"Blake!" Maeve's fist on the window startled me out of my daydream. "Tell me *right now.*"

"We erected Flynn's witch statue in the middle of the village greene." I swept an annoying black curl out of my eye. I left the window up for now, and the door locked. It seemed safer. Apparently Flynn had a death wish, because he jumped out of the car and raced around to her.

"What in Athena's name possessed you to do that?"

"Come on, Einstein. You've got to admit it's *brilliant*." Flynn's eyes danced. He grabbed Maeve's arms and turned her in a circle. She squealed as he dipped her down, holding her across the back then extending his hand out so she could twirl underneath it. She didn't twirl, of course. She yanked her hand out of Flynn's grasp and folded her arms again. *Fine.* I shoved the door open, grabbed Flynn's hand, held it up and twirled beneath it, pointing my toes in an elegant flourish. I finished by planting a wet kiss on his cheek.

"Ack, you wanker!" Flynn doubled over, gagging and wiping spittle over his face.

"Flynn!" Maeve yelled.

He scratched his head. "Sorry, Ma. You should be thanking us, though. We just created a big ole' vessel to collect all the belief in the village. After everyone wakes up and discovers a mysterious witch sculpture smack in the middle of the green that can't be removed no matter how hard they try, their belief is going to leap up like a dog with a stick up his arse."

"And what were you planning to do with all this belief?"

"Slay the fae, of course."

Maeve's face twisted. "Okay, so that is actually brilliant."

"It was all my idea," I said quickly.

"It was not!" Flynn shot back.

"Guys!" Maeve yelled. "I don't actually care. Did we not have a conversation this very morning about *not* going off on your own with hair-brained ideas?"

Flynn's smile froze on his face.

"It was all his hairy idea." I patted Flynn's shoulder, giving him a shove toward Maeve.

Flynn opened his mouth to protest, but Maeve plastered her hand over his mouth. "And would not you agree that this stunt is the very definition of a hair-brained idea?"

Flynn dropped to his knees in front of Maeve, his hands clasped in front of him, batting his dark eyelashes. "Please forgive me, O majestic one, O Maeve of the boundless bosom and arse that won't quit, O ravishing goddess, O mighty quoter of scientific theories and slayer of Arthur's mead. You're such a stunner, never in my life have I beheld a finer or more shapely behind—"

"Oi, keep it in your pants while the mother's around," Corbin said.

"Don't mind me, sweetie. I'm taking notes," Aline grinned.

"—of such heavenly and beddable physique, of the brain so big it's a wonder it fits in your noggin, would you find it in your big beautiful heart to forgive this wee poor bugger for his infraction…"

Maeve's face remained stern, but her shoulders shook. "Flynn…" she moaned, then a laugh burst out of her.

Flynn grinned and hugged her legs. "You laughed. I'm off the hook."

"Get up, you fool." Maeve lifted him to his feet. He threw his arms around her, nearly knocking her over.

"And me?" I lifted an eyebrow.

"Of course you." Maeve leaned in and kissed my cheek. "I know you weren't the brains behind this one. Or lack of brains, as it were. This is all Flynn. Come inside."

I slid my arm around Meave's waist as we trudged back through the inner courtyard into the Great Hall. Her sweet, spicy smell invaded me, mixing with the excitement of the car chase and the residual spirit magic that hummed in my veins. I'd given more than I'd meant to that statue, and my reserves were running low. Maeve hadn't been in the frame of mind for bedroom shenanigans since we'd returned, and I knew she'd last topped up from Rowan and Corbin in London, so she was good. I, on the other hand, was getting a serious case of blue balls (Flynn's phrase – descriptive and accurate). And although he was attractive enough with his floppy red hair and stupid grin, Flynn didn't want to 'cross-swords' (another delightful phrase I picked up) with me, and I didn't think the others would appreciate my advances.

Also, I missed Maeve.

I hadn't had a chance to be alone with her since the empty office in London, the day I realised she felt more deeply for the others than she did for me. The rejection prickled at the back of my neck. I knew she'd told Corbin and Flynn she loved them, and I'm guessing Arthur, too, since she managed to tempt him into the harem. She probably told Rowan about her feelings for him that night she stayed away with him and Corbin and they came back reeking of each other.

Maybe she didn't want me anymore, now that they'd figured out they were hot for each other? Maybe she had no use for me any more?

I hoped not. Even though Maeve didn't love me, I didn't want to leave her. She meant everything to me. As much as I tried not to think of Briarwood as home – because I knew I'd have to leave one day – the feeling of returning to the castle after all those nights away was like the first spoonful of hot curry. I was kind of attached to the decadent human inventions of beds and whiskey and indoor plumbing.

Briarwood and Maeve had wormed their way under my skin.

And the guys...

I hated to admit it, but I kind of liked them. Ever since Corbin made the stop at my parents' old house, they'd all been treating me differently – Arthur threw insults at me every chance he had, and Rowan still barely made eye contact, but it the insults and the silence were good-natured, comfortable. I was one of them now.

One of them.

Don't get used to it, the voice in my head reminded me. *Maeve's in charge – you're going to last as long as she needs your spirit magic, and then you'll be out of the harem, and her life.*

If you even survive the Slaugh.

We crowded into the Great Hall. The guys flopped down on to their favourite chairs. I went to sit on the bean bag I usually chose, but Maeve tugged me toward the couch.

"Sit with me," she whispered.

I grinned. Yeah, like I could refuse Maeve with her heavy eyes and cheeks still pink from her anger at Flynn. I dropped down into the soft couch. Maeve slid in beside me, wrapping my arm around her shoulders. My fingers grazed the side of her breast, and all thoughts of leaving and the Slough flew out of my head.

"We were about to have a meeting before you showed up," Arthur said from behind the bar. He opened a bottle of mead and poured out a goblet for everyone except Rowan.

"About our fae situation, I suppose." I accepted the goblet he held out to me and gulped back the sweet alcohol. By Oberon, that stuff was good. The fae had honey wine, but like all their food, I'd never been able to drink it. At least Arthur's gave me a decent buzz before I threw up.

"Thanks to the Banksy wannabes here, we have a growing vessel of power to use against them." Maeve sipped her drink. "But we still don't know if it's enough to stop the Slaugh. I think it's time we spoke to Daigh."

"You do?" That was a surprise. It wasn't like Maeve to change her mind once she'd made it up, especially not when she believed she had logic on her side.

"I do," Maeve yawned. "But not now. It's late, and I'm about done with emotional beatings today. Bedtime, all of you. We'll summon the evil fairy in the morning."

The evil fairy. She had that right, and she barely knew the half of it. I wasn't really sure I wanted to see Daigh again.

A sliver of hope worked its way into my chest. *Liah.* Maybe I'd be able to get Daigh to talk about her. Even though she was trying to destroy all humans, I still wanted to know she was okay. At the church, Liah could have shot me right through the chest, but she hesitated. She told Daigh it was so that Maeve wouldn't hate him, but that seemed weak reasoning to me considering Maeve had already made her feelings about Daigh clear.

Maybe she lied. Maybe there was still a way I could reach Liah.

The group split up. Rowan went to the kitchen for his night-time tea ritual. Aline trailed after him, holding up the hem of Rowan's jeans so they wouldn't slide down her narrow hips. Flynn and Corbin both gave Maeve long, lingering kisses. Arthur came over and held his arms out. "You want a lift up to bed?"

She shook her head, squeezing my knee, her fingers sliding along my thigh and springing my cock to life. "Not tonight. It's weird while Aline is here, you know."

"Sure." He wrapped his arms around her, pressing his lips to the top of her head. "Sweet dreams, Einstein."

Arthur's words sent a shiver through Maeve's body, but her face said it wasn't one of pleasure. Of course, *the dream.* She'd been having it more and more often.

A sickening thought occured to me as I watched her slink up the stairs. What if she'd snuck in a nap while I was busy being a guerilla artist? What if she'd seen whose body was on the sixth stake, and she knew I'd been hiding it from her?

What if that's why she'd been keeping me close by her tonight?

I sprinted up the stairs after Maeve.

"Hey Princess," I whispered in her ear. "You fancy some company tonight?"

She smiled. "I was hoping you'd be keen, but fair warning – I'm probably just going to fall asleep in your armpit."

I lifted my arm to display my pit proudly. "Consider it yours."

We climbed to the first floor together, my heart racing. In her bathroom under the curving staircase up to her bedroom, Maeve handed a bulk pack of toothbrushes. "Choose one," she insisted, elbowing me as she spat her own paste in the sink. "I want you guys to have what you need in here."

I took a black one and pulled it to my lips. Maeve watched me smear the paste across my teeth, rubbing it in the with brush the way Flynn had taught me. "That's way too much pressure. Try in circles, like this." She demonstrated and I copied. "Atta boy. Now you don't have that fae magic keeping you young and handsome, you want to keep this up twice a day, or you'll end up at the dentist. And if you think Daigh's torture was bad, wait until you need a root canal."

I rubbed my chin, where a few days of stubble had grown in. "At least I haven't slit my throat shaving yet. There were a few hairy moments there, haha."

"Urgh, that's a horrible pun. You've been spending too much time with Flynn." Maeve ran her hand along my jaw, her touch searing my skin. "I like it like this. It makes look dangerous."

"I *am* dangerous."

She flicked my ear. "Of course you are, cutie. Just don't go full-on beard. I don't think Arthur could handle the competition."

After we finished our teeth, we climbed the stairs to her bedroom. I inspected the stack of science books on Maeve's desk while she tossed her clothes off and settled into her bed. She rubbed her eyes. "I keep having the dream," she said. "The one you showed me, with Briarwood in ruins and the burned bodies and the six stakes."

"I know." I pulled off my own clothes and slid in beside her, copping a look at her naked body, sinuous and languid, ripe for picking.

"You know?"

"When you have it, Princess, so do I."

"Shit, I'm sorry." Maeve lifted her neck so I could slide my arm behind her head. Her warm body relaxed against mine. "I don't want you to have to live through that nightmare ever again."

"I'm not afraid of a dream."

"I am. I'm afraid it's really some kind of premonition, even though I don't believe in premonitions. I'm afraid that I'm looking at the deaths of five people I love most in the world, and I can't do anything to stop them. I'm afraid that I can't see the sixth body on the stakes. Have you seen it?" Her eyes narrowed. "Can you tell me who it is?"

The five people I love most in the world. My heart pounded. *Did she... include me in that list?*

Should I tell her? Maeve had made it clear she didn't want any secrets. I was pretty sure this counted as a secret. By keeping it I was disobeying her direct orders.

The sixth stake flashed in front of my eyes, and I set my resolve. *She's strong, but she's not strong enough for this. It will break her. Arthur and Corbin will protect her body. I have to protect her mind.*

I shook my head. "It doesn't matter. Either you're right and it's not a premonition, or it is a premonition, in which case there's no way we can change it."

She stroked my cheek. "Do you think it's some kind of fae magic planted by Daigh?"

"No. Dream magic is human magic. Faeries don't dream. Daigh used to ask me about my dreams. Sometimes he would paint what I described – vicious landscapes, tortured souls, weird creatures that didn't exist in the fae realm. He took great interest in this dream when I first had it. He painted the stakes, and the briar, and the castle in the background, exactly as I described."

"When did you first have it?"

"It was recent, maybe ninety days ago—"

"But those are fae days. How long was your solar day?"

"Huh?"

"The time it takes the planet the fae realm exists on to make one full rotation so the sun appears in the same position in the sky. Or the sidereal day, that's how long it takes for—" Maeve shook her head. "No, ignore that. It's too complicated. Here on Earth, our solar day is 24 hours, as you might have noticed. But since the fae realm is in another entire part of the multiverse, your day could be longer or shorter."

"It was longer, I think. We didn't measure it in hours and seconds, so I don't really know."

"Could you draw some of the constellations you saw at night? Maybe we could figure out where it's located, if it's even in this galaxy or—" Maeve smiled. "Sorry, I got distracted. What happened when you told Daigh about the dream?"

"Daigh was super interested in it, as I knew he would be. It was what made him start all the preparations to come to earth. It was why he sent Kalen to spy on the coven and follow Corbin to America, where he found out you were still alive."

Maeve paled. "Have the others been dreaming it, too?"

"I doubt it, otherwise they'd have mentioned it. Unlike your sexy dreams, I think this one is just for you and me."

"And Daigh."

"Hey, don't hate me – it was all in aid of getting to you," I stroked her cheek. "I had a cunning plan – I give the dream to Daigh, he decides now is the perfect time to launch an attack on the human realm. He starts testing the limits of the gateway so he can get his hands on the sacrifice. I prove myself in battle and seize my chance to escape."

"Great plan," Maeve said sarcastically. "Considering you'd basically be escaping into a land about to be overtaken by the Slaugh."

"I figured if the Briarwood coven had defeated him once, they'd be able to do is again," I shrugged. "I didn't count on the remarkable incompetence of its current ranks, present company excepted."

She punched me in the arm. "What about Daigh's plans for us?"

My heart stuttered. She was referring to Daigh's belief that I would wed her, and we'd produce strong spirit children he could mould to his will.

"I wasn't keen on it, but that was before I saw you in person," I said, one of the few honest things I'd ever spoken. "When you leapt over that wall to protect Flynn, I knew I dealing with a truly exceptional witch."

Maeve wrapped her arms around me. "Tell me a story."

"A story?"

"About the fae realm. I want to know what it's like."

"You saw it."

"I mean, what it's like to live there."

"What do you want to know?"

"Tell me about Daigh. Tell me something that might make me not hate him."

I cast my mind back, searching for a memory that fit her criteria. It was hard, not least because Daigh could be easy to hate. Fae have different ethics to humans, and I knew many of the stories I found hilarious would disturb her.

Finally, something came back to me. I couldn't believe I'd forgotten it. "Daigh had a celebration every year, on the day he took me from my parents. He called it my 'fae-day', because it was the day I became a fae in his eyes. As soon as the sun rose he placed a crown of rowan on my head, and I didn't have to remove it until sunrise the following day. It meant—"

"How long was your sunrise?"

I raised an eyebrow. "Is this your way of dragging me into a conversation about time in the fae realm? Because I can see through such an easy trick."

She laughed and threw up her arms. The blanket tugged down, revealing the swell of her naked breasts, and it was everything I could do not to grab her and devour her. "You got me."

I fluffed her hair instead. "You're ridiculous."

"And you're amazing." Maeve wrapped her arm around my neck and pressed her lips to mine.

Amazing.

I drew back from her kiss, breathing hard.

Amazing was not the word to describe me.

I continued with the story. "So when I wore this crown, the princes had to do what I said, no questions, no exceptions. God it was fun. I was drunk on my power."

"What did you do?"

"For the first ten years of my life, I did the revenge thing. I got the wankers back for all the things they'd done to me throughout the year. I made Airell burn his twin brother's face. I forced Pwyll to eat processed human food and he threw up for *six days.*" I grinned at the memory. "It was fun."

"The Unseelie have a weird idea of fun."

I grinned. "I didn't have a Flynn for entertainment."

"Is there more to this story, because so far I'm not really seeing this good side of Daigh."

"There's more. After a few years, the revenge thing got boring. So I decided I'd have an actual party instead – a party that included everything I liked about the fae realm. Daigh sent fae to the human realm specifically to bring me back some cake, and had his chefs prepare a fae version that they could stomach. I invited the Seelie fairies to our revel, and for hours we drank and danced and Liah and I laughed and talked and there was no violence or ill will. I declared that all grudges must be healed and all debts were wiped. Daigh thought it was such a great idea, he made the party an annual tradition – once a year all fae had to clean their slates. I always admired that decision."

Maeve nodded. "Okay, yeah. That's nice. It doesn't make up for kidnapping you and torturing you and forcing you to live in the fae realm without human contact and killing my parents and conniving to annihilate the entire human race, but it's *nice*."

I snorted. "You have very high expectations, Princess. Expecting your leaders to be kind and non-genocidal."

She laughed, her breasts bouncing against my chest. "In a weird way, we're almost like siblings, you know? In another life, in another multiverse, we might've grown up together, like Kelly and I. I might've called you my brother, instead of my boyfriend."

My heart leapt into my throat. "I'm your boyfriend?"

"Sure. That's what you call a boy who you're committed to. What do you call them in the fae realm?"

I grinned. "Lunch."

She punched my arm again. "Flynn has been a bad influence on you."

"Our father would be so proud."

"Don't say that. It's gross." She laughed bitterly. "Now that I know about the binding, I'm even sure about it anymore."

My heart hammered against my chest. "Not sure you love me?"

Maeve kissed me again. Spirit magic sparked from her lips, dancing over my tongue. "I'm more sure of that than anything. What I mean is, I don't see how I can possibly be Daigh's daughter. Not *scientifically*. Aline slept with Robert while Daigh was inhabiting his mind. So to her, Daigh's my dad. But that's not how genetics works." She broke off into a long explanation of chromosomes and DNA sequencing, which I didn't pay much attention to because I was distracted by her taste and her breasts swelling against me.

"You keep talking, Princess." I nibbled along her neck. "Don't mind me."

"Blake, this is serious. Do you have any idea if compelling someone would mean they retain some of your chromosomes..."

Maeve's words trailed away as I kissed a line across her collarbone. She leaned back against the sheets, pulling me on top of her. My lips crushed hers, my whole body lighting up as our spirit magic clashed against each other, rolling together inside of us and becoming one.

"I thought we were going to sleep," Maeve whispered, her mouth curling up into an enchanting smile.

"When beautiful women rub their naked breasts against me, sleep is the last thing on my mind."

More sparkling kissed landed on my lips. The room, the castle, the world faded away, unimportant against Maeve's unrelenting need.

She slid back, tucking a curl of black hair behind my ear.

"Did you know the last time we were alone together was in the bathroom at Jane's cottage?"

"I had so many evil plans for you in that bathroom."

"Oh yeah, like what?"

I grinned, cupping her breast in my hand and pinching the nipple lightly. Maeve sucked a breath in through her teeth. "Let's just say those candles along Jane's windowsill would've looked great dribbled across your skin."

"You'll have to show me some time," she grinned, pinning my lips with hers.

"I've been waiting for this for so long." I moaned, my hands roaming over her body.

"Me too." She wrapped her legs around my torso, pulling me closer as she arched up to kiss me.

Maeve's skin sizzled and melted under my touch. I swirled one finger around her nipple, extracting a deep rumble of pleasure from her. With the other hand, I pulled her against me, mashing our bodies together as if I might be able to crawl inside her. We went to that clinic in London a few days ago, and I didn't quite understand why but Flynn told me it meant we didn't have to use condoms anymore. My cock twitched with anticipation as Maeve moaned against my lips.

As we kissed, the spirit magic fluttered inside me, flaring through my whole body and breaking out of my palms. Maeve and I swapped magic as our bodies writhed against each other. Her tongue wound around mine and I nearly fucking lost control of my magic completely.

I drew away, kissing a trail down her body while I tried to wrestle back control. I didn't want to accidentally fall into her head, not without her permission. Maeve moaned as my tongue circled around her nipple. I licked and sucked as she arched beneath me.

My hands drew down...down...between her legs, cupping

her mound. My desire flared as Maeve's wetness touched my fingers. I slid a finger between her folds and drew it up, swirling it around her clit, pressing it against her until she came undone beneath me.

"Blake," Maeve moaned as her body shuddered with the remnants of her orgasm. I teased her entrance with the head of my cock. She tried to push her hips up to force me inside her, but I pulled back. She groaned in protest.

"If I really am part-fae, you must show me how the fae shag," Maeve whispered.

"As you wish, Princess." She yelped as I flipped her over. I grabbed her hips, yanking her on to her knees. "Brace yourself against the headboard."

Maeve wrapped her fingers over the top of the heavy wooden frame, bending her torso up toward me. She watched over her shoulder as I slid the tip of my cock down her back, resting it between her ass cheeks, admiring the shimmering quality of her pale skin. My cock twitched with irritation. It wanted to be inside her.

"Don't tease me, fairy." Maeve cooed, rocking her his back and tightening her cheeks around my cock. "I won't...oooooh."

I entered her with one stiff thrust. Nothing had ever felt as warm or sweet. Maeve Moore – skin on skin. Her scent swirled around me, pushing me closer to the edge.

Maeve's back curled as her hips shoved back against mine, driving me deeper still. The bedframe slammed against the wall as I pounded her body, binding myself to her with every shuddering thrust.

I reached around between her legs and touched the tip of my finger to her clit, so that every thrust would drive that sensitive bud into it. Maeve moaned her approval as she slammed her her hips back against me.

A wicked idea occurred to me and I withdrew my finger.

Maeve groaned in protest, but her groan turned to yelps of plea-sure as I opened the palm of my hand and sent a wave of spirit magic straight into her clit, exactly the way Flynn had taught me with the statue. I fed her all the shimmering heat she'd called up from inside me, until she slithered and slid down the bed.

"Blake...I...I can't..." Maeve gasped.

Her orgasm tore through her, and she thrashed wildly. I grabbed her waist and held her tight, bracing myself against the headboard so she didn't throw us both off the bed. Her walls closed around my cock, squeezing me until stars appeared in front of my eyes.

I lost control, and slipped through my magic, falling into Maeve's head. Her thoughts slammed into me – a wave of sensation and emotion rolling over me, plunging me deeper into her mind. With every fibre of her being, she reached out to me, her spirit humming as her sinapses converged on a single thought.

Love.

Waves of the stuff rolled off her and flowed into me, a whirlwind of warmth and comfort and devotion and passion and affection swirled through me, touching every part of me, inside and out. No one had ever expressed feelings like that about me, *about me.* I didn't even know it was possible to feel that deep about another person. But Maeve did. She loved with her whole heart and head and everything in between. She loved so hard her spirit magic loved, too.

She loves me. She loves me.

My whole body exploded. My own orgasm dragged me out of Maeve's mind and back into my own, which had turned to a mushy ball of primordial ooze. My limbs slackened and I collapsed against Maeve's body, sweat rolling down my back the last waves of warm pleasure coursed through my veins.

I was so spent, I couldn't even *feel* my cock any more. It was probably just as well, because my head was a complete mess of feelings.

Maeve rolled over, holding my head against her shoulder, her fingers rubbing lazy circles on my shoulder. "I'm yours," she whispered as her eyes fluttered closed.

She was mine. I'd never had anything I could call my own before, especially not a person as incredible as Maeve.

Mine.

And I was totally and utterly hers.

CHAPTER FOURTEEN

FIFTEEN: ROWAN

Aline's eyes burned into my back as I moved around the kitchen, filling the kettle and setting it on the element to boil. Every inch of my skin crawled with the sensation something terrible would happen if I didn't make the tea perfectly and count the Great Hall windows. Aline was watching me and I needed to do this on my own and why was she watching me?

My hand trembled as I reached for the cups. I dropped one on the flagstones. Ceramic sherds skidded in all directions.

"Oh, dear. Let me help." Aline hurried to my side.

"I've got it." I tried to grab the broom, but it fell through my fingers and clattered on the floor. Aline grabbed it up and swept the broken cup into a pile beside the counter.

"Do I make you uncomfortable, Rowan?"

"Yes." I stared at the mess on the ground. "Don't take it personally. Everything makes me uncomfortable."

"Did you want to ask me something?"

I nodded.

"About your parents?"

I nodded again.

"They died in the ritual." Aline closed her eyes. "I didn't know that before. So many died that night. So many children grew up without their parents. I'm sorry if I upset you earlier."

"Please...I really want to know."

"It's funny." Aline picked up two blueberries from the container on the counter and popped them in her mouth. "All those years I was trapped, I thought so much about Maeve but I never once considered what had happened to everyone else and what a mess we might've left behind for all of you. They were witches, of course. Dana was a water user, and Charles was earth. I'm not surprised you inherited his power along with his good looks."

"I don't even know what they looked like. There aren't any pictures."

"That doesn't make sense. Dana was always snapping away with a camera. She had hundreds of photographs of the coven in an album – our rituals, our parties, everything."

"Corbin's parents threw out a lot of stuff, after—" I caught myself. It wasn't right to tell Aline about Keegan. That wasn't my story.

Aline frowned. 'That's not right! They shouldn't be erasing our history like that! I can't believe Andrew would do that– he was always going on about how we'd know so much more about the mistakes of the past if we didn't burn so many books."

"He changed his mind."

"I don't believe it!" Aline glanced out the window into the garden. "Where does he live now? I'll ask him."

"No!" After Corbin's dad made such an effort to reach out to his son through Maeve, I didn't want Aline showing up at their house and scaring them away again. "I mean, he's not involved in Briarwood anymore."

"Now I really don't believe you. Andrew promised me he'd

watch over Maeve. He'd never back down from a promise like that."

"He has his reasons. That's why we're all here. We watch over Maeve now." The blueberries dripped juice trails down her fingers. I counted the trails as they twisted around her arm. "Can you please just tell me about my parents?"

Aline grinned, her own questions forgotten as she swept her hand in a dramatic flourish. She relished her role as the sage oracle from the past. "Let's see... I grew up here at Briarwood, as you know. Your mother Dana lived in Pembroke Hall just over the hills – on the other side of Holly Avenue, near Raynard Hall. We played together while our mothers did magical things. I didn't like Dana's mother much – she was always scolding me for having rumpled clothes and unruly hair. Sometimes Dana snuck over to Briarwood at night – I'd leave the kitchen gate unlatched and she'd sneak up the secret staircase and we'd stay up all night wishing on the stars." Aline popped five more blueberries into her mouth. "Sometimes when Dana came in the night, I could tell she'd been crying. She always had bruises on her arms and legs. She said she bruised easily. I believed her at the time."

My hands gripped the edge of the table so hard the knuckles turned white. I hated to think the violence that had been a daily part of my life had been my mother's reality, too. *I guess the apple doesn't fall far from the tree.*

"Dana's parents sent her away to a fancy boarding school. I stayed here at Briarwood. I didn't want to do anything except practice magic every day and build the new coven. My parents had a few friends they trusted – but it wasn't the coven I imagined; a true melding of kindred souls. My mother couldn't wait to hand it over to me so they could retire to the Maldives. When I was 21 my parents moved out and I moved all my friends in." She threw up her hands. "It was free love – any witch or weirdo was welcome. People in the village called us a commune. Rumours flew around about the orgies and naked dancing going on at the castle. I loved every moment of it."

I bet you did.

"By this time, Dana had started her law degree at Cambridge. She came back for the uni holidays, but her mother forbid her to see me. Imagine her precious daughter friends with the local witch? The scandal! But I guess Dana had enough. She appeared on the kitchen doorstep one night, her face bruised, a battered suitcase in her arms and a fierce look in her eyes. She moved in to my bedroom and we stayed up all night wishing on the stars and she told me she wanted to leave her law degree and Cambridge and join the Briarwood coven.

"The very next day she went down to Cambridge to submit her withdrawal paperwork, and returned a week later with a towering man with bright eyes and a kind smile. She introduced him as George, her husband. They'd married in secret that weekend. Your mother was so timid, I never expected it of her, especially not without consulting her parents first. Especially because..." Aline's face had that apologetic look people get when they know they're about to say something you won't want to hear.

Because my grandparents wouldn't approve, I filled in for her inside my head. My legs trembled. *Because my father was black.*

Because no one in your family is ever good enough.

My shoulders tightened as the anxiety clawed its way up my spine, lodging itself in my windpipe. My breathing slowed. I scrabbled at the edge of the counter for something to hold me upright.

No, not now. *I need to hear this. I need to know.*

If you dig into the past, you'll kill everyone you care about. Maeve will suffer if you don't stop asking about your parents. Corbin will die if you keep pushing. You think everyone accepts your rela-

tionship with Corbin, but you're wrong. You'll be ostracised from Briarwood. You'll have to go back to the streets...

I whipped my head up, fixing my gaze behind Aline's ear at my jars of herbs and spell mixtures lined up on the shelf. *One... two...three...*

The counting brought some relief. The tension in my shoulders loosened. The room no longer spun. But it wasn't enough, wasn't nearly enough.

If Aline noticed anything unusual about my behaviour, she didn't say anything. "Dana may have been quiet, but she was stubborn," she continued. "She and George moved into the room Corbin has now. She flaunted their marriage in the village, holding his hand and flashing her ring around so word got back to their mother. They had a screaming fight at the farmer's market one day. Dana made a pipe burst in the public bathroom, so a huge spray of filthy water hit her mother right in the face." She hooted at the memory. "I'd never seen Dana use her magic like that before, never out of anger. But her parents were cruel. They deserved it!"

...ten, eleven, twelve...

My nails dragged against the granite countertop. I strained to hear Aline's words over the screaming voice in my head.

"Your father was the chef here at Briarwood. More than that, he was the life of every single party. He was always joking and telling ludicrious stories at the top of his lungs. Anyone living in the castle spent most of their day in here, throwing whatever they could find into his pots when his back was turned and gorging themselves on all his amazing baking."

*...sixteen, seventeen, eighteen...*I gasped for air. My chest ached, a heavy weight squeezing my lungs.

"Dana had tremendous skill as a healer. She trained as a midwife and delivered every one of the babies at Briarwood, including Maeve. She acted as a midwife for any woman who needed her around the shire, even if they couldn't pay. I often woke in the night to the sounds of her collecting her things and driving off into the night. She used to sell soaps she made and infused with herbs from the garden at the castle gift shop. A cosmetic company in London wanted to give her forty grand for her soap recipe, but she refused because they couldn't assure her they wouldn't test on animals. I can't believe you didn't know any of this already."

"How would I know?" I choked out. *Twenty-two, twenty-three, twenty-four...*

"Surely your grandparents looked after you after your parents died? They knew all about your mother's powers, even though they never appreciated her."

"They told me I had no family left," I whispered. "That's why I went into the foster system."

Aline clamped her hands over her mouth. "That doesn't make any sense. I don't know about George's parents – I think they live on a Caribbean island somewhere, but Melanie and Richard definitely still lived at Pembroke Hall and they had so much money." Her face lit up. "I know. We could visit them. I bet they're still up at that hall, or another relative is. Melanie would've returned as a zombie before she let anyone else get their hands on their estate."

Visit them?

My legs jerked beneath me. My whole life I'd dealt with the crushing pain of being completely alone in the world. The care workers had never been able to locate my family. All this time, they had been right around the corner, living it up in a huge mansion while I drowned in my own private hell.

Did they even care when my mother died? Did they even know? They *had* to know. Why didn't they want to help her son? Why didn't they want me?

Because no one wants you. Your grandparents let you live in hell rather than take you in.

My vision blurred. The jars on the shelf melded together, impossible to count. I wrenched my neck around, searching for the comfort of something else to count.

Another thought occurred to me. *Corbin must know.* He'd worked his way back through the coven history and done extensive research to find me. The first place he'd have looked was my grandparents.

He knew they lived nearby – practically next door – and he never told me.

Because he doesn't care about you. He doesn't want you to have family. He wants you to be his broken boy, the brother he could save.

I swivelled my head back to the shelves, but the jars and bottles blurred into one. I grabbed for the counter, but my fingers slid off. Aline leaned toward me, her mouth moving.

"Help," I whispered, but it was pointless. No one could help me. No one wanted me.

My legs gave out from underneath me. My head hit something hard. Bright lights spun in front of my eyes, and a dark shadow loomed over me, before it consumed the light entirely, and the world turned black.

CHAPTER FIFTEEN

SIXTEEN: CORBIN

"Someone help me!"

Aline's shrill voice echoed up the staircase. I tossed down the book I'd been reading, threw open the door to my bedroom, and fled down the hall.

What now? Is it the fae?

Aline's yells came from the kitchen. I yanked open the secret passage and vaulted down the staircase in one leap. My naked torso slammed against the wall at the bottom. I shoved the secret door open and rushed into the room. The sight that greeted me turned my blood cold.

No.

Aline knelt in the middle of the kitchen floor, surrounded by squished blueberries and broken ceramics. Rowan slumped against the counter, blood gushing down his face. His eyes glassy, his body unmoving.

Rowan.

"He's not breathing!" Aline wailed, cupping his cheek.

I sprinted across the kitchen. Sharp sherds dug into the pads of my feet, but I didn't slow down. I grabbed Rowan and laid him down on his back. His legs and arms stuck straight out.

I tipped his head back to open his airway and checked for breath. Aline was right. Rowan had stopped breathing.

"Call an ambulance," I called out as I checked his pulse. He had one, which was a good sign, but it was faint and thready. With Rowan's intense anxiety and the medication he was in, a fall like this could throw his body into shutdown. I needed to try and get more blood and oxygen around his body.

I moved to his chest, placing the heel of my hand on the centre of his chest. With my other hand on top, I interlocked my fingers the way my mother had taught me when the twins were born. With my shoulders over Rowan's chest, I pushed down, feeling his sternum rock beneath me. I counted out the beats in my head. *One, two, three, four, five...*

After thirty compressions, I tipped Rowan's head back again, pinching his nose and blowing precious air into his lungs. *One, two... c'mon Rowan...*

He didn't respond. His glassy eyes stared back at me, cold and lifeless.

My whole chest collapsed. Air leaked from the hole where my heart had been. *Don't think about it. Don't panic. You have to focus for Rowan.*

Rowan would have found it funny that I was the one counting.

No, don't think in the past tense. Rowan is not going to die. Rowan is not Keegan. Rowan has a future.

"You hear that, Rowan?" I muttered as I compressed his chest again. "You're not dying on me, you bastard."

After another thirty, I tipped his head back, pinched his nostrils, and breathed into his mouth. A mouth that only hours before I'd kissed goodnight. Lips that had pressed against mine with such intensity and now hung slack against his teeth.

One...two...

Rowan coughed. My heart leapt. I lifted him up as his entire body convulsed, kicking sherds across the room. I clung to him as he sucked in breath after glorious breath, resting my head in his shoulder, my lips against his neck.

"Don't ever do that to me again," I whispered against his skin.

For the first time since I'd seen him lying there, I became aware we weren't alone. "God, Rowan." Maeve wrapped her arms around him, burying her head in his dreadlocks. I embraced them both, my body trembling with the knowledge of just how close I'd come to losing him. His fingers tightened around my bicep, then dropped.

"Ambulance?" I asked. Now that Rowan was okay, I didn't want them showing up and asking questions.

Aline shook her head. "I don't know how to work the... mobile phone thingie. I'm sorry."

"It's fine. What happened?" I glared at Aline.

"I don't know! We were just talking, and he was leaning forward. I thought he was just really interested, but then he seemed to be holding himself upright. Next thing I know his head bounced off the counter and he was on the floor and he wasn't breathing."

"Even if the fall knocked him out, he shouldn't have stopped breathing! His heartbeat shouldn't have been so weak."

"He was having trouble breathing right before he fell." Aline glanced at her arm, which was stained blue from berry juice. "Maybe he had an allergic reaction?"

"He's not allergic to anything except stress. My guess is you frightened him into a panic attack and he fainted before he hit the counter. Now he's probably got a concussion. What were you talking about?" I demanded.

"About the coven! He wanted to know about his parents."

My heart pounded in my ears. *No, don't let him find out about—*

Rowan's nails dug into my arm. "My grandparents..." he choked out.

Shit.

Rowan's eyes watered. "You never told me," he murmured.

"Because I was afraid that this would happen," I smoothed his hair.

"You should have said something. I had to find out...like this."

"Corbin, what's going on?" Maeve asked.

"My grandparents...they lived right *down the road*." Rowan's voice rose with every word. "They might still live there. Corbin knew, and he never told me. You never told me."

His words cut through me like Arthur's sword slicing through a Far Darrig. I glared at Aline. This was *her* fault. She should never have said anything, or let him get this upset. Couldn't she see how much her words stressed him out?

"I knew if I told you then you'd want to see them," I say quietly. "They're not nice people. I always meant to tell you, but you made so much progress and I didn't want you to relapse, and then months turned into years and it was too late."

"That was my decision to make."

"I know you. I know what you can deal with, and seeing them would've broken you. I visited them. They were the first people I tried when I went looking for you. Melanie told me she'd paid some officials a lot of money to make it appear as if you had no family. They changed your name, your story, every-thing." Rowan's face froze in an expression of such raw pain. My throat closed up. "They told me if you ever showed up on their estate, they'd have you shot."

"I needed to see them, Corbin. I needed to know for myself, but you kept me from my family."

"We're your family. I thought that was obvious. They don't give a shit about you and I do. I've done everything for you. I helped you get sober. I got you through the diagnosis and treatment. I protected you—"

"You can't protect people by sticking them in a bubble." Rowan's eyes flashed. His body shook so hard his foot tapped against the counter.

"Is that what I did?" my voice boomed. "I stuck you in a cage like an animal at the zoo? Or did I wipe your fucking arse and clean up your puke and hold you down so you wouldn't throw yourself out a fucking window?"

Flynn winced. I was being a total dick. I didn't want to yell at Rowan, but I couldn't stop. My hands trembled.

I nearly lost him. And it was like...it was like he was blaming me.

I already blamed myself enough for both of us.

"I'm not Keegan!" Rowan shouted. He kicked out with his leg, splintering the wooden cupboard door.

The crack of the wood breaking froze the room. Rowan never raised his voice, never yelled, never lashed out in anger. Not since he got sober. I sucked in slow, laboured breaths, trying to force some calm into my shattered body. Maeve's eyes bore into mine.

Rowan lowered his voice, choking out the words. "Corbin, you know I'm not Keegan."

The room spun. Rowan's face morphed into Keegan's – the last time I'd seen him alive, when he'd railed on me in a mighty rage, screaming that I was the favourite, that I wanted him out of the way so I could have Mum and Dad all to myself. And then he climbed up a tree with a length of rope and...and...

"I know you're not Keegan," I whispered.

"You don't, you don't! You think that I'm mad at you, so I'm going to off myself just to spite you. You think everything that's wrong with me could be cured if you just *work hard enough*. You think if you save enough of us, you'll be absolved of your guilt.

But it's not enough, Corbin. It's never going to be enough, because you have nothing to be guilty about. Your brother died because he was unhappy and his head was messed up. It had nothing to do with you. You think *I'm* the one who's messed up like that, but you're not going to get any peace until you forgive yourself."

My knees cracked as they hit the tiles. I barely registered the pain shooting up my thigh. A deep growl rose from my chest, tearing out of my mouth before I could stop it. Blake stepped back, his expression terrified.

Rowan shuffled forward. He rested a hand on my knee, and his eyes watered with shared pain. "It's not your fault," he whispered. "None of it is your fault."

"I..."

Nope, I couldn't do it. I couldn't dislodge the guilt.

It *was* my fault.

I'd been so angry at Keegan for all the things I said, I yelled back instead of trying to help him. I didn't go after him when he ran. I spent the last hours of his life hating him, and he needed me.

I nearly lost Rowan.

"Corbin, listen to us. I can see it in your face – you're still blaming yourself for all of this." Maeve knelt beside us both, her hands resting on our shoulders. "The same goes for both of you. The things that happened to you aren't your fault, either, Rowan. Being sick isn't a punishment. It's just a shitty thing that happened."

"I made those choices," Rowan's lips brushed against my shoulder. Wet tears rolled down my shoulder. "Corbin can't blame himself for my punishments."

"It's *not a punishment.*" Maeve glared at him. "You need to believe that."

"I don't really know what's going on here," Aline piped up. "But I think I know something that will help."

I glared at her, stroking Rowan's back. "It would help if you didn't fuck things up. If you hadn't said anything to him, none of this would have happened."

Aline winced. Maeve's hand grazed my other shoulder. "You can't blame her for this. She doesn't know the whole history of what's happened. But she's not going to fix it, either."

"I can!" Aline insisted. "Some of the witches in my coven came to Briarwood to escape bad situations, too. Rowan's mother Dana was one. Flynn, your mother was another. The first ritual we performed together was a cleansing. I wanted people to feel like when they entered the walls of this castle, who they were and where they came from and what they've done didn't matter. They get to start over. That what you all need – to cast off the past and cleanse yourselves of the negative energy that's corrupting your minds."

"Does it work?" Blake's voice dripped with interest.

"It did. Dana was able to make peace with what her parents did. Flynn's mother Bronagh stopped letting her hatred of the man who raped her corrupt her spirit." Aline pressed her hands to her heart. "I discovered the capacity to think of people other than myself."

I glanced around the room. Arthur leaned against the door-frame, naked from the waist up, his tattoos crossing his skin like the scars he covered with his hand. Flynn sat on the bottom step of the secret passage, his head in his hands, the weight of his own pain crushing the humanity out of him. Blake dangled his legs over the edge of the counter, his usual smirk invisible behind an unreadable expression, Rowan in my arms, his body trembling under the weight of his newest trauma.

And Maeve...kneeling beside me, her cheek pressed against my shoulder, that incredulous look on her face she got whenever someone talked about astrology or woo woo magic. I could practically *see* the cogs whirring in her head. "That sounds dumb. It's a fallacious attribution of the relationship between thoughts and deeds. Dancing around in a circle makes people *feel* like they've done something to help themselves, so they attribute any improvement to the magic when it's really the chemical changes in their brain. What Corbin and Rowan both need is to see a properly qualified psychologist."

Aline's face fell. "How can you say that? You're a *witch*."

"Transference of energy makes sense in a scientific concept, even if the rituals are hokey Gandalf the Grey stuff. But as the High Priestess, it's irresponsible of me to advocate chanting and crystals to cure real and deep psychological pain."

Maeve's jaw set in the firm line that meant she wasn't going to be argued with. But behind the incredulous stare, her own pain lingered. The grief of what she'd lost and the weight of protecting Kelly and Jane and Connor and the world that bowed her shoulders hovered over her like a cloud of darkness. Even though she didn't believe it would, she hoped this cleansing would help.

Maeve, Arthur, Flynn, Blake, and Rowan all carried burdens. They needed to be free.

I didn't want to let go of Keegan. I didn't know who I was without the shadow of him looming over me. But they all needed this, even if Maeve was intent on denying it. And I would do whatever they needed. I would keep them safe.

"I think we should do it," I said.

"Corbin, I'm in charge here," Maeve sighed.

"I know, and you still make the final decision. This is my opinion – I think there's no harm in trying the cleansing. Even if you're completely right and it does nothing except act like a magical placebo, if it helps, then that's a good thing. If it doesn't, then the only thing we've lost is a few hours sleep."

"I needed that sleep," Maeve grumbled.

"I agree with Corbin," Arthur said, rubbing his arm at the elbow. "It's worth a shot."

"It's not like you to be afraid of a little casual relationship, Princess," Blake grinned.

Rowan looked up, his eyes wide, his face streaked with dried blood and tears. "I want to do it."

"Fine!" Maeve threw up her arms. "The science nerd over-ruled by the hippie witches. Let's do this."

Unlike most rituals that were better performed outside in the open air, Aline insisted the cleansing take place inside Briar-wood. "These are the walls that protect us, after all. They can be symbolic as well."

We gathered in the Great Hall, pushing the furniture to the edges while Aline helped Rowan prepare another potion. This one was green and looked even less appetizing than the sleeping draught we'd used to dream travel to the fae realm – if that was even possible. Rowan brought in the tray of shot glasses and placed them on the small coffee table in the centre of the room.

"You have no idea how much I wish those were filed with whiskey." Flynn made a face that mirrored the way my stomach felt.

Aline arranged several objects on the table – sage incense sticks, a thick pillar candle on a large silver tray, a goblet of water, a ritual blade called an athame, and a small tray of salt. "As soon as Maeve's ready, we can start."

"I'm ready. How do I look?"

I whirled around. Maeve stood on the doorway, dressed in a flowing white dress that set off her dark hair and glittering eyes. The Briarwood pendant hung between her breasts and she held up her hand to show off the matching ring. The pink streak in her fringe reflected against the diadem in the centre of her forehead, giving the glittering stone a pinkish tinge.

"Enchanting." I wrapped her in my arms, kissing the top of her head and breathing in the fresh fruity scent of her shampoo.

"That's a relief, because I feel ridiculous." Maeve yanked up the skirt so I could see a pair of black-and-white striped socks and her boots underneath. "I'm the wicked witch of the west."

"Funny, I've never noticed any warts," I brought my mouth to hers. Our bodies melted together as we shared a deep, lingering kiss.

Another hand slid around my waist, and the familiar rosemary and flour scent of Rowan filled my nostrils as he pressed his body against ours. "Thank you for doing this," he whispered. "Both of you."

Maeve tipped her head to claim his mouth. I wiped his locs off his cheek so I could kiss his midnight skin. His long lashes tangled together as his eyes fluttered shut. Maeve and Flynn had done a decent job patching up the cut on his head, and a small bandage on his hairline was the only reminder of how close we'd come to losing him.

A throat cleared behind us. Aline held up the salt container, her lips in a tight line. "It's already well past midnight. We should get started."

My eyes locked on Aline's face as Maeve slid from our arms and moved across the room. Aline may be a powerful witch freed from a terrible spell, but she was still Maeve's mother. As far as I knew, Maeve hadn't told her we were all her magisters, but she hadn't exactly been keeping it a secret, either. I wondered how Aline would react when she discovered the true extent of her daughter's harem.

Judging by the pursed expression on her face, not great. But we could deal with that later.

Aline handed around the tray with the shot glasses and we all knocked them back. The foul liquid stung my throat and made tears burn in the corners of my eyes. Arthur caught my eye across the circle and screwed his face up, eliciting a choking laugh from Flynn.

Maeve moved to stand at the northern end of the circle, in front of the stone fireplace. The rest of us stood at points around the circle. Aline held up the salt and moved to the outside of the circle, then seemed to change her mind. She stood in front of Maeve, touching her hand to her daughter's cheek as she handed over the salt. "This is your job now."

To Maeve's credit, she didn't flinch from the woman's touch, although her eyes betrayed how uncomfortable she felt. She took the salt and used it to cast the circle, then followed the salt with the lit candle.

At Aline's signal, Arthur lit the incense with a wave of his hand. Smoky sage filled the room.

"Breathe deep of this magical herb," Aline said. "Bring forth the dark memories that taunt you, the shame and guilt that blocks the flow of magical energy and prevents you living in the full light of the Goddess."

It was all a little 'woo-woo' as Maeve would put it, but if it helped the guys, it was worth it.

Rowan stood directly opposite me, between Aline and Arthur, his eyes closed and his hands raised toward the ceiling. A wet trail marked his cheek. I hated that we even had to do this for him. Rowan shouldered the blame for all the pain in his life, and not a single bit of it was his fault. Beside him, Arthur stood with his arms folded, his fingers touching the scars on his arm.

How long had he been cutting again? That drove me wild. I thought he'd got over it.

Yet another person I couldn't save.

Arthur's gaze swivelled around to glare at me. *It's not your fault,* he mouthed at me. I shook my head. This ritual wasn't about me. I didn't need it.

After a few moments of silence, Aline said, "As Corbin moves the sage around the circle, hold out your hand to receive the blessing and say, "With air, I cleanse myself.'"

Happy to do everything I could to help, I held my palm out toward the table and called up the pillar of magic rising inside me. The air between my fingers sizzled as I grabbed it with my mind and twisted, pulling the trails of incense toward me. I breathed in the heady smell, memories of Rowan in the kitchen coursing through my mind. "With air, I cleanse myself," I muttered, for Rowan's benefit. I flicked my hand to shift the flow of incense toward Flynn.

"With air, I cleanse myself," Flynn said, his face unusually serious. Flynn was always hard to read – he never said much that wasn't a joke. But when I'd found him he'd been running away from a life in the Irish mob, and I had a suspicion that humour hid a dark past.

I passed the air around the circle, touching it to each person's skin. Now it was Arthur's turn. He held his hand out in front of him, palm up. His eyes narrowed, and a small ball of fire appeared.

I jumped as a fireball burst to life in front of me. The heat blasted my face. Identical fireballs hovered in front of every other witch in the circle.

I glanced over at Arthur in surprise. He could control that many files simultaneously? He focused on his hand, his gaze even, his beard framing pursed lips. He looked completely calm.

This is the same Arthur that nearly burns down the castle every time he gets agitated? It doesn't compute.

Aline nodded to Blake, who stood between Arthur and me. Blake waved his hand over top of the flame. "With fire, I cleanse myself."

My turn. I swept my hand over the flame, feeling the sharp heat on my palm. "With fire, I cleanse myself."

The air in the room shifted, heavy with the fragrance of sage and the weight of our pain. Magic sizzled in the air around us. For all Maeve's derision of this ritual (and a bit of my own too, I admit) it had raised a cone of magic more powerful than we'd ever managed on our own before. I sniffed the air. Behind the sage was a familiar scent – hyacinth and butterscotch.

My mother's perfume.

That's weird. At first I thought I was having some kind of reaction to the disgusting potion we'd had to drink. But as the smell grew stronger, bringing with it memories of my childhood at Briarwood – baking in the kitchen with Mum, translating books in the library with Dad, building forts in the wood with Keegan.

Flynn was next. He stepped forward and picked up the cup, waving his palm over it so the water curled up into a liquid ribbon that poured through his fingers. "With water, I cleanse myself," he said, and passed the goblet to Aline. Flynn's ribbon of water trailed around her fingers, looping between her bare hands. She passed it on, and the ribbon curled around each of our fingers as we all said the words.

As the cool water slid over my skin, a memory flashed in front of me. Keegan and I camping overnight in the woods for his tenth birthday. We found a little stream trickling down behind the Raynard estate, and followed it until we came to a flat area that was perfect for pitching our tent. Keegan splashed around in the water while I set up the tent and got a fire running. While my back was turned he found a rock the size of his fist and threw it at the back of my head. My vision swam and I passed out, toppling forward and burning my wrist on the fire...

My wrist flared with heat. A thousand needles jabbed into my skin. I yanked my hand out of the water, and the pain stopped.

Don't think about it. This is ridiculous. You haven't thought about that in years.

When the goblet returned to Flynn, he set it down on the table. "Rowan, your turn," Aline said.

At first I didn't think he'd heard her. He didn't move. "Rowan?" I asked.

Rowan blinked. He stepped forward, passing his foot in front of himself as if he expected a giant hole to open in the floor and swallow him. He grabbed the salt off the table and held it out in front of him, pinching the granules between his fingers. "With earth, I cleanse myself."

As I watched in awe, beneath his fingers a tiny shoot rose up from the salt, two leaves unfurling and opening up toward the light above.

Rowan passed the salt to Arthur, then to Blake. More tiny shoots sprung up from the white granules and wound around their fingers. Blake passed the dish to me. As I pinched the granules and muttered the words, magic hummed up my arms. Memories slammed into me – me waking up back in my room at the castle with a pounding headache. Dad explaining Keegan had run back to tell him I'd tripped and hurt my head. Keegan led Dad back to where I'd fallen and Dad carried me out of the woods. Keegan stood beside my bed, his wide eyes brimming with guilt and pain. My parents exchanged a troubled glance, as though they knew exactly what had really happened.

"With..." My voice wavered. "With earth, I cleanse myself."

Passing the dish to Flynn caused me physical pain – my arms ached to cradle it. Tears sprung in my eyes. Images of Keegan flashed in front of my eyes – all the violent things he did to me over the years, and to himself. All the sweet moments we'd shared. All the times my parents left me to look after the twins for days or weeks at a time while they took him to another specialist. And always his pale face and limp body swinging from that rope.

I want this stupid ritual to stop, now.

I blinked, trying to force away the memories. Only one more element to go.

Aline indicated that we take hands. I shoved my hands out, trying to keep my shoulders and elbows locked so no one noticed my hands were shaking. Flynn slid his sweaty mitt into mine. Blake squeezed my fingers and turned toward me.

"You okay, mate?"

"Fine," I growled.

"You don't look fine."

"Well, I am." I turned to Maeve. "Your turn."

"With spirit, I cleanse us all," Maeve said, narrowing her eyes.

It's okay. I can handle this. I can—

Heat flared down my arms. The memories rushed on me like a freight train, bowling me over with Keegan's smile, Keegan's laugh, Keegan's eighth birthday where Dad took us both for a ride in a real Spitfire, Keegan's scream, Keegan smashing paintings in the Great Hall. Keegan's body swinging, swinging...

Keegan's face morphed into Rowan's. Rowan, waking up and realising I'd effectively kidnapped him. Rowan smashing a priceless Wedgewood plate. Rowan on his second return from rehab, glassy-eyed and unresponsive. Rowan's gleeful grin when he plunged his hands into freshly turned-over garden beds. Rowan's shy smile when he presented me with his first ever batch of scones – sweet and light and wonderful, just like him.

My legs shook. Nausea welled up in my stomach, pushing against the back of my throat.

"The energies that no longer serve us, leave now," Aline said. "We have carried your presence this far. Now, we release you and ask you to leave."

The nausea hummed inside my head. My lips trembled. I forced my facial muscles to move, to form the words.

"Goddess, fill these bodies with your healing light. Give us the peace we desire so that we may continue our good works."

Light filled my vision, piercing my skull so I wasn't just seeing it, I dwelt in it. My whole body trembled and lurched and convulsed, as something dark and sickening welled up from my stomach and spewed from my mouth.

I slid into the light, and lost myself to the world.

CHAPTER SIXTEEN

SEVENTEEN: MAEVE

"Shit!" Arthur yelled.

My eyes sprang open. The light burning my retinas faded just enough to see Corbin hit the ground hard, his body bouncing as his neck jolted violently. I dropped hands and raced across the circle, battling the light that seared the interior of my skull.

"Corbin?" I knelt at his side, my heart hammering. *Did this stupid ritual hurt him? Is he okay?*

"I'm fine..." He sat up, blinking hard. He rubbed his head. "I think..."

"You're okay, buddy." Arthur slid his thick arms under Corbin and lifted him to his feet. Corbin stood for a moment, then his leg buckled and he slumped against Arthur.

Arthur wasted no time sweeping Corbin's legs out from under him and lifting him off the ground.

"Hey!" Corbin yelled, but he was in no state to protest.

Arthur moved toward the end of the hall. "His bedroom?"

"Mine, if you can manage it. All of you can go there if you want. We're done with magic for tonight."

Behind Arthur, Aline's eyebrows raised. *Screw her.* I was too tired and upset to care what she thought of me and the guys, especially not after her stupid ritual had made Corbin collapse.

That's two of my guys Aline's hurt with her presence already. I thought back to what she'd said about how that ritual had made her less selfish. *If this is her being less selfish, I'd hate to know what she was like before.*

"Maeve, wait...I should explain—" Aline's voice rose an octave.

"We'll talk in the morning," I snapped, my words harsher than I'd intended. Aline winced and stepped back. I followed Arthur up the stairs, the rest of the guys trailing after me.

In my bedroom, Arthur flopped Corbin down on the bed. "You alright, mate?"

Corbin rubbed his head. "Yeah, I don't know what happened. I got this rush of memories and then there was this light—"

"I got the light too. That was brutal," Flynn said.

I nodded. "I felt weird, all sick and gross. I don't want to sleep alone tonight. And we should take turns watching Rowan, if he does have a concussion."

"Come here, you fine thing. We're happy to oblige." Flynn flung his arm around me and pulled me in for a deep kiss.

I threw his arm off me. "As much as I love all of you, it is two in the AM. My mother has been alive for 24 hours, I found out my sister likes girls, and I've seen two of you unconscious. Right now, I just need to sleep."

"As you wish, Princess." Blake wrapped me in his arms and tugged me down on the bed. Beside me, Corbin looped an arm over Rowan's back. Arthur lay across the bottom of the bed. No one even bothered to remove their clothes.

The last thing I saw before I closed my eyes and slipped into sleep was the waxing moon peering in from the high gothic windows as it illuminated the pile of bodies that cocooned me. At that moment, I truly understood what it meant to be surrounded by light.

CHAPTER SEVENTEEN

EIGHTEEN: MAEVE

My eyelids fluttered open, then immediately slammed shut again. Bright light tortured me, pricking the blessed dark with bright orbs.

"Rise and shine, Princess," Blake whispered in my ear.

I moaned and slapped feebly at his chest. "What time is it?"

"After ten," Arthur mumbled from the end of the bed. "That's the best lie in I've had in *months*."

I bolted upright. "After ten? We don't have time to lie in bed. We need to talk to Daigh. I've got to try to get hold of Kelly—"

"Shhhhh." A hand rested on my shoulder. Corbin's voice tickled my lips. "If you're going to meet Daigh, you need to be magically charged."

When he put it like that, with his voice all gravelly and dark...

I leaned back, surrendering my body to their touch. Hands roamed over my naked skin, lighting trails of fire that had lain dormant for too many days. Skin slapped against skin as they tore off their clothes and mine and tossed them on the floor. The spirit magic flared inside me, hot and angry from her slumber, ready to pull in their energy and make it my own.

My eyes fluttered shut and I drew myself into my body, focusing on the sensations of wet lips closing over my nipples. Two tongues swirled around the sensitive buds, drawing up tendrils of fire from inside me. Another set of lips claimed mine, teasing out my tongue.

A head dived between my legs, coarse hair tickling my legs as a tongue thrust inside me. Arthur. He plunged his tongue deep, before moving to pound it against my clit while he slid a finger inside me.

Earth, fire, water, air, spirit – the five pillars of their magic reached inside me, feeding my own flaring heat that swept through my body like a forest fire. Arthur's rhythm on my clit was unrelenting, the machine-gun rapid fire of the heavy metal drumming he loved so much. My body responded, my back arching, the fire inside my burning my limbs into bright light.

The orgasm slammed into me, driving the air from my lungs and forcing my magic out through my body like a sonic boom. I floated in the moment, buoyed up by the pleasure rushing through my veins, before I could return to my body and my bed and the five adoring faces that watched me with a mixture of love (Rowan), bliss (Blake) and satisfaction (Arthur).

"Come to me, Einstein." Flynn pulled me on top of him. "I'm not going to let Arthur rule unchallenged."

My body still flared with warmth. I flung my arm out toward the bedside table, hunting for a condom, before remembering that we'd taken the tests in London. We'd all come back clean. We could do this without a piece of rubber between us, like Blake and I had done the other night.

My grin matched Flynn's as I settled myself on top of his cock and sank down. Skin on skin inside me. It felt *amazing*.

Flynn gripped my hips and slammed me down on his cock as he drove up inside me. He bit his lip in this totally adorable way as he focused on sending me to the stars and back.

Arthur moved around in front of me, kneeling beside Flynn. I tried to reach his cock with my mouth, but I couldn't quite bend that way. Arthur lifted his leg over Flynn, who pushed him off.

"Is it too much to ask that a fella gets to stare at Maeve's beautiful face instead of your hairy bollix?" he demanded.

Arthur grunted, but he shifted his leg back. He picked up my hand and placed it on his shaft. I tightened my grip and pumped him in time to Flynn's relentless rhythm. Arthur leaned down and claimed my mouth with his.

The familiar coolness of lube dribbled between my cheeks. Blake's fingers slid through the trail and over my back entrance, eliciting a groan from somewhere deep inside me. Flynn slowed his pace so Blake could position himself behind me, his cock rubbing against me. No finger this time – as Flynn drew out, Blake placed the head against my hole and pushed it home. I gasped as he filled me, working his full length inside me.

Blake's teeth dug into my shoulder as he slid all the way in. Flynn grinned up at me. "You're so beautiful when you take us all like this, Einstein." He pushed himself inside me, his cock rubbing along Blake's through the thin wall that separated them. I threw my head back, my breath coming out in hacking gasps as they started a slow, see-sawing rhythm that sent me to the stars.

So tight.

So full.

So perfect.

Something dark fell across Flynn's chest, tickling my throat. I glanced down to see one of Rowan's dreadlocks snaking across his skin. I rolled my head over. Rowan's head rested on the pillow beside Flynn. Corbin lay on top of him. His hand clasped Rowan's, their fingers knitted together, black-and-white. Their bodies moved in time with mine, their eyes darting between each other and then over to me.

"I don't know if I'm okay with this," Flynn frowned at Corbin.

"You'd better get okay with it, or we're kicking your homophobic Irish arse to the curb," Arthur growled.

"Don't tell me you're a prude when you've got another guy's cock practically rubbing against you," I breathed as Blake thrust inside me again.

"That's different. It's all about Maeve." Flynn pinched my nipple and I gasped as a wave of pleasure rolled through me. "That over there is purely selfish."

Flynn tightened his grip on my nipple, just as he and Blake thrust inside me, and I lost control. My fingers clawed at Flynn's chest as my orgasm slammed into me. Rowan's eyes met mine, swimming with joy, and I knew I reflected my own joy back at him.

"See? It makes Maeve happy," Corbin grinned. "How can you be against that?"

Flynn shrugged. "I guess I'm not. Fiddle-le-de." He grinned his compliance before devouring my lips with his own.

The five of us thrust and groaned and moved together, finding the rhythm of our hearts. Arthur shuddered as he came in my hand, squirting his load across my breasts. A few drops landed on Flynn's chest. I expected Flynn to squeal like a pig, but instead he gripped my hips tighter and thrust with renewed vigor, his expression tense and focused and totally adorable.

Blake came next, his body shuddering against mine. "Fuck, Princess," he gasped, his teeth raking my skin as he pulled out and collapsed against the bed. Beside me, Rowan and Corbin locked lips, Corbin holding Rowan tight as his body convulsed with his own orgasm. Seeing them like that, so happy with each other, and knowing the others accepted them and that what we'd created here was a family that loved and understood and gave pleasure selflessly made my heart swell in my chest and my body contract as yet another orgasm ploughed through me, shooting my spirit magic higher and hotter than I'd ever felt it before.

And to think some witches chanted over a cauldron.

As I stepped out from the spiral staircase leading down from my room, I noticed a dark shape standing in front of the mirror in my bathroom, leaning in so close it might've been kissing the glass. A voice murmured words too quiet for me to hear.

My heart thudded in my chest.

Is it Kelly, come back to talk to me?

"Who's there?"

The shape turned and waved a hand through the air. Aline's eyes watered as she met mine. She pulled the dark hood from her head and wiped her hand across her face. "I'm sorry if I scared you. I got bored waiting in the Great Hall by myself."

I wondered if she'd come up to check on me, and the thought of it made me feel both loved, offended, and mortified, especially when I thought about what she might just have heard. "This bathroom is off limits. Use the guest one downstairs in future. What's with the Dracula cloak?"

"Oh." Aline smoothed the fabric down, as if she only just realised she was wearing it. "I found it in a box in the cupboard at the end of the hall. There are a few old things in there from my coven. I used to wear this at rituals sometimes. I thought Daigh might recognise it."

"Good thinking." I stepped closer. "About last night, I'm

sorry I snapped at you about the ritual. I was tired and worried about Corbin and I—"

"Your magic," Aline whispered, her eyes widening. "I can feel it. "

I smiled. "Yeah. Let's just say I'm ready for anything Daigh throws at us."

Aline's eyebrows raised, and she gave me a knowing smile. "You do your ancestors proud, Maeve Moore. And your mother, for what it's worth."

Over a quick breakfast of toasted muesli topped with fresh cream and berries from the garden, Aline explained how we were going to contact Daigh.

I assumed we'd drink the same potion Blake had used to become a temporary shade and enter the underworld, but she shook her head. "This battle is all about power. I don't want to go to where Diagh is powerful. I want him to come to us."

"Hold on. We're currently safe from the fae, and you want to bring them here?"

"Not the fae, just your father. And he won't really be here. This kind of communication is part of my unique spirit magic. I know what I'm doing." She explained the steps of the spell that would open a portal to allow Daigh to talk to us without travelling here to the human realm. I had to admit it sounded like a far safer option.

We packed up our things and left for the sidhe. As I locked the kitchen gate behind us, a raven flew from the parapet above. It's beady yellow eye fixed on mine as it soared into the trees. It stopped on a branch overhanging the path and croaked three times.

Arthur shielded his eyes from the sun as she watched it's graceful arc across the sky. "An omen."

"Good or bad?" Flynn asked.

Aline gave him a sad smile. "Three guesses."

"Bad then." Flynn sighed. "Where's Obelix when you need him?"

"Sunning himself on the first-floor parapets, last I saw him," Corbin said.

"There are no such things as omens," I scoffed. But the bird's piercing eye stayed with me as I followed Aline through the orchard. I imagined it watching me from the trees.

We bypassed the sidhe and gathered behind it, in the shadow of the trees. Corbin had the idea that the villagers might be spying on the field, and we didn't want to give them any more fuel for their persecutions against us. Here there was a large enough clearing to hold our circle and we'd hopefully stay hidden from any prying eyes.

In the centre of the circle, Aline placed a round mirror and a knife. She stepped back between Flynn and Arthur, linking arms to join our chanting while I cast the circle. As soon as our magical protections were raised, she grabbed my hand and drew me into the centre.

"Do you want to do the talking, or should I?"

"He'll be expecting to see me first." I remembered last time I'd spoken to Daigh, how afraid I'd been. I didn't want to show him that same fear today. At least this time was different – I had the pull weight of my spirit magic humming in my veins. "You stay behind me. Don't let him see you at first. We'll use you to catch him off-guard."

"As you wish, daughter of mine." Aline gripped the knife in her hands. She winced as she turned the blade to herself and drew a shape on her skin, a rune. I glanced up at Blake, searching his face for recognition. He nodded, his eyes widening. "That's Daigh's rune," he whispered.

Aline handed me the knife. I stared at her blood coating the blade.

"You have to do it, too," she said.

My hand trembled around the handle as I touched the knife to my skin. As lightly as I could, I drew the blade to copy the lines Aline had done. The cuts stung as the cold air whispered over them, and faint lines of blood spilled over.

"King of the Fairies, Daigh the Chaotic, I call you to me," Aline intoned. She leaned over the mirror, smearing her blood across the glass.

"King of the Fairies, Daigh the Merciful, I call you to me." I copied her, dragging my own arm across the glass. I expected the mirror to feel cool against my hurt skin. Instead, the surface burned. I yelped and whipped my hand away.

From behind my back, Aline touched my shoulder, and a shiver of spirit power flowed through her fingers and jolted down my arm. I added a tiny piece of my own – I didn't want to waste the deep well the guys raised up inside me – and directed the stream of power into the mirror, focusing my will on the face of the fae king. I gasped as a dark mist rose from the surface of the mirror. The mist thickened, becoming long black tendrils, like the fog that seeped from the cracks at the church.

The mists shifted. Daigh's face appeared in the mirror, his emerald eyes wide and searching. The flowers in his crown had wilted, hanging off the twisted vines like the dry skeleton of fall. Instead, jagged bones jutted from the crown – talismans of his dominance in the world of the dead.

My spirit magic tugged at me, drawing me closer to him, holding me in his sway. The power he exuded even through the mirror terrified me. It took all my will not to sink back behind Aline and let her face him alone.

"My daughter, we meet again." His tongue flicked out and licked along his lips. I wanted to throw up.

"Hi. I actually don't want to talk to you, since you're trying to kill my coven and bring the dead back to life to terrorise the world and all. But I figured since you're doing this all the name of some new utopia you foolishly believe is going to happen, I'd better set you straight on a few matters."

"I know you've seen the vision," Daigh said. "You know that we are victorious. This castle crumbles to dust, and all the witches who stand around you burn at the stake."

Behind me, I heard a gasp. *I guess the guys know about the vision now.*

"You got the vision right, but you extrapolated your victory from it, and you got it wrong. That future is not your world. It will be Liah's."

Daigh snorted. "Liah is one of my most loyal fae."

"Is she? Or is she the fae plotting to steal your crown?" I pressed. "Liah knows that this battle your fighting isn't about returning the fae to their rightful realm or freeing the ghosts of long-felled trees. She knows you've dragged the fae to ruin for your selfish desires."

"And what desire is this?"

"You want your family back," I said. "You want to be a part of a family again. That's why you want me to join you. It's got nothing to do with my power. It's because I'm Aline's daughter, and you loved her."

"You've been reading too many fairy stories, daughter." Daigh laughed. "The fae do not love, least of all the Unseelie. Blake will tell you. I was nothing but cruel to him."

"What about his fae day?" I asked.

Daigh opened his mouth, and shut it again.

"If love is a weakness, then you're the weakest fae of all. You're losing them, *Father*," I grinned. "If Liah gets the other fae on her side, she'll never allow you to have what you truly desire. And she's already turning them. After all, her vision is purer than yours."

"If you called me here to gloat over some victory, then you call is premature."

"I called you because I think we can help each other. I think there's a way we can both get what we want, and no one has to die. Mostly, I called you because I met someone who wants to say hi." I stepped aside, giving Daigh his first look at Aline since the night she banished him back to the fae realm.

His reaction was...*interesting*. His expression remained the same – stony, ethereal. But he *blinked*. That blink said more than a gasp or a frown ever could.

"Hello, Daigh," Aline flipped her wavy hair over her shoulder and smiled that kind smile of hers and gave him a little wave.

"This is a trick," he growled.

"I am no trick." Aline slid her hands over her hips in a suggestive way. "I am flesh and blood again."

Daigh laughed. "Nice try. You're Blake wearing a glamour. You can't fool me."

Blake stepped forward so he stood between Aline and I. He wrapped his fingers around my hand. With his other hand, he gave Daigh the finger. *Flynn must've taught him that.*

I grinned. "No glamour. Here's Blake, and this is Aline."

Daigh's eyes widened. "You can't be real."

"I am."

"You told me that you and my mother had a single..." I searched for the right word. "Dalliance, down by the sidhe. But that's not true. You were compelling Robert Smithers for months and months. You tricked her into sleeping with you, into creating a binding. Why didn't you say that before?"

"Fae lie." he smiled, but the smile was thin. I wondered, did he not tell me because he wanted me to think well of him? That was also *interesting*.

"They do lie," I grinned. "You were in love with Aline here. You just can't admit it to yourself."

"How is this possible?"

Aline stepped forward. "During the ritual all those years ago, Robert Smithers sensed that you were trying to take me away with you, away from him, and so he used his own magic to trap me inside your portrait. I've lived there as pigment and spirit for twenty-one years, until our daughter freed me."

Daigh's eyes darted to mine. "But...how did you know of this?"

"I figured it out. It wasn't hard, given the evidence." I folded my arms. "The same way you figured out I was alive from the fae realm and sent your prince Kalen to kill my family and rob me of my scholarship."

"That was necessary to reunite us. I'm your father. *We* are blood." His eyes flicked to Aline again. "And now that Aline's returned, it's all perfect. We can be together in the new world we build."

"You *killed* my parents," I spat back at him. "If you think inhabiting someone else's head while his sperm impregnates an egg makes you my father, than you don't know anything about human genetics, either."

"We are bound magically. Our stories tell of a binding where our magic—"

"I know what the stories say, but human science has moved beyond your fairy tales. Genetic traits are passed on through chromosomes from the sperm and egg. You being inside Robert's head has nothing to do with that process. According to the science, you're not my father at all."

"Your science is flawed."

"There's an easy way to find out. There's a test we can do to determine whether you and I share any genetic material. All I'd need was a sample of your blood and I could have an answer in a couple of days from a certified lab. No cheating. No lies. I'm betting it's going to give a false result, because there's just no way we're related. But if it comes back true..."

Aline squeezed my arm. "Our daughter has every right to be angry. I remember what you said to me once – anger is just the other side of love."

I glared at her. *Daigh* told her that line she fed me? She'd better not be trying to suggest I loved Daigh, because that was *not* a thing.

Aline threw her arm around me. "Our daughter's very clever. She's explained this genetics thing to me, and I think she's right. I can't see how you can possibly be her real father."

Daigh drew a blade from his belt. His smile never left his face as he dragged the knife over his skin. My stomach turned as I imagined Arthur doing the same thing. A thin line of green blood spilled from the wound.

Daigh tossed the knife at the mirror. The glass shattered as the blade drove through it flew through the air. I froze as it sailed for my head. Arthur reached out and grabbed the handle.

"Keep that safe," I told him. "Don't let the blade touch anything else. Corbin's got a ziploc bag." Corbin stepped forward with a bag held open and Arthur dropped the blade inside.

"Was that all you wanted, daughter?" Daigh asked, his expression smug.

Aline looked at me for permission. I nodded. We might as well give it a shot.

"We propose an alliance," she said.

"An alliance with humans? How intriguing, especially considering your pathetic race is only days away from extinction at the hands of your own dead."

"We're not worried about the Slaugh," I said. "Aline stopped you once before, and this time we have a powerful weapon on our side – one you couldn't even conceive of."

"I think you're talking out of your arse, daughter." Daigh's eyes flicked over mine. I knew I had to hold his gaze at all costs. If I looked away, if I blinked, he'd never believe me.

"I know it's hard for you fae, but look at this *logically*. You've seen me dreamwalk into your realm. You now know I can bring the dead back to life. You tried to hurt my coven in the church, but I saved them all. I'm more powerful than you can imagine, and I haven't even got started yet. If you hurt anyone else I care about, you will find out what I'm capable of."

"These are empty threats," Daigh waved his hand as if he was flicking away a bug. Blake squeezed my hand. His dark eyes burned into mine.

You've got him, Princess. Blake's voice landed in my head. *He's worried. I can see it.*

"It's your prerogative to believe that. You can come at me with the Slaugh and be beaten back and have the fae turn on you and tear you limb from limb and devour your bones while they praise Liah's name." I shrugged. "It's all the same to me. You're not my father. I'm just offering you an alternative."

"Which is?"

"You call off the Slaugh and return the fae to *Tir Na Nog*. We will direct our weapon to destroying Liah and her faction of dissidents. You will rule the fae unopposed."

"Apart from my life, what's in this for me?" Daigh narrowed his eyes. "What good is a kingdom inside an iron box?"

"In return, we will give you back the wild places of the earth," Aline said. "We will throw open the gateway so the fae can return to dwell in the forests and on the glades and in the caves and upon the meadows. You will have dominion in these places, the only rule imposed on you that you may not harm a human."

"That doesn't sound like any fun."

"Fun is where you find it," Aline smiled at Daigh.

I glanced up at Aline. Could we really make an agreement like that, one that concerned the whole world, without consulting anyone?

Daigh threw his head back. "Why would I take this sorry deal, when in a few days I will have the entire world at my mercy?"

"Because this way you get exactly what you want – what you claimed this battle was all about." An idea popped into my head. I can't believe I never thought of this before. I pressed on. "I know Blake told you about the rest of the vision – the burned and cracked earth, the sky on fire, the air poison in your lungs. Do you know what that is? It's a nuclear weapon – it will turn the earth into an uninhabitable wasteland for at least five-thousand years. It's what the humans will hit you with once they see the Slaugh coming. I know fae live a long time, but can you really wait five thousand years before you ever hope to see a forest again?"

Nice one, Princess.

I know. I cast my mind back to the dream that had haunted me for so many nights. I'd been focusing on the stakes, I hadn't even considered the ruined landscape. Now that the idea had occurred to me, I knew I'd guessed correctly. The fae didn't have the power to do that kind of damage – and even if they did, they couldn't turn it against the natural world. I highly doubted it was the hand of a witch. No, it was the kind of destruction only humans were capable of.

"As dramatic as your tale is, I think I'll take my chances." Daigh swivelled his gaze to Blake. "You shouldn't have left, Prince. You chose the losing side."

"I think you did, old man."

"You will join me before this is over, daughter," Daigh

flashed me that cold smile of his. "We will be a family. You will see."

A black cloud rose from the sherd, tendrils swirling around us. Aline shoved me back just as one reached for my ankle.

Daigh's face disappeared into the black mist. The mirror shattered to pieces. I fell to my knees, my stomach lurching as his cold, cruel laugh rose from the mirror and echoed through the wood.

CHAPTER EIGHTEEN

NINETEEN: BLAKE

Only when Daigh's face disappeared from the surface of the mirror did I drop Maeve's hand. His evil laugh reverberated in my head, reminding me how important it was that we beat the bastard in this battle. Because if he won...we'd all be buggered, to borrow a phrase from Flynn.

Maeve bent down and picked up a long sherd of the cracked mirror, pinching it between her fingers. "It's hot."

"We did just hit it with a ton of magic," Aline pointed out.

Maeve tossed the sherd on top of the broken frame. "That was a waste of a perfectly good mirror."

Aline flopped down on the grass, wrapping the long sleeves of her cloak around her body. "Wasn't that exhilarating!"

"It wasn't. It was *awful*. And it was a waste of time – he didn't take our deal."

""Did you really expect him to?" Arthur frowned.

"I thought that was the plan."

Aline grinned. "Have faith, daughter. We're much more subtle than that."

"You did what you came to do, Princess." I kicked a mirror

sherd with the edge of my boot, sliding it on top of the rest of the glass. "You unnerved him."

Seeing Daigh again sure unnerved me. I hated the way he directed that smile of his at Maeve. I'd seen that smile too many times before, and it usually led to someone getting spikes under their fingernails or losing their head.

"We did," Aline grinned, twirling a strand of her hair around her long fingers. "I hoped we would also learn something valuable, and we did."

"We did?"

I nodded. Aline and I were the only people who knew Daigh well enough to read between the lines. "He denied practically everything else, but he never denied he was in love with Aline."

Maeve looked thoughtful as we trudged back to the house. Something rustled in the bushes as we made our way up the hill. "I think it's just a fox," Arthur said from further up the path. "Too small to be a human."

"I hope he's right," Maeve mumbled under her breath. I squeezed her hand.

"You're thinking something, Princess. You've got that constipated look on your face."

Maeve snorted. "Where did you learn that word?"

"Three guesses," I grinned, jabbing a finger at Flynn.

"He's a bad influence on you, or you're a bad influence on him. I haven't decided which." Maeve's hazel eyes bore into mine. "You're right, though. I'm thinking that I need to find out what's going on with Kelly and Jane. It's killing me that they're not here in the castle where they have some protection."

"I could visit Jane. One of us should go into the village anyway and see how much belief the statue's collected, and what the villages make of it. It should probably be me, since no one there knows who I am." I shrugged. "I'll stop by the cottage. I know where it is."

"You definitely do." Maeve grinned, remembering the day I snuck up on her when she was using the outhouse behind Jane's cottage. If looks could have killed, the one she'd given me that day would've had me dead and buried. She was lucky she was so hot when she was pissed off. "Thank you. She won't speak to me, but maybe you can make her see reason. Take Flynn with you – Connor loves Flynn. That might get you through the front door. But don't either of you *dare* do anything stupid."

"Your wish is my command." I wanted to speak to Clara, anyway. I needed to know what she made of the dream, and of the conversation we'd just had with Daigh. Flynn agreed to go into town with me on the condition we had lunch at the pub. I didn't think that was the cleverest of his ideas, but he insisted. I felt certain that fell under Maeve's definition of 'stupid.'

As we headed out the door, I noticed Flynn slide a knife into his sock.

Thick grey clouds hung low in the sky, and rain pelted us as we walked down the road into the village. We didn't encounter anyone else on the road, but as soon as we set foot on the high street it was clear we were even less welcome than we'd been a few days ago.

As soon as they say us, people ducked into nearby shops, or slammed their car doors and drove away. A woman lifted an enormous crucifix necklace and thrust it angrily toward us as she skirted around us.

"Maeve isn't going to like this," I said, as a young mother nearly drove her stroller under a car trying to avoid us.

"Don't be daft. This is exactly what we want." Flynn pointed across the greene. "Look."

I didn't even have to turn toward it to know what he was talking about. The statue hummed with magic – it rattled my bones and grated against my teeth. When I did lay eyes on the witch, I found it difficult to focus my vision. Something about the shape of it wouldn't hold my eye – I kept slipping off at the edges. Tendrils of pale blue light emanated from the witch's clawed fingers, snaking through the air as they reached toward the village.

Two blokes in orange vests stood behind the statue, watching a third man attack one of the legs with some sort of handheld torch that shot a jet of brilliant blue flame. From the way they yelled and cursed, I assumed the flame was meant to be doing more than just tickling the witch's feet.

The blue tendrils wrapped around the men, sliding over their skin, forcing their way into ears and nostrils. As they scratched their heads and muttered words about witchcraft and trickery, the statue pulsed brighter. Even as they tried to tear it down, they were feeding it with their belief, making it strong enough to resist their machines.

"What did I tell you?" Flynn patted my shoulder. "I'm a genius."

"Can we get away from the green, Mr Genius – I don't want to be nearby when they realise we're watching them."

"Right you are. We should find Clara."

"I hope this hasn't been affecting her too much," I said as we rounded the side of the bank that marked the halfway point of the high street. The old stone building hid the rest of the street from view. "They might be targeting anyone they suspect is a witch—"

I stopped short, my breath catching. We'd come around the front of the bank. The footpath glittered with broken glass. My boot kicked a bent tarot deck that had scattered over the road. A mangled dream catcher hung from the edge of the rubbish bin.

Someone had gone down the street and broken the window of every vaguely magical shop in Crookshollow. Lady Cordelia paced outside her tarot booth, railing down her mobile phone at some poor clot at her insurance company. The owner of the esoteric bookshop mournfully threw soaked volumes into a rubbish bag. Not even the *Bewitching Bites* bakery with its cartoon witch on a broomstick in the front window had been spared. Trays of pastries and cakes had been flung out the window and smeared across the footpath. The Asian woman who owned it knelt outside, weeping into her hands.

When we reached *Astarte*, we found Clara sweeping the broken glass off the pavement. She'd already taped a large black sheet over the broken window. It wouldn't do a thing to deter the weather or vandals. DIE WITCH had been scrawled across her shop door in bright orange paint.

"Don't fuss," she snapped when Flynn grabbed the broom out her hands. "I'm fine. I was at home when this happened."

"Go on up to the castle," Flynn said. "You're staying with us."

"I have a perfectly good home of my own, young man."

"Yeah? If they're capable of this, then you're not safe there." Flynn shrugged. "At least Briarwood is a fortress. It's designed to keep out invading hordes and low-level vandals. Or go to your son's house. Either way, you need to stay away from Crookshollow."

Clara patted his arm. "It's nice to hear your concern, seems as this is because of your little stunt."

"You saw my statue, then?"

"A creepy metal witch appearing from thin air in the middle of the greene? No, I completely missed it." Clara shoved his arm away. "You have moxie, I'll give you that, boy. It's been all anyone in the village can talk about."

"That *was* the idea."

Clara lowered her voice. "Turning belief into magic – it's clever. I wouldn't have thought of that."

"Oh, don't be modest now." Flynn teased her. "A clever

broad like you – the idea would have come to you eventually. Luckily, I thought of it first. It goes without saying that an Irishman knows his magical conduits."

"Indeed. It's becoming quite heavy with magic, if you don't mind my saying so." Clara's tone suggested she thought it might be *too* heavy. "I do hope you've thought through this plan of yours thoroughly."

"Not in the slightest," Flynn grinned happily. "Do you think it will be enough to hold back the Slaugh?"

"I don't rightly know, son. I guess we'll find out in seven days."

We helped Clara sweep up the glass. Flynn offered to go to the garden centre and pick up some MDF to fit over the window to keep more of the rain out, but Clara shook her head. "Gregory Stone owns the ironmongers and he's head of the church choir. They won't sell to any of us. You'd have to go all the way to the DIY store in Crooks Worthy, but I've already called my son and he's sending his driver over to fix it up. Luckily, my insurance company isn't local or superstitious."

"So you'll stay with your son?" I demanded.

"I will. And don't you boys worry. He knows how to keep an old woman safe." A shiny black car pulled up and a man wearing a black suit waved at Clara through the window. She climbed in. "Any time you need me, holler over the fence. Ryan and I want to help any way we can."

"I'll marmalise the bastards who did this," Flynn growled.

"Don't you dare." Clara wagged a finger at him. "I won't have violence in the village on my behalf. You boys be good and get back to the castle before you cause more trouble."

I touched my hand to hers, flicking a piece of my spirit magic under her skin, hoping it would calm her nerves. "If you can find out anything about using belief as magic, we'd be interested." She nodded. A shiver ran up my arm as she sent me a flicker back.

I ran a hand through my hair as the dark car drove away, disappearing around the side of the bank. Why had she done that? Did I look like I needed calming down? I wasn't the one who'd just had my business vandalised. "What do we do now?"

"Pub." Flynn marched off. I raced after him. Flynn's voice had this dark edge I'd never heard before.

"You sure that's a good idea, mate?"

But Flynn was on a tear. He stormed into the pub, marching past a table of locals and slamming the barstool on the flagstones as he pulled it out. "Hey Nell," he hollered at the comely girl behind the counter. "A pint each for me and my mate here. We've had a shitty morning and I'm hoping you'll cut us a little slack."

She waved at him to keep his voice down. "Aye, I'll serve ye," she whispered. "But only because the boss ain't here today. Just you sit right here where I can see you and stay out of trouble, Flynn O'Hagan. If you chance it with any o' my regulars, I be skelping ye and don't ye forget it."

"There's that warm Scottish hospitality I've come to love," Flynn grinned. "You'd better give us some scran as well. I'm right foddered. I'll have the bangers and mash, and Blake'll have the curry of the day."

I jabbed him in the ribs. "Do you order for me now like we're an old married couple?"

"Mate, we practically are an old married couple."

I leaned over and planted a sloppy kiss on his cheek, which he wiped away in disgust. Nell's laugh followed her into the kitchen.

Murmurs rose up from the nearby tables. My back itched from eyes boring into my skin. Flynn sipped his pint in silence, his gaze fixed on the wall. He sensed them, too. His whole body radiated rage.

What's going on with him? Why are we even here?

Nell came back a few minutes later with our food. We ate in silence. My curry tasted like dirt. Flynn kept his back to the door, but I snuck a look over my shoulder as two of the guys from the greene came in, orange vests glowing under the low pub lighting. Their faces set hard as they recognised Flynn. They stomped over to the bar, talking loudly about the statue. "The bastard thing won't come out. It's as if it's made out of kevlar or some shite."

"Graphene?" The younger one piped up. "That's the hardest substance in the world. A sheet one atom thick is two-hundred times stronger than steel."

"Yeah, well it ain't made out of no bloody kevlar." The old guy slapped him on the back of the head. "Ole' Mayer Scottson was out there in the wee hours with his concrete drill, but buggered if he didn't even get a chip out of the base. I'm telling you, that thing's enchanted."

"Why don't you try cracking your head against it?" Flynn piped up from the end of the bar. I punched him in the arm, but that didn't stop him from adding. "There's a pile of lead between your ears, so it might make a dent."

The entire pub fell silent. The guy's face turned red as a tomato.

"I'll make a dent in your face, *witch*." The guy slammed his fist down on the bar. At the back of the room, a woman whimpered.

"Are you startin'?" Flynn set down his glass and stood up, rolling his sleeves up. "I'm happy to knock your bollix in, give your wife something else to cry over other than your ugly mug."

"You wanna say that again, you fucking witch!" The guy shouted, reaching across the bar toward Flynn.

"Get him, Gus!" someone yelled from a nearby table.

Gus grabbed Flynn by the collar and slammed him against the counter. Flynn seemed to expect this, because he threw his arms against his chest and swiped them down, breaking Gus' hold. Gus moved to grab Flynn again, but Flynn was faster. He swung his fist and slammed it into Gus' cheek, flinging him back into one of the tables. Hot chips and sloppy curry flew everywhere.

"Fuck." Gus staggered to his feet, clutching his ear. Blood trickled down his shirt. Flynn swung again, but Gus ducked his hook and barrelled into Flynn, pinning him back against the bar.

"Oi, drop him!" Nell leaned over the bar and poured a pint over Gus' head. Gus yelled and spat, but he did get off Flynn. I grabbed Flynn under the arms as he surged forward, and his fist glanced off my shoulder as he thrashed and yelled. Nell frowned at me and pointed to the door. "I said *no trouble*. Get him outta here."

I dragged Flynn toward the door. Twenty pairs of eyes followed us. I was trying to shove Flynn through when Gus' young friend said loudly, "It's that new girl up at the castle behind all this. Calling herself the daughter of that weird lass who disappeared twenty years back. Looks like her, too, except with the short hair."

"You heard what young Bill Rilay's son said he saw up there earlier," someone else called out. "That weird lady is back."

Shit. Flynn and I both stiffened. *It wasn't a fox, after all.*

"Then he's a damn fool. Aline Moore's dead and buried," a woman said.

"He said it's her, all right. Looks just like the pictures in the old papers. They brought her back. Those witches rose her from her grave."

"It's that American witch who moved in," the first man

snarled. "She's behind this. We should go up to that castle right now and put the fear of God into her."

Flynn jerked his head around. He tore himself from my grasp and stalked toward the bar. His hands raised in fists. "You don't go talking shite about Maeve Moore."

"Flynn, let's go." I hissed. *We shouldn't have come here. The witch statue was one thing, but if they think we've raised the dead, they're going to get violent. It's like walking right into the middle of Daigh's court and loudly announcing all Unseelie were weak.*

"You heard him threaten Maeve?" he snapped, breaking my grasp and rushing back into the pub. "That's not right."

"What are you going to do about it, witch?" The young guy shoved Flynn. Chairs scraped back as several men stood up, hands balled into fists, faces twisted with rage.

Before I could grab him, Flynn had shoved the guy back, grabbing his collar to hold him still while he smashed his fist into his nose. The guy screamed as blood pissed from his nose and splattered across the flagstones.

Flynn hit the guy again, his eyes blazing with a fury I'd never seen before. Another bloke grabbed Flynn and tried to tear him off. Flynn flipped around and swung his fist, catching the second bloke in the jaw. With a roar, Gus launched himself into the fray, landing a hit in Flynn's gut as Flynn's foot connected with his knee. Gus went down in a barrage of abuse, and Flynn stomped on his neck.

"Bloody hell, Flynn!" I dived in, dodging a flying fist and grabbing Flynn's shoulders. I tried to tear him away, but Flynn was having none of it. He scrapped with three guys, sending two of them over a table and slamming another into one of the wooden pillars, which splintered with a mighty *crack*.

"Break it up!" Nell screamed.

"I'll hex the lot of you wankers," Flynn yelled. A jet of water shot between his fisted fingers, slamming into one of the men and knocking him to the ground.

Two blokes plowed into Flynn, who sprayed water all over the pub as they pinned his arms. Gus rolled on top of him and slammed his fist into the side of Flynn's head. Flynn went down like a sack of potatoes, and six angry faces turned toward me.

"Hi," I waved. "I'm Blake. I'm not from around here. Trust an Irishman not to know when to shut his gob, am I right?"

I managed to block the first fist that flew at my face, but the second slammed into my stomach, driving the wind out of me. A blow landed across my shoulder, and I went down on top of Flynn, the room spinning as a circle of feet closed in on us.

CHAPTER NINETEEN

TWENTY: ROWAN

After the talk with Daigh, Flynn and Blake went to town and the others all went back to the house. I stayed out in the garden, pulling on my gloves and picking up my shears. My head still felt a little woozy from my fall, but nothing cured me faster than being in nature. I cut back some of the herbs that were starting to look a little wild to encourage new growth, saving the nicer cuttings for drying.

Gardening was such an obvious pastime for earth witches, it was practically a cliche. If I'd known that when I'd started nursing seedlings on the edge of the old canal and growing potatoes on the roof of the squat, then I might've taken up crochet instead. But until Corbin, I had no one in my life to tell me what was normal for a witch. All I knew was that I could manipulate trees and plants and heal wounds and mix herbs together to make things happen, and that power terrified the foster families I was placed with. Terrified people tended to lash out with their fists. Or their cocks.

Gardening was a good skill. It meant I'd had something to barter at the squat. When I first came to Briarwood, the guys were living off takeout and microwaved fish fingers. Taking over the kitchen was one way I could start to pay back the kindness Corbin had done me. And I liked it – I liked the precision of gardening and cooking, the control, the easy access to things that could be counted and arranged. You raised the seeds, tended the soil. You added the ingredients in the right amounts, in the correct order, and something delicious emerged.

Rain pattered against my shoulders as I gathered a selection of herbs into my trug. I was low on some of the key ingredients for the poultices that healed magical attacks. I wasn't sure what we could expect in the coming days, but my remedies had saved us before. The more I had on hand, the better the chances I could help anyone who got hurt when the fae attacked.

My stomach twisted at the thought. Seeing Daigh through that mirror, hearing him talk about the destruction of humankind as if it was nothing, was like stepping into a cold shower, it brought home just how precarious our situation truly was, just how little control we actually wielded. We were only seven days away from the full moon, and we still didn't have a solid plan. If Daigh didn't take the deal Maeve offered him, we'd have to fight. Even if we did manage to beat the Slaugh back with our belief magic, we wouldn't escape unscathed. People would die.

You're useless. What's the point of collecting all those herbs? What's cooking going to do to help fight the Slaugh? They're all going to die. Everyone you love is going to die.

My skin itched and crawled, like it was about to slide off my bones. My muscles tightened, desperate to stop what I was doing and fulfil one of my counting rituals to relieve the tension and feel like I was doing something, anything, that might actually *help.*

No, I told myself, and the voice relented, just a little. Ever since the ritual in the early hours of this morning, I'd been feeling calmer, like I had more control over the rituals and the tics and the voice. I told it to go away and it did, for a few minutes at least.

In the kitchen, I set down the trug and ducked under the sink to pull out my drying racks and paper bags. When I stood back up, I wasn't alone.

"Hey." Corbin leaned against the doorframe. "What are you doing?"

"Replenishing some of my stores," I said, as I set one of my drying racks down on the island and started laying out the herbs. They needed to be dried for a few days in the airing cupboard. I separated out seven sprigs of rosemary, tied them together with string, and looped the string around the top of a small paper bag. I punched five air holes in the bag (always five. It had to be five), and tied it to the rack.

"Good idea. We never know what scrapes Flynn might get into next," Corbin grinned. He stood opposite me at the counter and rested his hands on the countertop. I stared at his fingers, at the mythological tattoos swirling down his forearms. "What's the paper bag for?"

"It speeds up the drying time, and it also catches any seeds that fall, so I can use them, too."

"Clever. But then I'm not surprised. You know exactly what to do with all this stuff." Corbin shuffled on his feet. "Rowan, I want to ask you something."

I picked up seven sprigs of thyme and wrapped the string around them. I couldn't force myself to look up at him. Tension flared between my shoulders, beckoning me to count and dispel the nerves that shot through my body.

He regrets last night. He doesn't want to be with me any more. It was the most amazing night ever but he thinks I'm disgusting—

"I noticed that last night you didn't come down to count the window panes. Is everything okay?"

I dropped the sprigs on the floor.

He's right.

I *hadn't* counted the window panes last night, or the night before, or any of the nights since the one Corbin and Maeve and I spent together in London. In the two years I'd been sober at Briarwood, I hadn't gone a single night without counting the window panes in the Great Hall while drinking my tea. I had to do it, or something horrible would happen to Corbin.

But I hadn't done it last night. I hadn't even *wanted* to do it after that ritual. It never even occurred to me.

What does that *mean?*

"Everything's fine," I whispered. And it was.

That fact was terrifying.

The voice had never been silent for so long before. Usually, if I was even a half hour late for the window-pane counting ritual, the fear would twist in my gut. But I hadn't even *noticed.*

Panic shot through me, and I had to give in to the urge now. *One...two...three...*I counted out seven stalks of feverfew. I couldn't look at Corbin.

"When you were talking to Aline, you got so anxious you fainted. You stopped breathing. Your pulse was so weak I could barely feel it. If I hadn't known how to perform mouth-to-mouth, you'd be dead right now."

"I know," I whispered. "It was a mistake. I shouldn't have asked about my parents. I should have counted the window-panes."

"Rowan." Corbin's voice dropped half an octave. It sent a shiver down my spine. "I think you should see a doctor."

"No doctors. I'm fine."

"This isn't going to be like rehab. They'll—"

"I don't want to." I knew what would happen when I went to a doctor – they'd give me all these horrible tests that would confirm what I already knew – that I was broken, messed up on the inside. They'd put me on drugs that made me not myself, that made me forget about how much I loved Maeve, and Corbin. Or worse – they'd lock me away like Robert Smithers, and I'd never see them again.

Corbin sighed. "It's your decision."

"You're not mad?"

"Disappointed, but not mad."

"After last night...do you still feel..." I couldn't finish the words. I couldn't bear the idea that he might have changed his mind about me, about us.

'Come here. I'll show you how I feel." A hand touched me under the chin. I jerked my head up.

Corbin's lips met mine, hot and ferocious.

Herbs scattered around me as he leaned across the counter and pulled me to him.

The kiss seared me inside, waking up parts of me that had laid dormant for so many years. The pressure inside my head fled, replaced by the heat of Corbin's lips.

"Out of the way, lovebirds," Blake yelled from across the garden. "Injured man coming through."

Corbin and I flew apart. Blake stumbled through the kitchen door. Blood trickled down the side of his head from a cut over his hairline. The sleeve of his leather jacket had been torn.

But he wasn't as bad as Flynn, whose body lay limp in Blake's arms. Blood poured from his nose and lips. His t-shirt had been torn in several places, revealing cuts and bruises all over his body. He groaned as he clutched his arm across his torso, like it couldn't move on its own.

I backed away. "I've got yarrow. It will help stop the bleeding."

"We'll need a whole bloody yarrow forest for this eejit." Blake swept my trug and drying racks off the counter and dumped Flynn on top.

"You should have called an ambulance," Corbin scolded. "He needs a hospital, not herbs. He might have internal damage. What's wrong with his arm?"

"I didn't see what happened because I was being stomped on by Gus and his cronies at the time, but I think he might've broken it," Blake shrugged.

Flynn leaned over the side of the counter and coughed. Blood splattered across the kitchen floor. "I'm *fine*. It's just a flesh wound. Besides, I saw Doctor Lewis while Blake was dragging me out of the pub, and he did nothing. Ain't no one in that village going to help us now, not after they saw...ow, Holy Mother of Mary, that fecking *hurts*."

I'd barely touched his arm and he was screaming like a banshee. Definitely broken. I ran through the remedies I had available...yarrow, of course, and comfrey leaves to help knit together the break...and feverfew, to stimulate healing...

Anxiety flared inside me as I laid eyes on the herbs and racks scattered all over the floor, and the blood puddling under Flynn's body. *Push through it, Flynn needs you.*

"Put the kettle on," I said to Aline, who'd just entered the room. She went to the stove while I ran over to my herb shelves and grabbed several jars. I tipped ingredients into a strainer and added that to a large mug. While I waited for the kettle to boil, I grabbed a handful of yarrow leaves and a dash of water and crushed them up in my mortar and pestle, all while Flynn moaned and writhed.

"Rub that into his worst cuts," I said, thrusting the crushed yarrow leaves into Aline's hands.

The kettle whistled. I took it off the element and filled the mug with hot water, and covered it with a tea towel to keep the vapours in. I covered the top with my hand, pushing my magic through my anxiety to speed up the infusion process and imbue the herbs with my own unique power. A warm hand pressed into my back. I opened one eye and saw Maeve's concerned face staring up at me. A flicker of spirit magic flared against my palm as she leant her own power to the remedy.

"This is ready," I whispered, closing my hands around the cup. Maeve took it from me and went over to Flynn.

"Where's Rowan?" Flynn's eyes widened as he saw Maeve coming. He knew he was in trouble.

"Rowan's right here. We're all right here. And we want to know what happened. What did the villagers see that made them do this to you?" Maeve demanded, holding the glass at an angle so Flynn could drink.

He coughed as the hot tea poured down his throat. "You should be thanking me, Einstein. I was only defending your honour."

"Some guy at the pub made a comment about you, so our Flynn here punched him out. Then the whole rest of the pub jumped in." Blake wiped blood off his face. "We only got out of there because Nell called the police and everyone scrambled."

"Jesus, Flynn," Maeve growled, splashing hot tea all over Flynn's face.

"I'm fine, Einstein," Flynn coughed. "You should see the other guys. But they know about Aline."

Panic surged through me. If the villagers saw Aline back from the dead, that would frighten them more than the statue. But how could they know about her? She hasn't been outside the castle except to talk to Daigh, and we were well hidden in the trees...

The fox.

Maeve must've had the same idea, because she turned to Arthur. "That rustling you heard in the trees the other day, did you see for sure it was a fox?"

"No, but it was low to the ground, too small to be a person hunched over."

"So it couldn't have been a kid?"

Arthur's face turned stony. "Shit."

"Don't slash yourself up over it, Arnold," Blake said. "We've got enough blood from Flynn."

I gasped. Corbin looked mortified. But Arthur just laughed. "I never thought you'd be the one calling me on that shit, fae." He rubbed his arm. "I'm not doing that anymore."

Just like that. I wondered if it was Aline's ritual affecting him. It sure was affecting me. And Corbin too, judging by the way he'd kissed me last night and what he was willing to do and the fact that he was trying to get me to a doctor again.

And Flynn...had the ritual got under his skin, too? Could it somehow explain his strange desire to pick a fight in the pub?

"In the pub, people were talking about Aline," Blake said. "A kid saw us talking to Daigh through the mirror, and they all put it together after they recognised Aline from old photographs from her coven days."

Maeve paled. "So the village knows about Aline."

"Aye, and now they think we're necromancers as well as witches."

"You're a damn fool," Maeve scolded Flynn, who winced. "You've made everything worse."

"Leave him be for now," I said, taking the mug from Maeve. "You can yell at him later."

I managed to get the rest of the tea down his throat, and Aline and I packed his wounds with yarrow leaves and bandaged him up. Corbin helped me to lift him so I could tie a sling around his arm. Hopefully, the magic tea would knit the break back together in a few days and he wouldn't need to go to a doctor. I slid to the floor, exhausted, as Arthur scooped Flynn off the counter. "Up to bed with you."

"Not bed, the couch. I have a mind to watch some action films and take my mind off my imminent castration at the hands of Einstein." Flynn grinned at Maeve, who folded her arms and glared at him. He probably wasn't wrong about the castration.

Arthur rolled his eyes. "Fine. As long as it's not *Commando* again."

"I'm the one who got marmalised. If I want *Commando*, I get *Commando*."

Arthur and Blake settled Flynn on the couch, placing a blanket over his knees and the TV remote in his hands. I brought him some snacks and set them on the table in front of him. Aline went to the kitchen to make tea. I got up to follow her, but Maeve grabbed my wrist and pulled me into the hall. She beckoned Corbin to join us.

"So..." she gave each of us at stern look. "Blake mentioned that when he came in you two were locked in a rather passionate embrace."

Corbin looked guilty. "It was all me. I'm sorry I—"

"Don't think that. You're not in trouble. I know you've got this thing going on that's much older than me. I like it. I *love* it, in fact. Seeing you guys last night made me so happy, you have no idea. I have all of you, so there's no reason why you shouldn't have each other, too. But I'm going to need all the magic I can get if we're going to defeat the fae, so this is a warning – don't fuck it up for the next eight days, got it? Because I need both of you at my side and in fighting and fucking form, and if I can't have all five of you because the two of you are fighting, then it's not going to work."

Corbin slipped his fingers through mine. The smile he flashed me melted my heart. "We're here for you, no matter what."

I nodded, unable to find words.

Maeve grinned, and wrapped her arms around us both. Her sweet, spicy scent hit my nostrils, mingling with Corbin's dusky, heady aroma and bringing me back to the night under the bridge, the night I'd poured out all my secrets and found the love I'd never believed could exist.

"I love you both so much," Maeve whispered. "Now, get out of here. Go do something useful. Trust me, you don't want to be around for the bollocking I'm about to give Flynn."

TWENTY-ONE: FLYNN

"Okay, tiger. You've had time to gird your loins. We need to talk."

Maeve plonked down on the beanbag in front of me, her head blocking the screen so I couldn't see who Arnie was shooting at. I had a smart comment ready to rip, but the expression on Maeve's face said I'd better not chance it. I paused the movie with my good hand, and raised myself up, the movement sent a splitting pain through my injured arm.

"Hit me with it, Einstein."

"Do I need to tell you what a monumental idiot you were, dragging Blake into the pub and then picking a fight?" Maeve said.

When she puts it like that...

I shook my head. "You don't need to tell me. I was a fecking eejit. I was just so *angry*. They threatened you and I snapped."

"You get this was your idea to stir up the villagers with your statue? Now they're all stirred up you can't go getting mad at them for the hysteria *we* created. And the fact they know about Aline is all the more reason why you shouldn't have been in there. This is dangerous, Flynn. They broke your arm. You could have gotten killed."

"I don't care what they do to me. I'll scrap 'em all if I have to. But if they hurt you, I'll—"

"You'll what, Flynn? You'll turn into Arthur? Don't do that. I can only handle one warrior with a Lancelot complex. What's going on with you?"

I shrugged. "Dunno."

"You do know. Spill it. Do you remember what we agreed to only yesterday? No more secrets. No more keeping things hidden away."

"You're going to think it's so dumb."

"Try me."

"Did I ever tell you when I first decided I wanted to be an artist?"

Maeve shook her head.

"I was living in Dublin with my uncle. He trafficked drugs around Ireland – the hard shite like horse, crack, yokes for the clubbers. This one day, he had a bigwig from the Irish mob coming over to negotiate a deal, and he kicked me out of the house because 'your ugly mug'll turn him right off' or some shite. I didn't have anywhere to go, and it was pissing down so I couldn't just sit at the dog park and pretend all the dogs were mine. So I went to the Irish National Gallery."

"I thought you hated art galleries."

"Easy on, let me finish my story!" I took another sip of Rowan's tea. It was weird, but the heat from the drink seemed to warm right through my body, especially my throbbing broken arm. Rowan was a right healing genius. "As I was walking around, gawping at Caravaggio's *Taking of Christ* and Morisot's *Le Corsage Noir* and feeling absolutely nothing, I noticed this large class of art students sitting down in the main gallery for a lesson. I had a sketchbook in my bag, so I pulled it out and hovered at the back and tried to look like I'd paid a gazillion quid to be there like the rest of them."

"The tutor lectured on about Caravaggio – how the artist pioneered the strong light contrasts and moved his figures close to the picture plane to really pull the viewer in and create dramatic tension. And even though I think Caravaggio is fecking shite, my hand moved across the page. I couldn't help it. In minutes I had this sketch of the figures, only I'd given them all dog heads."

"Of course," Maeve said.

"This girl was standing beside me, watching me sketch. 'You're really good,' she whispered. I kept my head down. I didn't want to say anything. 'You're not supposed to be here, are you?' I shook my head, hoping she wouldn't rat me out. Instead, she grabbed my hand and dragged me out of the gallery.

"She took me to an abandoned shoe factory, where a bunch of artists had set up a workshop and gallery. It was wicked – just this big warehouse where people hung out and made art and swigged bottle-shop whiskey. I started going there every day, helping the girl – her name was Moira – finish a big mural on one of the warehouse walls. Most of the artists were like me – from the wrong side of the tracks, mixed up in gangs and street fighting. There were tensions, because some artists are territorial wankers, and no one trusted outsiders. Some of them were mad as a box of frogs at Moira for bringing me along. But they tolerated me because Moira liked me and I wasn't some rich Trinners kid slumming it. In that warehouse, we were friends. We had hope."

"So the day Corbin showed up asking about me, there was trouble. He looked like a rich Trinners kid. He got the shit kicked out of him and I wasn't even there that day. They told me about it later. But he came back a week later, and the week after that, and finally he cornered me and told me who he was and what I was and that he wanted me to come back to England with him."

"What'd you do?" Maeve leaned forward.

"What do you think I did? I laughed in his fecking face. I didn't need no fairy godmother in a Blood Lust t-shirt dragging me back to some draughty castle. I'd found my people. I was going to be a street artist. I had Moira. I sent him packing."

"A few days later, I showed up at the warehouse to work on another mural project with Moira, and she wasn't there. I waited around for ages, but she never showed, didn't answer her phone or nothing. She didn't show the next day, or the next. The other artists told me they didn't want me coming around no more. I asked about Moira, and they told me there'd been a fight downtown between two rival gangs, and she'd been down an alley working on a mural and got shot in the crossfire. The man who shot her? My uncle."

"Shit, Flynn," Maeve breathed.

I tried to wave my hand, to show her it wasn't a big deal, but I forgot my arm was broken, so when I moved it I dissolved into pain-filled whimpers. "Ow, serves my right for acting the maggot. So yah, I packed my things and left with Corbin the next day. I threw myself into Briarwood and protecting you. I went to Arizona for that year and met you in person and made a right fecking mess of things. I haven't thought about Moira in a long time, but last night during that ritual, these memories kept flashing in my head. I feel like she left me a legacy, and I've been failing her. And you."

"You're right," Maeve leaned down and kissed my forehead. "That is dumb. Tell me about the memories. What did you see?"

I gave a one-armed shrug. "My uncle and his friends telling me to stop acting the maggot while they smoked crack in the kitchen. Having a paint fight with Moira while we were painting a mural out the back of the warehouse. Moira smiling, always smiling. Moira's gravestone – cold and grey, just the opposite of her. The way I turned my art into a joke, like I turn everything into a joke, so that I didn't have to face my feelings about her or about leaving Dublin. But it never felt like a joke, especially not after I met Moira."

"Your art's not a joke. That statue of yours might save us all."

"There's a piece of me inside that statue. But it doesn't say anything, you know? It just makes people afraid and angry. I always thought that's kind of what I wanted, the way Banksy's stencils piss off the authorities. But..." I shrugged. "I dunno."

"You think maybe you want your art to say something else?"

"Maybe."

"It can, Flynn." Maeve grinned. "Just think, if the belief that statue collects actually ends up helping us defeat the Slaugh, you'll be famous for something else entirely."

"Yeah," I one-arm shrugged again. "I guess."

That wasn't what I wanted, though. I wanted to do right by Moira, give her art that was worthy of the gift she gave me. I wanted to do right by Maeve, too – the second woman who ever loved me and changed my life for the better.

Robert Smithers managed to use art to stop Daigh from taking Aline away from him. In a way, it was an act of love, although the act was selfish. Even Daigh, the evil fairy king, made art that moved people.

I didn't know the first thing about how to make art like that. Maybe I never would. And I couldn't explain it to Maeve the scientist.

She came over and settled on the couch beside me, perching gingerly on the edge so she wouldn't jolt my arm. "What did you see at Jane's house?"

My heart thudded. "We didn't get there. We were going to

go after the pub, but then..." I sighed. "I'm sorry. I'm guess I'm nothing but a disappointment today."

"It's okay. I shouldn't send you guys to do my dirty work, anyway." Maeve curled in beside me. She ran her fingers over my arm. Spirit magic pierced my skin like needles, seeping into the bones and spreading warmth down my arm. With her other hand, Maeve reached for the chocolate guinness cake Rowan had made me. I reached for the remote to turn the TV back on, when Corbin's voice boomed through the castle.

"Maeve, everyone. Clara's here!"

"We're in the Great Hall!" I called back.

Clara bustled in, hugging a heavy old book against her chest. A tall bloke with tousled reddish hair and paint-speckled black clothes trailed in behind her. Clara didn't even say hello. She just dumped the book on the table – sending up a cloud of dust – and announced. "I've found it."

"Found what?" Arthur asked from the doorway. Rowan and Blake appeared behind him, and Aline after that, her face flushed and a small makeup compact in her hands.

"The answer we've been looking for." Clara stood back, her tiny chin held high, like the Queen ready to greet her subjects.

"Is the answer Bela Lugosi over there?" I asked, jabbing my good arm toward the bloke hovering behind Clara.

"Oh, yes! Forgive me. I was so excited." Clara grabbed the man's arm and shoved him forward. "This is my son, Ryan Raynard."

Ryan Raynard.

Mary Mother of Jesus.

Ryan Raynard the infamous reclusive modern impressionist artist who lived in the ancient hall just over the hill from Briarwood. Ryan Raynard whose paintings fetched millions of pounds at auction even though no one had seen him in public for ten years.

Ryan fecking Raynard is standing in my living room. And I'm lying around in my boxer shorts, covered in bandages, and wearing a t-shirt that said "Irish Whiskey Makes Me Frisky."

The famous artist gave a weird little half-bow, as though he wasn't quite sure what to do with himself, and stepped back behind Clara. He seemed to be more comfortable hiding in the shadows. I could kind of relate to that.

Except I couldn't, because he created brutal paintings that stole hearts, and I did Sweet Fanny Adams.

"Flynn, you okay?" Maeve waved her hand in front of my face. "Your eyes have gone all glassy. Does Rowan need to—"

"No, no, I'm fine," I croaked. "Fiddle-le-de. Clara said she found the answer to our prayers. I'm just giddy with anticipation. What's happening with your shop, Clara?"

"Oh, don't worry about that. I want to show you what I found. It's all thanks to you," Clara beamed at me.

"Me?" *Unlikely.*

"When I saw Flynn's statue this morning, it reminded me of something I'd read in one of my own family spellbooks. I wasn't always a lone witch. I used to be part of a coven in London – the Soho coven, as it happened."

Maeve's eyebrow shot up. I remembered what she'd told me about what she and Corbin had seen at the coven's headquarters. It was hard to imagine lovely old Clara mixed up with that lot.

Clara laughed. "It wasn't always as sterile and...pompous. Back in my day, it was a real party house. They were good to me. I had to flee from Raynard Hall after Ryan's father...well, that's a story for another day. When I came to London I was a single mother with nothing, but they helped me find my feet again. I came into my own as a witch thanks to their guidance. I left shortly after Isadora took over as High Priestess – she and I didn't see eye to eye, as I'm sure she'd delight in telling you.

When I left, I took this book with me. I shouldn't have it, but I had this idea that if Isadora got her hands on it, bad things would happen. Anyway, your statue made me remember this. Look."

She flipped through the book until she came to a page of tiny writing, the letters jammed close together. Maeve pulled the book toward her, scanning the words.

"This is a diary entry from one of the Soho coven who used to entertain army officers during World War I. During the Blitz, the coven would hide in a certain exclusive air raid shelter – imagine the scene, these whores trapped underground for hours and sometimes days with some of the top minds in England. The coven became a repository of all sorts of useful knowledge about the war effort.

"Eliza Flaharty was one of those whores. She was a songstress – she used to entertain the soldiers with cabaret-style performances at the house. Sometimes she'd be invited into the officer's barracks for private entertainments. As her lover held her in his arms, she asked him to tell her a story. He wanted to be a writer when he left the war, and so he was always inventing tragic and beautiful tales. This tale was about an officer in the British Army who was a double agent. He was loyal to Germany, but in his guise, he met and fell in love with a beautiful English woman. Torn between the two worlds, he didn't know what to do. The idea turned itself over and over in Eliza's head, and she wrote a song about the officer's divided loyalty. The problem was, the song was so haunting, so evocative, that fear spread through the regiment there was a double agent. They hanged Eliza's boy for a crime he never committed – a crime that was entirely imagined – all based on the power of belief."

"That's a horrible story!" Maeve slid the book back across the table.

"This horrible story tells us one key thing, that belief is a powerful form of magic that can make its own truth. It has the power to invert the world as we know it – fictions become fact, and facts a fiction. When the fae come, the world will see their own dead walking the earth. They will know that magic is real and deadly and powerful. And to whom will they turn to save them?"

"Witches," Rowan whispered.

"Exactly." Clara jabbed the book triumphantly. "Their belief in us is all we need to make fiction a fact, to bring about the result we desire – the banishing of the Slaugh, and the return of the fae to their realm. We have to make their belief in witches powerful enough that it will create the result we desire. Flynn has the right idea – witches exist now only in pop culture, as fragments of mythology turned into Halloween candy. We can make them real again through art."

I leaned forward, my chest tightening. *Who knew art had such fierce power?*

And then Moira's face flashed in front of my eyes, and I realised I'd known all along.

"There are many artists in the covens, as well as artists like my son here who aren't witches but have a connection to our cause. If we got them to flood the market with art that challenged and confronted, art that spoke of the destructive power of witchcraft, art that couldn't be explained away, then we will be able to create and channel that belief." Clara touched her son's arm. "Ryan here has just finished a beautiful painting about the witches of Crookshollow. He will release it into the market. It might draw some attention to what's going on in the village."

Might draw some attention? If a new Raynard painting hit the market it would send the entire art world on a tear. And if the subject made the press look at witches in Crookshollow...

They'd look at my statue. A statue that mysteriously appeared overnight, and couldn't be moved or destroyed. A statue that hummed with a mysterious power...

I glanced over at Maeve. The muscles in her face twitched as she worked through Clara's words. *She doesn't believe Clara. It's art, not science. It's too irrational, too open to chance. It's—*

"This is it," she breathed. "This is the weapon we have. This is how we can stop the Slaugh."

CHAPTER TWENTY-ONE

TWENTY-TWO: MAEVE

"I need the bathroom!" I yelled over the noise of the welder.

"What?" Flynn yelled back.

"Bathroom!" I threw down the box of screws I'd been holding for Corbin and raced off toward the house.

Ever since Clara had come knocking with her book and her famous artist son, we'd all moved into Flynn's studio. He sat in a chair in the middle of his piles of junk, directing us to drag out bits of scrap from his collection and cut them up and solder or screw them together. Occasionally, Ryan Raynard would pipe up with a suggestion, and Flynn's face would go as red as his hair and he'd stammer a bit and change to Ryan's way.

Even Clara and Aline were pitching in, although their contribution was mostly running back and forth from the kitchen with endless cups of tea. Between all of us, the statue was taking shape in record time – a male companion to Flynn's female witch with a wild mane of wire-brush hair. He cast both his arms wide, an arc of lightning surging between the hands. I had the idea of making the statue into a Tesla coil so the lightning would be real, but Corbin overruled the idea in the interest of public safety.

"Spoilsport," Flynn muttered. I had to agree.

I wiped my greasy hands on my jeans before pulling open the kitchen door. It was fun getting dirty with the guys. Arthur tossed around the heavy scrap metal like it was made of paper. Flynn loved bossing everyone around for once, and he and Blake kept us all laughing with their antics. Shy Rowan contributed a couple of really creative ideas, and of course, Corbin was good at making everyone work together.

Once this statue was finished, we'd sneak out and plant it somewhere else in the village. Flynn thought we might even be able to get a third one up before Ryan released his painting and the press went crazy.

We spoke to Gwen at the Avebury coven earlier this afternoon. She had all her artists working on another piece. "I'm astounded we'd never thought of this before," she said. "There are many documented instances where belief magic has been used effectively. Combining it with art objects to store that magic makes perfect sense."

"Do you think it will be enough to stop the Slaugh?" I said.

"And then some!"

I'd also packaged up the knife Daigh had used along with a sample of my blood, and typed up a letter to send off to a DNA testing lab I found on the internet. I explained the sample was green because of a rare genetic condition, and hoped that would be enough to encourage them to go forward with the test without any further questions. Corbin wrote out a check for the lab fee from the Briarwood fund we all shared for expenses. According to the lab website, we'd get a result back in 3-5 business days.

Then we'll find out just how related Daigh and I really are.

In the bathroom, I smiled at my reflection as I washed my hands. My dark roots had started to grow back into my fringe, and my short pixie hair now completely covered my ears. Bits stuck out at all angles, streaked with dust and grease from the shed. A black stain smudged my cheek.

I was a completely different person to the girl who'd first set in this castle a month ago. Was it really only a month? It felt like so much longer. The bond I shared with the guys felt like it was forged decades ago. In a way, it was. I carried pieces of them around inside of me, and they each held a piece of me.

I'd fallen apart in this castle. I'd come undone after the death of my parents. I'd discovered a side of myself I'd never even imagined, and I'd met and fallen in love with not one, but five incredible men. The girl in the mirror wasn't someone old Maeve recognised – she was entirely new – a quantum leap in Maeve-ness.

I smiled despite myself. *Maybe Aline's ritual had a bigger impact on me than I thought. Maybe it was good for all of us to cleanse away the guilt of the past.*

Maeve Crawford was dead and buried. Maeve Moore – she was ready to kick some serious fae ass.

I rubbed at the grease smudge on my cheek, but that only smeared it further across my skin. I scrubbed it with soap and water.

The mirror fogged up. I couldn't see. *Odd.* I'd only been running the hot water for a few minutes. I rubbed at the fog, but it didn't clear.

A pair of crystalline eyes emerged from the fog, followed by two long, full lips leering at me out of the mirror. I screamed and leapt back.

"Hello, daughter," a dark, familiar voice echoed through the bathroom.

An invisible hand slammed my body against the shower wall. My heart leapt into my throat as the features coalesced into a face. Daigh stared back at me, his lips curling into his usual expression of carefree nonchalance.

"You can't do this," I said, fighting to get my pattering heart under control. "You can't be inside the castle like this."

"Can't I?" he smirked. "I spent months within those walls when I was inside that insufferable painter. Do you not think I made sure there was a way I could get back in this castle if I needed to?"

"I don't believe for a second you were that clever."

Daigh laughed. "You got me, daughter. I am, of course, not really here. I used a variation on the spell your enchanting mother used to call me, only this time I sought you out. I thought we could have a little heart-to-heart without the others around."

"A heart-to-heart is what you do with people you care about, and I don't care about you. I sent away the DNA sample this morning. In only a few days you'll see how superficial our connection really is."

He let that one slide. "You made me an interesting offer yesterday."

"Which you rejected."

"I did. But maybe I'm reconsidering."

I tilted my head to the side. "I believe your words were that you'd rather die than ally with us witches."

"That was before Liah became a problem. While I was speaking with you, Liah spied on our conversation. She's gone to one of our gracious hosts and told them I was thinking of selling them out to the humans. The underworld is in uproar. My fae are no longer listening to me. I'm in hiding lest a demon strike me down. Our hosts are considering giving Liah control of the Slaugh if I can't rein in the fae. Liah's building a resistance – soon she'll be too strong for me to oppose. I'd rather give up the earth than live under her reign."

Everything he said was good news for us. Hope surged inside me. "Then accept my proposal. Call off the Slaugh. Go back on the deal. Bring the fae to earth to live in the wild places."

Daigh shook his head. "I wish I could, but if I bring this to the fae now, they will not accept it. They will see me as weak, trying to save my family at their expense. It will send them all to Liah. If she controls the Slaugh, they have no reason to follow me."

"You have another idea, I'm guessing?"

Daigh nodded. "Liah needs to fail first. My fae need to know that the world she envisions can never be. I need the fae to see the vision you and Blake have seen – of the world broken and burning from this 'nuclear' weapon. Only when they realise there is no hope with her will they accept the offer you propose."

"And how do you plan to show them our vision? You haven't even seen it. You only know about it because Blake told you."

"*You* will show them, dreamwalker. You and Blake."

"If you think I'm setting foot down in wherever in the cosmos you're mirroring in from, you can think again," I warned. The words 'hell no' danced on my tongue, but they seemed a little on-the-nose, so I held back.

"We will come to you. I can make that happen. I will bring a few of my most trusted and loyal fae. I know you and Blake can communicate through your dreams. You will draw my fae into the dream, show them the truth of it, of what will happen. They need to feel their lungs closing over, and the ghosts of the trees clutching at a dying world."

"When do you want to do this thing?"

"As soon as possible. I believe I can be ready at midnight tonight. We'll meet you beside the sidhe."

"Midnight, of course. How mystical." I yawned in the mirror. "I'm never going to get a decent night's sleep. Sure, let me talk to the guys and we'll—"

Daigh frowned. "It must only be you and Blake."

"Why?"

"Because if my fae see the Briarwood coven closing in around them, they'll suspect a trap."

"For your most loyal fae, they're untrusting."

"They *are* fae. You and Blake must come alone."

"The guys aren't going to let us do that. They'll be hiding in the forest, watching. That's the best I can offer."

Daigh sighed. "You drive a hard bargain, daughter. Fine. They will hide, but if they are seen, this will not work."

"I'll tell them to be extra careful. What happens once we've convinced these fae of the truth of the vision?"

"They will spread the word amongst the rest of our kin. Once the fae have returned to my power and Liah has been dealt with, I will call off the Slaugh."

"Let me get this straight – Blake and I take a huge fucking risk by stepping outside the protective boundaries of Briarwood to show your fae this vision, and the only guarantee we've got that it's even going to stop the Slaugh is your *word?* The word of a lying fae."

"Why do you care? If The Slaugh comes, the humans detonate this nuclear weapon." Daigh steepled long fingers against his chin. "Problem solved."

"War against the Slaugh means *humans die too*. We can't breathe in that poisonous atmosphere or live without nutrients any more than you can. It's mutually assured destruction, not the best-case scenario."

"Then you'll help me?"

I thought of Flynn's statue drawing power from the village's hatred of us, and the other artworks that would soon be joining it.

If Daigh is lying, then we still have a way of stopping the Slaugh and sending the fae back to their realm. But if he's telling the truth, then we might be able to end the feud between fae and humans once and for all.

"We're helping each other. If that makes you uncomfortable—"

Something crunched out the window.

I spun around. What was that? Because this was the ground-floor bathroom, and the window looked into the inner courtyard, the glass was frosted. A shape moved in the corner of the frame, but I couldn't make out what it was.

I raced to the window and flung it open, squinting into the courtyard and straining my ears for a sound. I thought I heard something scrape against stone, but no other sound followed it. *It's probably Obelix, chasing some small defenceless furry creature.*

I turned back to the mirror, but Daigh was no longer visible. "Hey, come back!" I pounded against the glass, but he didn't show his face.

Another scraping sound outside. *Okay, that definitely wasn't a cat.*

I ran to the window again, shoving my shoulders through and leaning right out so I could see around the edge of the inner gate. I could just make out a long shadow retreating down the drive. I shoved the window open further. "Hey, who is that?"

The shadow didn't answer. It sped up, disappearing around the corner of the drive. I flung the bathroom door open and ran through the kitchen, shoving my head out the kitchen door. "Guys, come quick!"

Hopefully, they heard me over all the banging and soldering.

I didn't have time to find out. I tore back through the house, flung the front door open and raced across the courtyard. As I rounded the first corner of the drive, my chest heaving, I caught a glimpse of a car parked over the front of the drive. Someone – the shadow, I guessed – yanked the passenger side door open and climbed in. The tyres squealed as the car sped off, heading back down the road toward Crook-shollow.

"Bloody hell, Maeve." Arthur puffed as he came up next to me, his sword clattering against his leg. "You gave us all a heart attack. We thought the fae had got you."

"Someone was in the courtyard," I said.

"Who?" Corbin appeared on the other side of me, his expression grave, his hands clenched into fists.

"I didn't see, but they made a run for it as soon as I saw them. They had a car waiting at the bottom of the drive."

"Maeve, look."

We turned around. Flynn stood under the portcullis at the entrance to the inner courtyard. He pointed a shaking finger at the high wooden door. A message had been scrawled across it in red.

DIE, WITCHES.

CHAPTER TWENTY-TWO

TWENTY-THREE: MAEVE

"The fuck?" Arthur growled, touching the sword at his side. He must've grabbed it on his way out to see what I was yelling about. Thank God...I mean, thank *Athena*, Arthur was never too far from a sword.

"How did the fae get behind the wards?" Aline asked.

"It wasn't the fae," I whispered, my stomach clenching as understanding dawned. "It's the villagers."

"How do you know if you didn't get a proper look at them?"

"They wouldn't have come here by car if they were fae."

"It could have been a human compelled by the fae," Blake pointed out. "Like Robert or Dora."

Clara shook her head. "The fae believe they've already won. They don't need to skulk around the castle hoping to scare us. But angry villagers who think we're raising the dead would do this."

Rowan touched his finger to the message and sniffed. "This isn't paint," he whispered. "It's blood."

"A warning." Corbin glanced around us.

"But whose blood is it?" I whispered.

I dug my phone out of my pocket, my heart beating. *If*

they've got to Kelly, I'll never forgive myself. As I dialled Jane's number, I noticed Corbin punching something into his phone.

Jane picked up on the second ring.

"Jane. Thank Athena, you're okay. Is Kelly there?"

Jane's voice was stern. "She doesn't want to talk to you."

"But she's there? No one hurt her?"

Jane sighed. "Yeah, she's here. Maeve, what happened?"

"Someone wrote on the door at Briarwood. *Die witches.* But it's written in blood. I thought..." I sank against the stone wall, holding my chest as if I might be able to shove my heart back inside.

"Well, it's not us."

The phone clicked off. *Jane hung up on me.*

Rowan sank down beside me and wrapped his arm around my shoulders, his eyes questioning.

"Kelly's fine," I breathed. "It's not her."

"I'll have Ryan's butler check the grounds for anything unusual," Clara said, fishing her mobile phone out of her purse.

Rowan's face crumpled. "What if they hurt Obelix?"

Flynn gripped his knife. "I'll cut those wankers."

"Obelix!" Rowan cupped his hands over his mouth. "Come here, boy!"

"Obelix, you wanker. Show yourself. Obelix?" Flynn joined in the call.

Something rustled in the flower garden under the ticket office. Rowan bent down and pushed aside the hydrangeas. "Obelix?"

The tubby cat waddled out with his nose in the air and plopped down on top of one of the beanbags. "Meorrrw?"

"Some guard cat you are," I scolded, picking him up and rocking him in my arms. Rowan came over and tickled his belly.

Flynn grabbed Obelix from my arms and rocked him like a baby. "Whose blood is it, then?"

"It's probably sheep blood," Corbin said. "The farmers around here would have easy access to that."

"They're just trying to scare us."

"It fucking worked," Rowan said, nuzzling Obelix's fur.

"What do we do now?" Flynn asked.

"From now on, no one goes into the village," I said. "We know these people are capable of violence. Corbin, is there anything we can do to magically propel them away from the house?"

"I know some protective charms we could make," Aline piped up. "Rowan can help me with the ingredients."

"Get it done," I said. "We've got something else we need to focus on. I just spoke to Daigh."

"You...what?" Corbin looked horrified. "But how?"

"He was in the mirror in the bathroom. That's where I was when I saw a shadow in the window." As quickly as I could, I explained how Daigh had appeared in the mirror and what he agreed to. Everyone listened with rapt attention, but their response wasn't what I expected.

"How is he communicating via the mirror inside the wards?" Aline asked, her brown furrowing.

"It wasn't really him – it was just a projection in the mirror."

"Last time we spoke with him, it was also a projection, but we still had to go outside of the walls to call him," Aline said.

"Maybe it only works if he calls us, but not the other way around?"

"Maybe," she said, but she didn't look convinced.

"I can't believe I'm saying this, but we don't have time to worry about the mechanics of Daigh's appearance." The rules of magic didn't seem to follow any logic I understood. If they did, Aline would be in a box in the ground and not standing in front of me arguing about this *exact* point. "The fact is, we have a chance to stop the Slaugh before they walk. Even though we have the belief power, it's completely untested. We have to take the chance to stop fae before they're able to hurt anyone else, especially if it means a permanent solution."

"I agree," Corbin said. "But I don't like the idea of you and Blake meeting him alone."

"Me neither," Arthur growled, touching his hand to his sword again.

"I knew you'd say that. That's why I told Daigh you'd be hiding in the trees, watching the whole thing. He knows he can't pull one over on us. What's the worst he can do?" I said. "We're all baptised now. He can't drag us down to the underworld with him."

Corbin didn't look convinced, but he wasn't in charge, I was, and I needed to believe that we could solve this without getting the souls of the dead involved. I looked around our little group. With the exception of Clara and Ryan – because I didn't really know them – every one of us had lost someone special to us, someone who we didn't want to see resurrected as a ghoul to terrorise and scour the earth. We had to take the chance that Daigh was at least considering the plan.

Back in the house, Flynn, Ryan, Arthur, and Corbin went back to work on the statue. Rowan grilled sausages and made a salad and fries (chips, in the English vernacular), while Aline chopped herbs and made small pouches out of some old velvet curtains. She filled the pouches with herbs and stones, and waved her hands and chanted over them like a fairground fortune teller. I hoped like hell she knew what she was doing.

Aline added a drop of blood from each of us into the charms and sealed the bags. "No human will be able to pass through these charms except for those whose blood has touched them," she explained. "They will work alongside the wards that protect you from the fae entering, and will also stop most magic – fae or witch – from penetrating the walls. There is a catch."

"Spill it," I said, holding my head in my hands. *Great, one more thing to worry about.*

"You'll still be able to use your magic inside the castle grounds, but you cannot send magic over the boundary. Any spell you cast or attempt to will come up against an invisible barrier. The barrier won't last forever. Enough power or muscle thrown at it and it will crumble, same as any wall. But I've made it as strong as I dare."

"I just *know* this is going to bite us in the arse," Corbin said, gathering up an armful of the pouches. "But we'll take what we can get."

Arthur and Corbin went to place the charms at the corners of the estate. When they returned and reported no other villagers nearby, we sat down for a tense dinner, punctuated by a long stream of Flynn nonsense as he tried to impress his new artistic hero.

After dinner, Clara and Ryan left to return to Raynard Hall, and the boys decided to teach Aline how to play video games. Since the last time she saw a computer game the graphics were still in two dimensions, she was awestruck as soon as Flynn handed her a controller. I laughed along with them watching her die three times in quick succession, when I noticed Corbin had disappeared from the Great Hall.

"I'll be right back," I told Flynn and headed up to my room to grab something I wanted to show Corbin, which I folded up and hid under my shirt. Back on the first floor I found him – of course – behind his desk in the library, poring over Clara's ancient book.

"Find anything important?" I asked. Corbin set down his magnifying glass.

"Not important, just interesting. I knew the history of the Soho coven was sordid, but it turns out I don't even know the meaning of the word."

"Oh yeah?" I raised an eyebrow as I slid onto the arm of his wingback chair. My leg brushed his, and a shiver ran through my body as I remembered the first time we'd been in the library alone together, when we'd ended up shagging on top of the Briarwood grimoire.

"Look at this." Corbin turned the book around. "This was a drawing from one of the coven members, who was a relatively well-known London artist."

I glanced at the sketch, which looked pretty similar to the orgy pictures in our own grimoire, except...*woah*. Some of the men in the picture weren't really men. "Those are—"

"Werewolves and vulpines – fox shapeshifters," Corbin grinned. "It seems humans and witches aren't the only races with peculiar tastes."

It was on the tip of my tongue to ask if shapeshifters existed, but I decided it wasn't something I wanted to know at this point. "Are you worried about the villagers?" I asked.

"Not as much as I'm worried about Daigh. You know he's up to something with this meeting tonight, don't you?"

"Of course. But what's the alternative? Even if we did stop the Slaugh and send the fae back to their realm, we'd take casualties. I think we can all agree enough people have died."

"More than enough," he agreed, his voice grim.

"All we do, if we win, is banish the fae back to their realm, where they'll fester their resentment for years and come to attack us again. Only next time they might not have Daigh's desire for his family to temper their rage. And for all the evil Daigh and Liah have done, they have a point. Humans treat the earth like crap. We burn fossil fuels, poison the oceans, and bulldoze the forests to make way for more cities when we can't even feed all the people we have now. We were the ones who invaded the fae lands first, and we haven't exactly been the best caretakers."

"Are you agreeing with the fae?" Corbin asked with a smirk.

"If we can make this alliance work, it's the best for everyone. I'm just trying to see the good in both sides, the way a good leader should," I flicked a strand of hair from his eye. "Like someone taught me."

"I've been thinking about what you said yesterday," Corbin ran a hand through his dark hair. "About going to university."

I waited. It was something I noticed Corbin did – instead of asking questions or giving his opinion, he waited out the silence until people opened up and said the things that were burning in their minds. It was time someone turned that trick back on him.

Corbin stared at the wall of books – the one Rowan always counted before he sat down. He stared for a long time, not saying anything. I was just about to give up and ask him if he was serious when he said, "I think...I would like to go to university. Maybe to Oxford, if I can even get in. It's not a guarantee, even though my Dad teaches there. You have to be good at writing essays and shit, and I haven't done that stuff since high school, which was a long time ago."

"You'll get in." I reached my hands around his waist, kissing his smooth lips. "You're amazing. You can do anything if you set your mind to it."

"I don't think so," he scoffed.

"You brought all of us together, didn't you?" I thumped my hand on the stack of books on the desk. *Bad idea.* A column of dust kicked up and tickled my nose. "You put all the pieces together from all these old books and followed the clues all the way across the country – across the world, in my case. You're like that famous detective whose picture was in all the Oxford pubs. Detective Semaphore—"

"Inspector Morse?" Corbin's lips curled back.

I waved my hand. "Whatever. You should write about him in your application essay."

Corbin laughed. Then his face turned serious. "It would mean I would have to live in Oxford, at least for the first year. It's only ninety minutes on the train, but I don't like the idea of leaving Briarwood, and you—"

"Maybe you don't have to. I've been thinking about Oxford ever since we visited, too. We'll go together."

Saying that out loud was worth it 100 times over just for the shocked expression on Corbin's face.

"You...but..." His eyes widened. "What about MIT?"

"Oxford is just as fancy and prestigious as MIT." I pulled the folded papers from under my shirt and tossed them down on the desk, revealing the Department of Physics prospectus I'd taken from the Ashmolean. "I've been doing some research into their astrophysics program, and I think I'd learn just as much here as I could in America. And, as you say, it's only ninety minutes by train from Crookshollow. Think about it, Corbin. We could get a room in one of the colleges together, and come back to Briarwood on the weekends. The guys could visit us whenever they wanted."

"Rowan could send us care packages of biscuits and scones," he grinned.

"So you like the idea?"

"Are you kidding?" He wrapped his huge arms around me, his lips meeting mine for a searing kiss. "I love it. But you'd better not make me sign up for any more theoretical physics papers. That one you did at community college nearly did my head in."

"You of all people should know a good education is a well-rounded one," I grinned back.

"Fine. If I'm doing theoretical physics, you're studying Farsi."

"What in Athena's name is Farsi?" I was enjoying swearing by my new patron goddess, even though I didn't believe in her.

"The language of countries that historically identify as part of Persian society."

"Great." I rolled my eyes. "That sounds *really* useful."

"You never know – maybe one day we'll all be speaking Farsi on Mars."

My stomach fluttered with sudden nerves. "Do you think we can do this? Leave Briarwood to study?"

"I think it's worth a try." Corbin smiled, but his smile was tinged with sadness. "I know I need to let go of this idea that I have to look after everyone, that Briarwood is my sole responsibility. The other guys have more than proven they're capable of managing any problems while we're away, and as you said, we'll be back on weekends. It might just be possible to be a Briarwood witch *and* have a life. That is, if we can stop the Slaugh and survive the next week."

I sighed. "We just made plans to study astrophysics and obscure languages next year. It's going to be hard to do that if the university becomes a fairy grotto. We've got no choice now."

Corbin glanced over my shoulder at the grandfather clock. "It's nine o'clock. You're meeting Daigh at midnight. How do you propose to pass the time?"

I slipped my hands down the front of his shirt, popping open the buttons one by one. "I dunno... maybe we should bone up on our Farsi..."

CHAPTER TWENTY-THREE

TWENTY-FOUR: MAEVE

"You're not going with us." I folded my arms, spreading my feet wide to block Aline from the kitchen doorway.

"Daigh said he didn't want any of the other *guys*," Aline insisted, her voice rising into what was rapidly approaching an irritating whine. "But he didn't say anything about *me*."

"He said it had to be only me and Blake or the whole thing was off. I'm not going to risk this deal just so you can ogle your old sweetheart."

Aline's face fell. Guilt panged in my stomach, but I pushed it aside. She was acting irrational, and a bit childish. She reminded me of Kelly chasing after her latest crush.

Kelly. The pangs in my stomach intensified. I hadn't seen or heard from her since our horrible fight. *Will she ever talk to me again?*

Aline wasn't going to let me forget that she existed. "I know Daigh better than any of you." She grabbed my arm. "I may be able to read some treachery you can't."

"I think I know his treachery when I see it," Blake murmured behind me.

"You're not coming, and that's my final word as High Priestess of this coven. Stay in the castle. We need someone to watch out for any of the villagers approaching. Call on Corbin's mobile if there are any problems."

"But—"

I turned on my heel and headed toward the orchard, not waiting for her to finish.

"You don't seem happy to have your mother back," Blake said as he caught up with me.

"She's only my mother in the biological sense. Another woman raised me, wiped my tears, put Bandaids on my skinned knees, and bought me astronomy books for Christmas. Right now she's a whiny houseguest with a penchant for trying to fix everything with woo-woo hippie stuff."

Blake grinned, like he didn't believe me. "If you're sure, Princess."

"What?" I growled. Behind us, I heard the creek of the kitchen garden gate as the boys snuck out behind us and headed toward the topiary maze, where they could cut through to the wood and hide without Daigh's fae seeing them.

"Nothing. Nothing at all." Blake's grin infuriated me.

"If you think she's so awesome, how come you haven't asked her about your parents?" I demanded.

Blake shrugged. "Never thought about it."

"Bullshit. I saw your face after all those things she said on the night we freed her from the painting. Rowan needed to know. Why don't you?"

Blake shrugged again. "It's not going to bring them back."

"But you never knew them at all. Don't you at least—"

"Do you want to know anything about Aline?" Blake shot back.

"I've asked her lots of things." I thought back to our private conversation in the library the first day she was here with us. I'd been wary of her presence, but I caught glimpses of her life before through the things she said and left unsaid. I didn't like thinking about Aline too much because if she'd been my mother – *really* my mother, the way Louise Crawford was – my life would have been different. I didn't like to think about the person I might've become – and the fact that Kelly wouldn't be part of my life – if Aline hadn't been trapped in that painting. "It's my job to be suspicious of her, especially now that she's trying to talk to Daigh and making charms that confine our magic to the castle. But I guess…I really do believe she's who she says she is. I just don't know how I feel about that yet. Hearing about the past is nice, it makes me feel weird, but good, you know? I just can't let it distract me from the present."

"Hm." Blake wrapped his arm around my shoulder. I leaned in, letting his bright, spicy scent strengthen me for what was about to happen. "You and I feel much the same, only I don't want to know anything. I never had loving adoptive parents like you did, Princess. If I go digging into my real parents' pasts and start finding out how kind and wonderful and amazing they were, then I might go postal."

I snorted at his terminology. Blake grinned. "I heard that on Flynn's video game. And you said those things rot your brain."

"They do."

Blake ran his fingers through my hair, messing it up. He kissed my cheek, his lips so deliciously soft and warm. "You keep being suspicious and asking your questions, Princess. That's who you are. But don't expect me to keep focusing on the past. I'm trying to enjoy my time at Briarwood while I have it. I don't want to think about the past or I might end up hating you or the others because of what you had that I didn't. No way do I want that to happen, okay?" He kicked a loose stone on the path. "Can we forget about Aline and focus on Daigh and that pox-ridden dream?"

I remembered Blake's face from a few days ago, when Corbin took us to visit the home where his parents lived. Or where that home *had* been, since Daigh compelled Blake's dad to burn it down after he killed her mother and before he killed himself. I thought Corbin was nuts taking Blake to a place tainted by such vicious, insidious crimes, but Blake seemed to appreciate it.

Now I wondered if that house was all Blake needed to know about his past. Maybe it was too much.

On our right, Corbin shushed the other guys as they fanned out through the forest, moving into their hiding places around the sidhe. Blake pushed open the orchard gate and we jogged down the hill to the stone wall that marked the barrier of Briarwood with the field and sidhe beyond.

My head darted down the length of the wall. We hadn't bothered with a flashlight since the moon shone cold and clear, uninhibited by clouds. It cast a blue haze over the dry grass covering the sidhe, highlighting the charred patches where Arthur's fireballs had wasted the fae. Was that only a week ago? It felt like another lifetime.

My cell phone beeped. Corbin:

> The forest and meadow are clear. Good luck.
> We're all watching out for you.

Blake took my hand. Together, we clambered over the low wall – passing through the protective wards and charms that surrounded Briarwood – and made our way down to the sidhe.

At least now we can use our magic freely to defend ourselves, if we need it.

Please, Athena, don't let us need it.

The entrance to the largest mound loomed like a black mouth into the earth. Blake squeezed my hand. Tendrils of black smoke curled through the grass, lifting into the still air and forming narrow smoky shapes.

From the smoke emerged four figures, their bodies wrapped in a black film that melted from their skin like hot wax. Daigh's face appeared – his pale skin luminescent in the moonlight, his mouth set in that characteristic carefree smirk that Blake emulated too well. However, the glittering eyes that set their sights on me were a mirror image of my own.

Three stony faces materialised behind him, each one with the glassy eyes and smooth, alabaster skin that marked the high-born fae. They regarded us warily, scanning the hills, their hands darting to their weapons.

"I sense other witches nearby," one said, raising his bone blade and pointing it at my chest. "We've been betrayed."

"She was hardly going to come here unprotected," Daigh said. "I wouldn't expect anything less from my daughter. They will not hear our conversation from here. Or do you not wish to proceed?"

He delivered the words casually, as if it mattered not to him whatever happened. But the fae's skin got even more pale, and he stepped back, shaking his head. He didn't take his hand off the hilt of his sword.

Daigh beamed at Blake. "We meet again, my Prince. You're looking well-fed."

Blake's smirk twitched a little at the edges. "The curry is good here."

"I'm glad." Daigh swivelled his gaze back to me. "You have the potion?"

I dug my hand into my jeans pocket and pulled out a small vial of the same sleeping draught Rowan had made for our journey to the underworld. "Here's how this will work. I will pull you into the dream, and Blake's magic will amplify mine and ensure we're all able to come back again. To do this, I'll need a lock of your hair. Each of you."

The fae grumbled. Daigh glowered at them until the first fae raised his knife to his hair and sawed off a lock. He handed it to Blake, who plaited it into a strand that he wound around my wrist. I followed with plaits of the others, holding my wrist up to the light to admire the gossamer threads of fae hair that glimmered in the moonlight.

"We don't have much time," Daigh said.

I uncapped the vial, tilted my head back and swallowed the draught in one go. I leaned back into Blake's arms. "Maybe this time I'll see who's on the sixth stake," I murmured.

He kissed my cheek. Spirit magic fluttered from his lips, piercing my skin. "Sleep well, Princess."

My eyes fluttered shut and the world faded into darkness.

CHAPTER TWENTY-FOUR

TWENTY-FIVE: MAEVE

I woke up face down on the parched earth. Heat and steam rose through the cracks, scalding my skin. I gasped for breath, but the air in my lungs tasted foul. My stomach heaved, burning up my oesophagus as acidic bile rose through my throat.

I looked up with stinging eyes. Orange flames streaked across the sky. A towering wall of impenetrable briar rose up, blocking me from the blackened castle beyond.

I'm here.

I scrambled to my feet and tugged at the bracelets on my wrist, unravelling them one by one as fast as I could. I wanted to get this over with so I could go back to where I could breathe. A hand fell on my shoulder.

"Welcome to hell, Princess," Blake's voice reverberated against my ear. He might've sounded sexy if he hadn't broken down into a coughing fit of his own.

"Where are we?" Daigh demanded, peeling his lanky body from the ground. His fae scrambled to their feet and brushed the dust from his clothes.

"This is it," I whispered. My words fell away as I choked on the acrid air. I pointed up at the wall of briar, to the castle beyond. Orange fire streaked across the dead sky. The only sound was the crunch of our boots on the parched ground and my gasping, hawking breath in my ears.

I was so used to Daigh's indifference that I wasn't prepared for the strangled sob that escaped his throat. His facade crumpled with horror, and for the first time, I glimpsed what it was to be a fae connected to the earth and the seasons. His grief flowed out of him, sizzling in the air around me – a raw and vengeful magic.

One of his fae raised her hand to her mouth, but her thin fingers did nothing to hold in her dry scream. Another dragged a bow from his back and pointed it into the sky, as though he might slay the demon we now breathed into our lungs.

Daigh cried, "This is *torture.*"

"It's what will become of the earth if the Slaugh ride," Blake said.

"Take us to the stakes," Daigh ordered.

My whole body trembled. I didn't want to move, didn't want to see my boys strung up like that again.

Daigh's hard gaze bore into my back.

I stepped forward, moving along the briar hedge, crawling through the pain in my body and the tears stinging my eyes until I came to the entrance to the maze. I turned into the briar, relishing the cooler temperature inside the briar, although it could provide no relief from the poison air.

The others followed behind me, coughing and hacking as we made our way deeper into the briar. We emerged into the clearing. The six stakes rose from the earth, circles of charred dirt beneath them. A sob escaped my lips as the bodies came into focus – twisted forms that had once been human but had been brought to ruin by the cruelty of the fae. Flynn's clear blue eyes bulged from the charred skull of the first, Corbin with his face cut and mutilated, Arthur wearing his severed hands around his neck like a grisly necklace, Rowan with his ears cut off and his black hair matted against his burned skin, Blake's white teeth leering from his ruined face. The sixth figure was too far away and at an angle for me to recognise.

The sixth…I have to see the sixth…

I tried to lift my leg, but it was rooted in place. I flung my arms out, trying to propel myself forward, but I barely managed to slide an inch. Panic rose in my chest as I fought against the invisible barrier. Why won't the dream let me see? Why does it never let me see?

"The dream's breaking up," Blake choked out from behind me.

He was right. The dream cracked at the edges. Black tendrils curled through the vivid orange sky. The stakes wobbled in front of me. Arthur's collapsed beneath him, sending up a cloud of dust as his body crashed to the ground.

Blake grabbed my arm. "We have to go back," he yelled. Spirit magic leaked out of his skin as his whole body trembled. Pain arced through his voice. He couldn't hold much longer.

I need to know.

My magic hummed and crackled, protesting my defiance. I collected the well of spirit magic inside me, sucking it from the dream and balling it up. The sky cracked and shattered like glass, sherds of the broken heavens plunging into the earth around me like porcupine quills.

"Maeve, no!"

I ignored Blake and threw the magic in front of me, tearing through the invisible wall. My legs broke from the vice that held them and I toppled forward, my hands slamming into the earth. I leapt to my feet and ran toward the sixth stake. Just as I glimpsed the corner of the face, the entire dream collapsed and I ran into a giant black void.

My body slammed into hard earth. My fingers clutched at blades of grass. I lifted my head, and pain surged along my neck. I gasped for breath, and the air tasted deliciously cool and fresh and sweet. Beside me, Blake moaned and rolled over.

"Did you see?" I gasped at Blake. "Did you see the figure on the sixth stake?"

Blake dug his hands under my shoulders and hauled me to my feet. He wrapped his arms around me, holding me upright. Warm spirit magic flowed from him into me, easing the pain in my shoulders and back, calming over the horrors in my mind. "I didn't see, Princess," he whispered. "I'm sorry."

Daigh watched us, his mouth twisted into a strange expression that might have been half terror, half satisfaction. His fae clutched each other, sobbing and keening for the broken earth.

"So you'll do it, then?" I demanded. "You will accept our deal?"

The fae exchanged glances with Daigh. Their pale skin was even lighter than usual. Their eyes flickered with unease. What they'd seen had horrified them.

Good. It had bloody near broken me.

"We will take this dream back to the fae realm with us," Daigh said. "We will spread word amongst the fae of the consequences of the Slaugh. As soon as the fae are in my control again, I will send word that we accept the deal. Wait for us at your castle, if it still exists."

I started at his words. "What do you mean, if it still exists?"

Daigh tilted his gaze up toward Briarwood. I followed his eyes, and my heart leapt in my throat.

A glowing, flickering light moved across the meadow toward the castle. I could just make out the snatches of chanting and shouting on the still air. Angry voices. The light drew closer and I made out the shapes of individual torches held aloft.

Torches. The kind peasants burned witches with.

The villagers. They'd worked themselves into a frenzy over Flynn's statue and Aline's presence, and now they were approaching the castle to do what? It couldn't be good.

But why hadn't Aline warned us?

Corbin and Arthur burst through the trees and raced toward the castle. Corbin yelled something, but I didn't catch it. Blake's face twisted.

"Come on," he yelled as he bolted toward the house. "The bastards are coming for us!"

TWENTY-SIX: CORBIN

I raced up the hill after Arthur, blood pounding in my ears. As we pounded across the garden, voices drifted up from the meadow. Angry voices shouting at the top of their lungs. I caught snatches of the words; "...witches...necromancers...cast out the devils..."

We've been so busy worrying about the fae, it never occurred to us that we'd have to fight other humans.

But it should have. History has shown us this exact situation time and time again. I should have predicted this the moment we started talking about belief magic.

Yet another way I'd failed the coven.

Arthur was the fittest, so he reached the kitchen garden first, slamming the gate back against the stone wall so hard I heard it splinter. He held it open for me. I skidded into the heavy kitchen door and flung it open.

"Come on!" I yelled, holding the door back as the others raced across the garden. "We've got to get inside!"

Flynn was next, slowing his speed as he came through the gate so he could give a Ministry of Silly Walks performance on the way to the kitchen door.

"Get in," I growled, shoving him through so Rowan could slip in behind him. This was no time for Flynn's nonsense.

Blake dragged Maeve along by the arm. Even in the gloom of night, I could see how they both staggered with exhaustion, their eyes ringed with red from the huge amount of magic they exerted to pull Daigh and his fae cronies into the dream.

I flicked my eyes toward the meadow. The tall hedge and kitchen garden wall hid it from view, but I could make out the flicker of the torches through the leaves. Loud, angry voices met my ears, still too far away to understand more than a few words, but I could gather the gist of it. No one brought pitchforks along to a peaceful sit-in.

They're not hurting my coven. I'll die before I let them into this castle.

Maeve and Blake staggered through the kitchen gate. Arthur moved to bolt it when another voice cried, "Wait, don't shut the door!"

I turned back to the garden. A figure in white raced from the orchard. Aline. Her skirts flapped around her and her face was drawn with fright. She crashed through the open doors and we slammed and locked them behind her.

"Right," I hissed, leaning my bulk against the door, and faced the room. "We have a problem."

"Mary Mother of God, never in my life did I think I'd see a lynch mob," Flynn whistled, gripping the edge of the counter. "What are the chances they're here just for you protestant infidels?"

"Not the time, Flynn," I yelled. My mind reeled, compiling all the things we'd need to do to secure the castle. *The protective charms we set out earlier today will hold them back for a while, but not even they will stop a fire, and we can't use our magic against them until they're inside the walls, which means we've got no way out—*

"Why weren't you in the house?" Maeve yelled at Aline. "You were supposed to watch for something like this and warn us."

"I'm sorry!" Aline sobbed, throwing herself against the island. "I wanted to see Daigh again. I wanted to help."

"And because of you *trying to help*, they got a jump on us. If we hadn't seen them when we did, we might not've made it back in time." Aline shrunk away from Maeve's anger.

"This isn't important right now," I growled, pulling myself off the door and racing into the hall. We couldn't just sit here and argue while the villagers approached.

"Corbin, where are you going?" Maeve called after me.

"Rowan, bolt the kitchen gate," I called back, as I hit the hallway and kept on running. Behind me, wood scraped against wood as Rowan slid the heavy bolts into place.

"Corbin, hold up, mate." Arthur grabbed my shoulder, yanking me back so hard he wrenched my arm and we bumped against a heavy medieval dresser.

"What are you doing?" I demanded.

"You can't just run off like that. Remember, you're not the leader any more."

"Our enemy approaches. We've got to prepare ourselves for a siege – bar the gates and strengthen our defences."

Arthur looked confused.

I clench my fists with exasperation. "Come on, Aragorn, you know this stuff. Unless they've brought equipment for scaling the walls, the only two ways into the inner courtyard and the keep is through the main portcullis and Rowan's kitchen garden."

Understanding dawned on Arthur's face. "Right. I'll help you."

The portcullis was operated from a locked gatehouse near the gift shop. I grabbed the key from the rack beside the door and raced across the courtyard, Arthur at my heels. Inside the gatehouse was an old-fashioned crank, installed during the Victorian period to replace the medieval one that had finally given up the ghost. We'd often talked about getting something modern we could operate from a switch in the house, but we lowered the portcullis so infrequently it wasn't worth the expense.

Arthur and I leaned on the enormous winch, and after a bit of grunting and sweating, we managed to unlock it and lower the portcullis. We shut the wooden inner doors and slid the bolts true.

Once we were back inside, I slid the heavy bolts over the keep doors. "They can't get in that way."

"They've got flaming torches," Maeve whimpered, knocking her knuckles against the wooden door.

"And we've got a human power hose who can work magic as soon as they're inside the grounds," I grinned, jabbing my finger at Flynn, who took a deep bow. Maeve didn't look convinced.

"Don't forget, the majority of the castle is made of stone. It's not as easy to burn," Arthur added.

"If I had to be trapped in a medieval castle with anyone, I'm glad it's you guys," Maeve smiled.

I clapped my hands, and six heads turned toward me. "Okay, next line of defence. If they manage to break through to the inner courtyard, we're vulnerable because of the windows that face inward. But the windows on the first floor all have the security bars over them, so we're good there. Our big problems are the kitchen windows and that huge glass panel in the drawing room that could be broken. We need to bar the doors to those rooms."

"I'm on it," Arthur said. "I'll shift those heavy dressers in the hall in front of the doors. I'd like to see them shift those."

"Go," Maeve nodded. Arthur ran off.

"What about the secret passage in the kitchen?" Blake asked.

"We'll block the top of it, but I think we leave the bottom alone. It might be a useful escape route for us. We just have to hope like hell none of them notice the door in the back of the pantry."

"What about the Great Hall windows?" Maeve asked. "The ones overlooking the gardens could also be broken."

"The ditch is right underneath them. To get at those windows they'd have to either be giants or have access to some seriously sturdy ladders." I thought of the garden shed down by the orchard, and all Flynn's tools in the stable buildings. They might find a ladder in there. "Just to be safe, we'll seal off the Great Hall, too. But we should get all these weapons off the walls. If they manage to get in here, I don't want to give them access to an arsenal."

"Should we move the tapestries?" Maeve asked. "Dora said they were valuable."

"Not as valuable as our lives. We don't have time."

Maeve and I started tearing the swords off the walls and piling them on the ground. After ten minutes of grunting and scraping in the hall, Arthur came into the Great Hall with a handful of blades and swords. "Ah, you've had the same idea." He dumped his haul on top of our pile.

"I don't think we did," Maeve said. But Arthur had already made his way to the bottom of the stairs.

"Everyone, come choose your weapon," he bellowed.

Before I could protest, footsteps clattered through the house as the boys and Aline converged on our weapon horde. "I want this one," Flynn declared, grabbing for an enormous curved scimitar.

I clamped my hand over his wrist. "No weapons. We're not

fighting the fae this time – these are *people*. They bleed red, just like us. They're only outside because we frightened them, and they think it's the only way. Having blood on our hands isn't going to help us win the war with the fae."

"I agree with you, mate, really I do," Flynn said, swinging the scimitar around like he was in a video game. I winced as he sliced off a corner of the tapestry. "But what if one of those bastards out there tries to kill me? I'm too virile and handsome to die tonight."

"You've got your magic," I pointed out.

"Only once they're too close for comfort, thanks to those charms. Besides, I don't think fighting them with magic is going to help dissolve this situation," Maeve added, taking a sword and scabbard from Arthur and belting it around her hips.

"Fine," I growled, picking up a small blade and shoving it down the side of my boot. "But these weapons are *only* for self-defence, got it? We don't want any more innocent lives on our conscience."

Everyone nodded vigorously as they swept over the pile, strapping swords to their hips and across their backs and shoving daggers down the sides of their shoes. Aline held up a beautiful narrow blade, while Flynn stuck a mace into his trousers. Arthur hefted a large pike between his meaty fists, testing the weight. I shook my head. He tossed it into the hall and shot me a disappointed stare.

"What do we do now?" Maeve asked, her big eyes staring up at me. She'd completely given over command to me. All other eyes in the room faced mine.

This is all on me now. Keep everyone safe.

"We need to hole up somewhere we can see what's going on," I said. "We don't know how long the charms will hold them back."

"Maeve's bedroom?" Flynn raised an eyebrow.

"Perfect." The tower room was the highest point in the castle. We'd be able to see right down over the meadow. It would give us our first clue if our defences had failed. "Let's go."

We clattered up the stairs. Arthur lifted Maeve and carried her in his arms, the way he'd done when she first arrived at the castle. Aline trailed along behind us, looking like she didn't know if she was invited or not.

"Rowan, can you go and grab the mattress off your bed for Aline?" Maeve asked. Rowan darted off and Aline's shoulders relaxed a little bit. Maeve didn't know how to act around her mother, but when it came to the crunch she wouldn't make her fend for herself.

I stood in front of the arched window. From here, I could see over the briar hedge at the bottom of the garden and into the meadow beyond. A crowd of fifty or so people had gathered around the entrance to the right-of-way. As I watched, two of them ran at the gate but bounced back into the grass as if they'd hit a trampoline.

The charms are holding for now.

But how long that would last? More torches moved along the road, heading for the front gates to Briarwood. Eight figures broke off from the main group and started down the boundary, heading toward the sidhe to try and get through the back of our property. My breath caught in my throat – what would they have done to us if they'd caught Maeve and Blake there earlier when they were in the dream world and powerless to stop them?

Beside me, Aline whimpered. I wondered if she was thinking the same thing. I tried not to feel anger toward her. We'd made it back in time, that was what mattered. Now we had to focus on what came next.

"I'll take the first watch," I said. No way was I going to get any rest tonight. "The rest of you try and sleep. We need to be strong and rested."

"Okay, but you need to actually wake us up, " Arthur growled. "No being the martyr and staying up all night so we can sleep. We need you to rest, too."

"Deal." I had no intention of waking them up, but Arthur didn't need to know that. We shook hands. He crushed my fingers under his grip.

Rowan collapsed on the bed, his eyes boring into mine. An unspoken message passed between us. He was afraid – for Maeve, and for me. I was afraid, too. Aline collected blankets from the box at the end of Maeve's bed and made up the mattress for herself, while Arthur, Flynn, and Blake lay down beside Rowan.

"Corbin, I'm scared." Maeve wrapped her arms around me, her deep hazel eyes watching the scene outside the window.

Me too. I squeezed her shoulders, wishing on all the gods that I had the power to protect them all. Briarwood had seen too much pain and death. I was all that stood in the way of ruin, and I wouldn't turn my back on my loved ones.

Me too.

CHAPTER TWENTY-SIX

TWENTY-SEVEN: MAEVE

A chorus of snuffles and snores rose up around me. Warm bodies pressed against mine, limbs tangled together like a hot bowl of Mom's spaghetti bolognese. My head rested against Flynn's chest, which rose and fell in a steady rhythm. *This is the* best *way to sleep.*

If I could actually sleep.

I'd been staring at the ceiling for hours, straining my ears as though I might somehow be able to hear what was going on outside. How could I sleep while people stood out there with torches ready to burn us alive? How much longer would the protective charms hold us?

I sat up, my bladder screaming. Arthur stood at the window. He'd cleverly set his alarm clock so he could wake up and relieve Corbin. That exchange had happened a half hour ago. Corbin hadn't looked happy to leave his post (clearly, he never intended to wake Arthur up), but he'd snuggled down into Rowan's arms and fallen asleep in minutes. He didn't stir as I slid out from under Blake's arm and joined Arthur at the window.

"No change," he said, wrapping his huge arm around my

shoulder. His eyes never left the scene outside. "We're still holding. Why are you up?"

Far below, figures surrounded the walls of the cottage, their glittering torches still glowing. At the front gate, a tow truck and a couple of tractors had torn the iron gates off and now banged against the invisible barrier, trying to break it down.

"I need the bathroom," I said.

"You should wake someone to go with you. None of us should be alone, even in the castle."

"It's literally at the bottom of the stairs. I'll be fine." The boys weren't able to build an ensuite into the tower without extensive plumbing work, so they'd given one of the bathrooms on the second floor over to me. They'd decorated it in the same jewel tones as my room, and a brand new claw-foot bath took up half the impressive floor plan. I'd already filled it with Rowan's handmade soaps and organic skincare products from Clara's shop. It smelled like a rose garden and I loved it.

I did my business, then sat on the edge of the bath and stared out the narrow arrow slit beside the vanity at the sky beyond. Stars glittered across the sky like torches in the heavens. For the first time, they didn't fill me with wonder – only dread.

How long until the villagers break through?

Out of the corner of my eye, I noticed movement on the vanity. The mirror swirled with a dark mist that congealed in the centre. After a few moments, it settled into Daigh's face.

"You're hiding inside your castle, instead of fighting them?" he sneered. "That's not the daughter I raised."

"That's right. I'm not the daughter you raised, because you didn't raise me. Enough people have already died," I shot back. "That's the whole reason I'm trying to get you to take this deal – to save lives. We can't go around dishing out justice just because the villagers are scared of us."

"Why not? When people fear you, they obey you."

"I don't want people to obey me. I want them to leave me and my guys the fuck alone." I glared at him. "Present company included."

Daigh tilted his head to the side. "Such righteous anger. And yet, if the enemy outside were fae…"

"Same deal. Maybe in the past, humans have been cruel to the fae, because they were greedy or afraid. It doesn't mean we can't try another way. But you have to stop trying to slaughter us all first. I don't want to hurt the fae, but…" I touched the dagger I'd carried down with me. "We will defend ourselves."

"I'm not trying to slaughter you, my daughter." The rhyme sounded lyrical, intentional, on his lips. Daigh laughed. "I'm here to help save your skin. And maybe the skins of all your fellow witches, since you seem so attached to them."

"You can do that by telling me if you've secured the loyalty of the fae, if they'll support our agreement."

"It's too early to say, but the evidence is compelling. The fae see now that the dream cannot possibly be any future I bring about."

"There's no way to know that."

"But there is. Because I'd never impale my own daughter on a stake and burn her flesh off."

Air leaked out of my lungs like a punctured balloon. *It was me on the stake all along.* I ran my hand over my cheek, imagining the skin peeled away, the muscle and tendons below exposed to fire and carrion birds, my body burning while I screamed for mercy. My stomach churned.

Burned alive, just like my parents in the Ferris Wheel fire.

"You saw the sixth stake," I choked out. I tried to remember where Daigh had been standing in the dream, but it wouldn't come back to me. I'd been too focused on the scarred and broken bodies of my guys, pierced through the chest and blackened with fire. *Why did Daigh see it and not me?* Perhaps my subconscious had blocked me from seeing it, knowing that it would distress me.

I dug my nails into the enamel rim of the bath and leaned forward as my stomach heaved. Bile rose in my throat. I coughed, fighting to hold back my dinner. Through the mirror, Daigh made tutting voices.

I pressed my hands against the tiles. Their coolness brought me back to the present. To Daigh in the mirror, and the mob outside.

Do your duty, I reminded myself. *Protect the coven. Protect the earth at all costs.*

The urge to puke subsided, and I rose shakily to my feet. I stood at the window and gazed down at the mob outside. *Surely they didn't intend to—*

The door to the bathroom flew open. "Maeve, are you—" Aline's eyes widened when she saw the face in the mirror. She tripped over the hem of Flynn's pyjama pants in her haste to scramble to the basin. "Daigh! What are you doing talking to Maeve—ow!"

"Get away from him," I grabbed her wrist before she could touch the glass and yanked her away. "You don't know what touching that mirror might do."

"He wouldn't hurt me!" she whimpered.

"Don't be so sure of that. It's kind of your fault he's stuck in the fae realm in the first place."

"Just let me talk with him. I can help you."

My body twinged with indecision. On the one hand, this was my mother, the woman I'd wanted to get to know my entire life. On the other hand, the only connection we had was our biology. She was technically only a couple of years older than I was, and she was a complete flower child who believed in *astrology* of all things, so she wasn't exactly a mature, sensible influence. Her presence at Briarwood had unsettled everything. And I wasn't entirely convinced she'd make the right decisions when it came to Daigh.

"Ladies, as much as this display amuses me, we should continue our discussion before your friends upstairs start to miss you. I came tonight to deliver an important warning about a discovery I made upon returning to the underworld."

"Why didn't you say this before?" I demanded.

"You didn't ask."

By Athena, fae were so infuriating. "Okay, fine, what's this top-secret thing you discovered you couldn't tell me before."

"My spies reported Liah and some of her main guard were missing. I've been trying to figure out what they're doing. Finally, I captured one of her sprites and managed to wring the truth out of her – they're up on earth."

"I thought none of you could return to the earth now you were in the underworld," I threw my hands in the air. "You bounce between lies like a yoyo."

"Anything can be had, for a price." Daigh sighed. "What's a yoyo?"

I answered his question with another. "What price did you pay to bring those fae here tonight?"

"Nothing you need trouble yourself with, my dear. You should be more concerned about Liah. The sprite says she wants the coven out of the way before the Slaugh ride."

I gestured to the window, where the villagers continued to ram the gates with their tractors. "She can join the club."

Daigh laughed. "She will do just that."

Right, that made sense. If Liah joined with the humans, they could work together to get through our defences.

Except, it didn't. "Liah hates humans. Will she accept their help?"

"She doesn't need to," Aline said, squeezing my thigh.

Of course. Fae can use compulsion. I can't believe I'd forgotten. Liah would be able to force the humans outside to do her bidding. They might even be under her control right now. My chest tightened with fear at the idea.

"Liah knows she won't be able to cross the wards of the castle," Daigh said, as if I needed it explained to me. "But she will use the humans to draw you out."

"Yes, yes. I've got it now," I snapped. I sank my head into my hands. What could we do? We couldn't fight the fae without leaving the castle, but we couldn't risk hurting the villagers trying to get through them. And if they fought us with the fae behind them...

My mind flicked back to the image of the guys impaled on those stakes.

It's not going to happen. We've got to find a way. Think, Maeve.

"If you want to stop her, you have one path open to you, and you need to choose quickly. Turn back the magic on the defensive charms. Allow the villagers entry into Briarwood."

"Why would I do that? Isn't that giving Liah exactly what she wants?"

"It creates a distraction. The villagers surge forward, eager to get their hands on the evil witches. Liah and her fae lie in wait for the humans to deliver you into their hands. Meanwhile, you have escaped to a safe location far from Briarwood, such as your friend Clara's family hall, where without restriction you can attack her at your leisure."

"This isn't *Star Trek*. We can't just beam ourselves to another location." *I think.* I looked to Aline for confirmation, and she shook her head.

Daigh gave me a puzzled look, but continued. "There is a secret passage in the cellars. The last wine rack contains a spring-loaded door. Push it in the right place and it will swing open, revealing a narrow passage that will admit one witch at a time. It will bring you out in the forest near the Raynard estate."

"How do you know about this?"

"I lived in this castle for many months," he said. "I was here specifically to hunt for weaknesses the fae could exploit. Many times I used the tunnel to return to the sidhe without the witches knowing. It's your only chance to escape the castle without the humans capturing you. If Liah compels a human to capture you, she can get close enough to your boys and compel them to break the wards that protect the castle."

Shit, shit, shit.

"You're telling me we have to abandon Briarwood Castle."

"To save your skin and give you a chance against Liah, yes."

"But it's not a solution. It's only a delaying tactic. They'll eventually figure out we're not in the castle and they'll find us and we'll be in exactly the same situation."

"Think of it more as a tactical retreat. You buy yourselves time and room to move. You can sneak up behind them and take Liah by surprise. I recall you saying you have a weapon that will stop the Slaugh," Daigh rubbed his chin, his eyes sparkling. "One wonders why you haven't used it yet on the humans."

Dammit, he's right. I hated that Daigh had seen through us like that. Even though he didn't know about the belief magic, he knew there was a reason we hadn't used our weapon on the fae. We couldn't harness the magic because the statue was outside the castle grounds, but even if we could, there's no way we'd use it. If we hurt the villagers or drove them away or did anything to disrupt the flow of belief magic that was going to Flynn's statue, we could lose our shot at defence against the Slaugh. The angry mob outside our gates were probably driving up the belief magic to stratospheric levels. In case we couldn't make an agreement with Daigh or, more likely, he double-crosses us, we needed to keep that magic flowing until the Slaugh came if we wanted any hope of defeating them.

If we could hold out it until Ryan's painting came out and the press descended on Crookshollow, then the villagers wouldn't be able to pull stunts like this – not without the whole of England looking on. Without our magic throttled, we could hit Liah with some of the belief power, try and get her out of their heads, maybe take her out completely. If we hid out a Raynard Hall, we'd at least have a chance.

But when they got in here...we would lose the castle, we'd lose the wards. We'd most likely be dead.

But we can't leave Briarwood. Memories flashed through my mind – of the first day I'd arrived and the boys literally fell over themselves showing me around and trying to impress me. Of the first time Corbin and I shagged on his desk in the dark panelled library, of the delicious smells wafting from the kitchen whenever Rowan was at the stove, of climbing over Flynn's piles of crap in the garage, and swinging swords with Arthur in the orchard.

Briarwood was *my* castle. It was the only place in the world I'd ever considered home. No way did I want to give it over to a horde of villagers to pillage and ruin.

"Forget it," I said. "We're not letting them in here. For all I know, you could be lying about Liah even being here. I'm not giving up Briarwood based only on your word."

"If you don't stop Liah, then what you showed us tonight will come to pass," Daigh insisted.

I sighed. "You're basing this hair-brained scheme on that stupid dream? You're more deluded than I thought."

"If we've seen it, then we must try to change it," Daigh insisted. "Isn't that our responsibility to the earth and her inhabitants?"

"Either predestination exists, or it doesn't. You can't have it both ways."

Aline smiled at the mirror. "Our daughter questions everything, even the evidence of her own eyes."

Daigh grinned back. "What monster have we raised?"

"Neither of you raised shit," I snapped. "I was raised by two amazing people in Arizona who you *killed with a Ferris wheel*."

"Temper, temper." Daigh grinned at Aline. "She is most definitely mine."

"The DNA test will confirm that," I growled, wrapping my fingers around Aline's arm and dragging her toward the door. "I'm just going to consult with my mother here. Don't go away."

Out in the hall, I yanked Aline through the doorway of Rowan's room and flattened us both against the wall. "Okay, I give in. What's his game?" I hissed. "Is he telling us the truth or what?"

"I was going to ask you the same thing," she whispered back. "You've been around him a lot more recently than I have."

"I've only had a handful of conversations with the guy, and from what I can gather, precisely 82% of what he says is lies."

Aline smiled, her white teeth catching a glint of the "For Daigh, that's a pretty good percentage."

"Is this funny to you?" I snapped. "Lives are in danger here, and you're flirting with the enemy."

She rubbed my shoulder. "Woah, hey, calm down, honeybee. We're going to figure this out."

I cringed at her saccharine pet name. "You lived in this castle a lot longer than I did. Do you know about this door in the cellar?"

Aline shook her head. "But that doesn't mean he invented it. I never did go down in the cellar much. It's dusty and grotty and full of spiders! We have to remember that Daigh's got nothing to gain or lose personally by coming to warn us. He's safe in the fae realm. His safety is not in danger."

"We have no idea what he might gain by this, that's the whole point. At least there's an easy way to confirm his story," I said. "We go to the cellar and look at this secret doorway. If we can find it we can conclude at least that part was true."

Aline glanced up at the ceiling. Heavy footsteps moved across the floor above. Arthur's voice called down from the top of the stairs. "Maeve, are you okay down there?"

"I'm fine," I called up. "Aline's down here, too. Can we talk to you about something?"

The stairs creaked under Arthur's weight. Aline reached behind me and shut the bathroom door. A few moments later, Arthur appeared in front of us.

"What's up? I don't want to leave the post for long."

"Aline will go and watch the window for a few minutes. I need you to go down to the cellar."

"You thirsty?" Arthur used the cellar to brew and store his mead and other alcohols.

"Not really. But Dai—" Aline stomped on my foot, shoving me out of the way so she could face Arthur.

"I just remembered there used to be a secret passage in the cellar," she breathed. "There was a spring-loaded door in the last wine rack, and the passage behind led into the woods."

"I've never seen it," Arthur said.

"Not many people knew about it. I don't even think Andrew and Bree knew. It might be a good escape route if we need it, but we need to know it's still there." Aline batted her eyelids in a flirtatious way. "Can you go down to the cellar and check?"

Arthur glanced over at me, a questioning look in his eyes. I nodded. I didn't like that Aline was lying to him about how we found out about the tunnel, but we needed to know it was there. It was better for him to go down there than me. No way was I leaving Aline alone with Daigh.

"You'll both watch the window?" Arthur said. "Don't take your eyes off it. I think the protective wall is starting to buckle."

My stomach churned. I nodded again. Arthur shot me a final dark look and hurried off down the stairs. As soon as he was out of sight, I grabbed Aline.

"What did you do that for? Why did you lie about Daigh?"

Aline's eyelids fluttered. "Because if Arthur found out Daigh was here, he'd rush in with his chest puffed out and we wouldn't get anything else out of Daigh. And then your Sir Lancelot would probably go straight back upstairs and wake everyone up, and that's not what you wanted, is it?"

She's right. That's exactly what would happen.

I let go of her. "Sorry. I'm just a bit—"

"It's okay, Maeve. I understand." Aline wiped her eyes. I noticed the sheen of tears on her cheeks.

"Go upstairs," I told her. She didn't move. I didn't have the heart to tell her again.

A few moments later, Arthur's footsteps beat a path up the stairs and down the hall. "You were right," he huffed when he saw us. "There's a door and a tunnel behind it. Has there been any movement on the border?"

"Not that we could see," I said.

"You coming up?"

"I want to speak with Aline privately for a bit. I won't be long. I promise."

Arthur looked ready to protest, but what could he do? I was still his High Priestess. "Hurry up," he called back as he vaulted up the spiral stairs.

Aline pointed to the bathroom door. "Shall we?"

"Fine, let's get the over with." I re-entered the room. Daigh swivelled his face toward me. His features appeared eerily solid for being only an image in the mirror. I longed to touch him and see if his face felt real, but I didn't dare. "Okay, so you were telling the truth about the tunnel. Say I believed you that Liah was outside compelling the humans, if we wanted to stop her, what would we have to do?"

Daigh grinned, showing two rows of beautiful white teeth. How did he get his teeth so white? They can't have dentists in the fae realm. "That's my girl."

"I'm not your girl. Just answer my question, or I'll have Arthur down here to smash that mirror into a thousand pieces."

Daigh shook his head. "You can't involve the giant knight, or the coal-coloured one, or any of the others. This has to be just between the three of us."

"Why?"

"Because Liah is coming for you. We know she has the power of compulsion. She can leap from mind to mind like a frog. We can't have this inside their heads if she tries to get in. Only spirit witches like you and your mum can withstand compulsion."

"And Blake," I said.

"Probably best you don't run to him with this, either. He doesn't exactly trust me, and he's likely to go to the other guys with this information, is he not?"

He was right. Damn, I hated that. I didn't want Daigh to be right. I wanted him out of my life.

But that wasn't my role here. I had to work for the good of humankind. I thought of Corbin — of how he felt trapped at Briarwood, and of all the amazing things these guys could do if they had freedom, real freedom. How even if we managed to defeat Daigh, we'd still go through this again and again and again until the fae got what they wanted.

And as much as I hated to admit it, Daigh and Liah had a point. Climate change, deforestation, genetic vulnerability of crops, fossil fuels...all the science points to humankind wiping itself out and taking the earth and her ecosystems with us. I could see how they concluded the earth would be better off without us.

I had to show the fae another way, a new future. I had to try. And that meant surviving tonight, no matter the cost. It meant losing Briarwood – a symbol of freedom, hope, and power. But it was worth it for true freedom.

I have to do this. It's the only way.

"Fine," I sighed. Daigh beamed at me through the mirror. "Tell me what we have to do."

CHAPTER TWENTY-SEVEN
TWENTY-EIGHT: MAEVE

"I don't like this."

"What did you say?" Aline yelled over the wind. Her long wavy hair whipped around her face.

I shook my head. It didn't matter what I thought now. We were committed to this course of action. I didn't see any other choice.

We stood on the parapet overlooking the gardens at the side of the castle, and the meadow beyond. My foot slipped into the internal gutter running along the narrow ledge. I pressed my back against the slate roof, my eyes focused on the flickering torches along the boundary and the village of Crookshollow in the distance.

After Daigh disappeared back into the mirror and we'd gone back to my room, Aline and I fell into bed. I pretended to sleep, my ears prickling for any change in the noise outside. After half an hour, Arthur woke Flynn up and crawled back into bed. In a few minutes he was snoring, and Aline and I could get up and go to the bathroom again.

My stomach churned with guilt and disgust that I was deceiving the guys to break the wall. But Daigh was right about the fact that Liah couldn't be allowed to get her hands on our escape plan.

Shouts and cheers blew into my face. I gripped the edge of the crenulation and peered over the wall. Arthur was right – the tractors had made it half a length closer. The wall bent back under their onslaught. Soon it would break anyway.

"I hope this works," I yelled at Aline. "I hope Daigh's right."

She squeezed my hand. I couldn't hear her words, but I read her lips. "Me too, sweetheart."

Sparks of her spirit magic flickered against my hand. I closed my eyes and focused my attention on drawing up my power. My magic flared inside me, and I pushed it through my fingers, sending it to Aline so she could deactivate the charms.

After a few moments, she dropped my hand. "It's done," she mouthed, and picked her way back along the ramparts to the low-arched door leading back inside.

I dared a final look over the parapet. At the front gate, the tractor's wheels spun against the gravel as it crashed through the invisible barrier and skidded up the drive. A roar of triumph rose from the villagers, spreading along the wall as the lights moved through the trees and up the curling paths toward Briarwood.

It was downright Shakespearean.

I've brought this ruin upon my house.

Shouts echoed up the stairs. I raced down, slamming the door to the roof behind me. As I made my way across the first-floor landing, Flynn slammed the bathroom door open and screamed my name. Even the the gloom, I could see his face had gone pale.

"I'm here!" I cried, rushing around the covered porch.

"There you are!" Flynn crashed into me, his arms engulfing me in a tight hug. "I thought your tiny arse got sucked down the loo."

Flynn's silly words belied the raw panic in his voice. I clung to him, not wanting to let him go. I hated that I'd worried him and that I was still lying to him.

I hate this. I'm so scared.

The other guys crashed down the stairs. Rowan carried a struggling Obelix in his arms, and Arthur already had his sword strapped around his waist. "They're broken through the barrier," Corbin said. "Arthur tells me Aline remembered a secret passage in the cellar that leads out to the forest. Our best shot is to make it there."

Corbin flung open the door to the secret passage. It would get us downstairs quicker. "Last person through needs to pull this shut," he said, jabbing the secret door hidden in the panelling. I followed him as he vaulted down the narrow steps and pushed the small door in the pantry open. In front of the pantry was a small square wooden door cut into the flagstones. Corbin pulled it up, revealing a rickety staircase leading down into the gloom. He gripped my hand and led me down the steps, shining the screen of his phone in front of him to illuminate a tiny square of light.

"Meeoorww!" Obelix yowled from behind me. He didn't want to go into the cellar. *That makes two of us, buddy.*

A loud bang crackled through the castle. My heart leapt into my throat. Arthur shoved Rowan down the steps after me. "Hurry," he growled. "They're ramming the portcullis with that tractor. It won't take long until they're inside the castle!"

CHAPTER TWENTY-EIGHT

TWENTY-NINE: MAEVE

"Someone pinched my arse," Flynn squealed.

"Meeorrw!"

"Shut up, Flynn." Corbin shot back.

"But it's such a bloody nice arse," Blake said. "And Arthur won't move up and give me more room."

"My shoulders are stuck," Arthur groaned, grinding his enormous arms into the rough walls in an attempt to dislodge himself. I winced as my arm scraped against the sharp stone. The passage was too narrow for me to walk straight ahead. I had to shuffle sideways. I couldn't imagine how uncomfortable it was for Arthur.

"Everyone, quit your bickering," Corbin said, his voice stern. "I'm shutting the door now. Arthur, we need light. Flynn, we need absolute fucking silence."

"Aye, Aye, Mussolini," Flynn shot back.

Corbin pulled the cellar door shut behind him, plunging the tunnel into darkness. "I'm on it," Arthur said from in front of me. A moment later, a small flame flared to life, casting a flickering glow over the rough walls and Arthur's strangely calm expression.

"Hold out your hand," Arthur told me. I complied, and he rolled the tiny fireball onto my fingers. Heat flared in my skin, but the fire hovered an inch above my palm as I moved it back and forth. *Cool.*

"Pass that back," he said. "I'll make you another one."

I rolled the ball onto Flynn's palm. The firelight caught Flynn's features. His usually bright eyes were wide and terrified. His red hair flopped over one side of his face – a complete mess. He turned and passed the fireball to Blake, while Arthur rolled another on to my fingers, and cast a third for himself.

"Three will do," he stage-whispered.

Arthur started to move along the tunnel, sliding his bulk along the rough walls. I followed him, carefully planting my feet on the uneven ground. Above our heads, the castle groaned and banged. *What are they doing to Briarwood?*

Tears stung my eyes. I blinked them away. I couldn't think about it now. We were alive. We were getting out of here. We'd live to fight another day. That was the important thing. Even if they tore down every single stone, Briarwood would live on inside us.

The bangs and bumps above us faded as inch by inch we made our way further from Briarwood and deeper into the dark tunnel. I wondered how far we'd have to run on the other side to make it to Raynard Hall. *I bet Flynn will love hiding out in his artistic idol's house—*

Ahead of me, Arthur groaned – a deep, inhuman sound that made my blood run cold. He stopped dead in his tracks and I crashed into him. My hand slammed into the wall, snuffing out the flame and plunging my section of the tunnel into darkness. Behind me, Flynn's body slammed into me, his elbow digging between my shoulder blades.

Rowan grunted. Blake yelped. Corbin yelled something, but

I couldn't make it out. Blood pounded in my ears. I settled my hand on Arthur's shoulder. He trembled – was that rage, or fear? "Arthur, what happened? What's going on?"

"The tunnel is bricked up," Arthur growled. "There's no way out."

CHAPTER TWENTY-NINE

THIRTY: CORBIN

"There's got to be a way through," I moaned, standing on my tiptoes so I could see over everyone's heads to where Arthur stood at the front of the line. "Have you looked for a spring?"

"It's a solid brick wall." Arthur held up his fireball and checked every corner. "It's not fucking springing anywhere."

"A loose brick then?" I held up my own fireball, scanning the walls on either side of the tunnel. "Maybe there's a side passage we missed—"

"There are no side passages," Arthur growled. "It's like we've been deliberately led into a trap!"

"I swear I didn't know—" Aline whimpered.

"Meorwww!" Obelix cried. A clawed hand swiped across my arm, raising three stinging cuts. *Great. Thanks, cat.*

Arthur kicked the brick wall. Fire flared from his hand, bouncing against the brick and flying toward us. Maeve screamed and dropped to her knees. I grabbed Rowan and yanked him down. Flynn bent over Maeve and slammed a jet of water into the fireball. Cold water splashed over my face as the water hit the wall and sprayed us. The fireball sizzled and went out.

"Bloody hell, Arthur!" I cried. "Do that again and you'll burn up all the oxygen in here, and then we're all goners."

"We're goners any way you bloody look at it," Blake muttered from in front of Aline. "We never should have trusted her."

"Let's not fight," Rowan said. His voice sounded calm, steady. But the hand that gripped mine trembled. "What are we going to do?"

"We've only got one choice," I said, with more bravado than I felt. "We've got to go back out there."

"That's a stupid idea," Flynn said. "The pitchfork mafia are out there, remember? Why don't we just hide in here? It's cosy and unless you count Arthur, no one is trying to kill us."

As much as I wanted to agree with him, I shook my head. "Arthur has a very good point – I'm not liking being trapped in here. I think we stand a better chance if we get out of this tunnel and hide in the castle. We're just dealing with the villagers, so we may be able to scare them off with our magic."

"I agree," Maeve said. Even in the dark, I could see her skin was pale, her expression shocked and terrified. I wanted to hold her and calm her, but no way could I push past the other guys in the narrow tunnel. Flynn had an arm around her, streadying her, and she took strength from his touch, drawing herself up to her full height. "I never liked the idea of leaving Briarwood, anyway. This is our castle. We can't let them hurt it."

"I want to fight. Get me the fuck out of here," Arthur growled.

I raised my fireball so I could see the others' faces. Rowan gave a small nod, his eyes wide. In his arm, Obelix let out a "meorrw", as if agreeing. Blake was already turning to head back.

We all shuffled around, and Arthur made Maeve another fireball. Blake passed me his and I led the way back to the tunnel entrance. The tiny ball burned bright against my skin, it's heat doing nothing to thaw the chill that had settled in my bones.

As soon as my hands pressed against the secret door, I dropped the fireball, snuffing it out from my boot as I reached for the dagger in my sock. Rowan's breath fluttered across my shoulder, giving me the strength to face the unknown. I held the dagger to my cheek and shoved the door open, half expecting Daigh's grinning face to greet me on the other side.

Instead, I stepped into a dark room. The noise overhead suggested they hadn't broken through the portcullis. I beckoned the others out of the tunnel, and Maeve shut the door. She moved beside me, her hand searching for mine. On the other side of me, Rowan whimpered, probably because Obelix clawed him. Bloody cat. My arm still stung.

Arthur climbed the stairs, a fireball swirling in his hand. He lifted the lid of the cellar a crack and peered out. I held my breath. A few moments later, he set the lid back down and leaned toward me and Maeve.

"There's no one out there, and I can't hear anything from inside the castle," he said. "They haven't made it inside yet, but it can't be long now."

"How do we know for sure?" I whispered.

"We go up there and see." Arthur tapped my shoulder. "You and Blake will go first. If anyone is hiding out there to ambush us, you take them down. Don't kill them – just take them out of the fight."

I nodded. That made sense. Blake and I had the most control over our powers. I could remove just enough air to make someone unconscious without killing them, and Blake could do that creepy showing them their nightmares thing that had once left Flynn in a bit of a state.

"Everyone else, once Corbin and Blake give us the signal, make a run for the secret staircase," Arthur growled. "Get up to the first storey. Move onto the walkway, but stay low, so they can't see you. We'll launch our attack down on the courtyard. If at all possible, we need to stop them from entering the castle."

"I'm going first, too," Maeve said, trying to push her way toward us.

"No." Arthur and I said in unison.

"This is no time for your chivalry. Blake and I can do more damage with the 'creepy dream' thing if we work together." Maeve held up her hand, which was entwined with Blake's. "I'm not letting go, and that's final."

No, no, no, no, no. I hated it. Maeve shouldn't be putting herself in the line of danger like that. But that fiery look in her eyes told me she'd just follow us anyway. *Impossible woman.*

Incredible woman, more like.

I sighed. "Let's go."

I shoved past Arthur and grabbed the handle for the cellar door, lifting it up a crack so I could see into the kitchen. We'd turned all the lights off when we secured the castle, but the moon – less than a week until full – shone brightly through the window, casting a pale glow over the space. I couldn't see anything move.

Fear rose through my chest, but I pushed it back. I threw open the cellar door and leapt forward, holding my palm out in front of me like a weapon, the dagger in my other hand. The cellar door clattered on the flagstones, the sound like that *CRACK* of a rifle shot. Maeve yelped.

No one rushed at us. The banging and shouting continued outside, but the house was as still and silent as the night.

"Come on." I hissed, beckoning the others forward. Maeve

and Blake guarded the door to the kitchen as I yanked open the secret door and ushered Rowan upstairs. From outside the window, torches flickered over the top of the garden wall. They were out there, trying to break down the kitchen gate. Wood splintered with a sickening crack.

"Hurry!" Aline ducked through the door. At the rear, Rowan struggled up the steps with a yowling Obelix in his arms. He was a bloody fool, his arms had been cut to ribbons, but he wouldn't put that cat down. I dropped the cellar door in place and pulled and locked the secret passage behind me just as the kitchen gate crashed open and villagers poured into the kitchen garden.

At the top of the passage, I slid the door back into place. Bending low, I crept through to the covered walkway, where the others all huddled at the base of the parapet, their backs against the stone crenulations. Arthur had his sword in his hand, pointing the blade to the roof, as if drawing power from the sky.

I slid down beside Rowan. Voices rose from the courtyard below, yelling horrible things, jeering about what they would do to our bodies once they caught us. They screeched in high-pitched crackles and warbled incoherent nonsense. Someone screamed, joined by another. Something heavy pounded against wood, again and again and again.

I leaned close to the edge of the crenulation and dared a peek over the edge.

I couldn't believe what I saw.

The tractor lay in pieces beneath the mangled portcullis, completely useless now. But that hadn't dissuaded the villages. People threw *themselves* at the inner door, using their bodies as battering rams. Halfway through their flight, their bodies wrenched around as they tore themselves away and slammed into the pavement without touching the door at all.

They'd drag themselves to their feet and do it again, and again.

They moaned, they screamed, they howled. A woman clutched her bleeding head. Another man raked at his eyes. What was going on? Why were they acting like this? As if they would sacrifice themselves one minute, and wanted no part of it the next?

Compulsion, I realised. Terror welled inside me. A battle of wills was going on below us. In all the scenarios I'd imagined for tonight, I'd never considered this. The fae were in the underworld. They couldn't compel shit.

This can't be happening.

I crawled over to where Blake was sitting. He too was watching the scene below with horror. "It's compulsion, isn't it?" I whispered.

He touched his temple and nodded. "It's Liah. I can touch her mind, but I can't stop it. This was their plan all along. They all think we're in that tunnel. They knew we'd be trapped. All they have to do was go in and drag us out."

"But how would Liah know we'd be in the tunnel? She couldn't know it existed. We didn't even know under tonight when—" My blood ran cold.

Aline.

She was the one who told us about the tunnel. And she was the one who kept trying to get us to trust Daigh. Maeve was suspicious of her but I didn't listen because I thought it was all about her coming to terms with her mother being alive, but all this time...

I glanced around the porch for her, but couldn't see her anywhere. Come to think of it, I didn't remember seeing her on the staircase. *Where is she? What has she done?*

"Shit," I whispered.

Blake nodded. "You came to the same conclusion I did. But

there's something else – I read *two* minds out there. Someone else is compelling the villagers, telling them that they don't want to be here, that they want to go back to bed and forget tonight even happened."

"What?" *This is insane.*

"That's what makes them so violent. Their minds are being tugged two different ways. What I don't know is who that other mind is and why they're trying to help us." He rubbed his temple. "It's hard to tell anything, there's so much horror in there."

Warm fingers brushed mine. I whirled around. Rowan had crawled beside me, his eyes wide. "What do we do?" he mouthed.

Good question. This compulsion changed everything. We weren't just fighting humans anymore. Did we reveal ourselves and hit them with the full force of our magic? Or did we let them think we were in the tunnel for a bit longer?

"Can we break compulsion spells?"

Blake nodded. "With two spirit users, probably."

"We need to try it."

Blake crawled behind me to where Maeve cowered with Flynn. As quietly as I could, I explained what we thought was happening. Maeve's face grew even more pale when I told her about the compulsion. "Where's my mother?"

"She's gone, Maeve. My guess is she had some way of sneaking out and meeting the fae. I'm sorry. But she was the one who led us to that tunnel, which turned out to be a trap."

Maeve shook her head. Tears rolled down her cheeks. "No. That's not it. She didn't betray us. There's something else. She—"

I wiped a strand of pink hair out of her eyes. "We can't worry about her now. I need you and Blake to break the compulsion spells that are holding them. Blake knows how to do it. Just lend him your power."

Maeve nodded. Blake leaned in, entwining Maeve's fingers in his. She whimpered as he pressed his mouth to hers.

I'd never paid much attention when Blake and Maeve worked their spirit magic before. I was usually too busy fighting the fae or burying my cock into Maeve. But this time, I was right up close and personal. The wave of magic slammed into me, knocking me backwards. Strange thoughts swirled in my head – flickers of memories that didn't belong to me. Warmth spread up my arms and through my limbs, carrying with it a sense of serenity, of finality. *Whatever will be, will be.*

"It's working!" Rowan whispered.

I crawled beside him and peered down. Sure enough, One by one people picked themselves off the ground and shook their heads, like dogs shaking off water. Eyes rolled, fingers twitched, and the inhuman cries turned into moans and sobs as the foreign powers were forced from their minds.

"What was that?" someone cried.

"There were voices inside my head!"

"I'm bleeding," sobbed another.

"It's the witches!" The vicar screamed. He sat near the inner doors, clutching his bleeding temple. "They sent demons to terrorise us, but the Lord has banished them. God will protect us as we perform his righteous works."

"Get them!"

"Burn them all!"

"And we're back to square one," Flynn groaned. "Always with the burning."

"Stop moaning and get to your battle stations," Arthur growled.

Maeve elbowed him in the ribs. "You always wanted to say that, haven't you?"

"A little bit, yeah."

We spread out around the covered walkway and along the ramparts. Someone shoved a ladder up against the wall. Arthur threw it back down. "We don't want to hurt anyone," he shouted down.

"Then why did you plant evil demons inside our heads," a woman with dried blood down her face called up.

"That wasn't us!"

"Their tongues are red with lies," the vicar called up. "Come down and face your judgement. Thou shalt not suffer a witch to live!"

Flynn groaned as he shoved another ladder off the wall. "They're setting fire to the garage," Blake yelled from further down the ramparts.

I ran across to the other side where I had a clear view. My heart sank as flames leapt across the buildings. The garage and workshop was a Victorian wooden addition, and it connected to the house via a small wing of servants' quarters. Flynn had both hands trained on the blaze, jets of water battling back the tallest flames, but if he couldn't hold it back...

Even if the fire doesn't do much to the stone, it'll tear through the interior and gut Briarwood.

Panic rose in my throat. I bit it back. Oxygen. The fire needs oxygen to breathe. I stood beside Flynn and pointed my palm toward the castle, calling up the air around me to shift and mutate. The flames petered out as I sucked the oxygen from around them.

"They're using their foul magic against us!"

"The Lord is on our side. We will triumph!"

"Look what I found!" Three men ran up, carrying one of Flynn's sculptures on its side – a large metal plate he used as a stand.

"Stand clear!" People flattened themselves against the walls of the courtyard. The men lined up the statue with the door of the keep, and at the count of three, they rushed forward, ramming the doors so they groaned on their hinges.

"Think about what you're doing!" I yelled down at them. "No one in this house has hurt you. If you came here to do violence, then are you any better than the demons you say we are?"

"Silence, witch!" The vicar called up. "We answer to a higher power. I saw you at the church. I saw you call up those beasts from beneath the ground to steal away twenty-two innocent souls."

"We didn't do that! It was—"

Maeve grabbed my collar and yanked me back. "It's no good, Corbin. You won't change their minds. Flynn did too good a job on the belief magic. It's rolling off them in waves. It's like talking to Flat Earthers. Even if we gave them a reasoned argument, they wouldn't listen."

The full horror of what we'd clung to my skin like a rash. We'd fed the superstition in the village, building their distrust and belief for our purpose. We did it to save them from a foe they could not see, a foe they believed was a harmless fairy tale. Their belief in our hands could have saved them. Instead, it would doom us all.

Briarwood will fall tonight, and it's all our fault.

It's all my fault.

"No!" Rowan cried.

The men slammed the statue into the door. With a sickening crack, the wood gave way, and the villagers poured inside the castle.

THIRTY-ONE: MAEVE

My heart broke as the wooden doors splintered and the villagers pushed their way inside Briarwood. Our castle wasn't ours any longer. We'd lost. I watched in horror as people shoved each other in their haste to be first through the doors to attack us.

Not for long. There was a loud thump, followed by a scream, and the crowd surged back as those inside struggled to get out again.

"Got 'em," Flynn grinned.

I glared at him. "What did you do?"

"You remember there's a hole just above the door where the castle's inhabitants could throw burning pitch down on any marauding forces who made it inside?"

"You didn't! We swore we wouldn't hurt anyone—"

Flynn's grin spread wider. "How little you think of me, Einstein. I rigged up a huge pot of Rowan's scone mix. They're covered in sticky, gloopy, dough, and the floor will be pretty slippery. That will slow them down."

I slapped his shoulder. "I love you, you mad Irish bastard."

"Don't say I never listen to Corbin's boring history lectures."

"Why are you standing here gabbing?" Corbin shoved us toward the door. "Flynn, get downstairs. Hit them with whatever you can. Don't let them start another fire. We can't lose the castle. Maeve, you're with me."

"Where are we going?" Corbin dragged Rowan and me down the steps from the roof and into the library. He scrambled for the bookshelf, releasing the secret panel that hid the priesthole.

"Hurry, get inside!"

"Corbin, no. I'm not hiding while the rest of you fight."

"Maeve, we don't have time to argue. We need to keep you safe so you can use your spirit magic. Rowan's here to protect you. Both of you, get in."

Corbin shoved me inside. My back hit the back panel. Pain shot down my spine. Rowan crammed in after me, wrapping his arms around me and planting his legs against the opposite wall.

"What about you?" There was barely enough room for Rowan and me inside, let alone his bulk as well.

"I'm hiding somewhere else. Don't worry, I've got a plan. I'm going to get us all out of here. I promise." Corbin blew us a kiss and slammed the panel shut, plunging Rowan and me into complete darkness.

My heart pounded against my chest. Rowan searched out my hand and squeezed it. Corbin's footsteps padded out of the library, leaving us with the company of our own breathing and the faint sounds of fighting and shouting from downstairs.

It wasn't long until the air inside the hole grew stale. My limbs cramped from not moving, from the fear clawing its way down my spine. Rowan's body shook, and he gasped against the stale air. *Is he going to have a panic attack here? Is he already having one? How can I help him when I can't even straighten my legs?*

I didn't know what to do.

Desperate for some activities to take my mind off the horror, I felt around the top of the compartment, figuring if the stories Corbin told me were true and priests had hidden inside this cramped space for hours while the castle was searched, they must have thought to put in an air vent. Sure enough, a tiny hole above Rowan's head emitted the slightest rush of cool air. At least we wouldn't suffocate.

"Rowan," I whispered against his trembling cheek. "There's an air vent. We won't suffocate. Rowan, we're going to be okay."

He trembled harder, his whole body jerking. He let out a strangled sob. I squeezed him as hard as I could, pushing spirit magic into him to try and calm him. I counted silently backwards from a hundred, then from a thousand, then I listed all the elements on the periodic table and moved on to the names of all the different constellations. Bangs and thuds and shouts sounded from outside, closer now but still muffled like I was listening from underwater. *What's going on? Are we winning? Is Briarwood ours again—*

The door flew open. "I've found two of them," an unfamiliar voice called.

I guess we're not winning.

Terror gripped me. I froze. Rough hands reached inside the priest's hole and grabbed my arms, dragging me out into the light. Rowan's arm was wrenched from mine. He howled and thrashed like a wild animal as they tore him from me.

After being in the dark for so long, the bright light from the library's chandelier made my eyes water. I blinked, waiting for the white welts to disappear so I could get a look at my attackers. Beside me, Rowan thrashed about, knocking one of them in the teeth so she fell back in pain. I copied him, kicking out with my feet, pooling my terror into fighting against whoever held me.

"Restrain them!" A familiar voice barked. I was pushed to

the ground, and my hands were yanked behind my back and tied with something coarse and rough. A knee jammed into the small of my back, keeping me in place. Beside me, Rowan was getting the same treatment. His eyes had gone dark, feral, and he bucked and thrashed and even made a run for the door before they jumped on him and got his hands tied, too.

The vicar stood over us, his robes torn and filthy. The light of righteous justice glowed in his eyes.

"We got ourselves a couple of witches," he snarled.

"Better a witch than a murderer," I shot back. "Isn't that one of the Ten Commandments?"

"Silence, witch!" He kicked me in the side. I gasped as my breath left me. "Take them to the meadow with the others. It's time for them to face God's final judgement."

CHAPTER THIRTY-ONE

THIRTY-TWO: ROWAN

They marched me and Maeve downstairs and out the main doors. People swarmed through the castle, taking axes to the beautiful wooden mouldings and smashing the ancient furniture. As we were dragged across the courtyard, someone tossed an end table from one of the upstairs windows, where it smashed against the cobbles with a sickening crack. Panic rose in my chest, settling on me like a familiar weight.

They're destroying our home.

Everything I'd loved in my life was tied to this house. For all of us, Briarwood was more than stones and wood and windows. It was the place where we'd uncovered our true selves. Corbin had taken five broken people and given them the magic of Briarwood, and this castle wormed its way into all our hearts. I loved it the same way I loved Maeve, and the guys, and Corbin.

Corbin...where is he? I twisted my head around, trying to see him on the ramparts, fighting amongst the crowd. *If they found us, did that mean...*

And the others, where were they? Was this it – the end of Briarwood coven?

I'm glad I let Obelix go back on the roof. I hoped like hell the little rascal had the sense to hide up there somewhere, and that he'd escape unscathed. At least one of us would.

"You can't do this," Maeve yelled at the men dragging us down the narrow path toward the meadow. "This is illegal. It's vandalism and assault and you'll go to jail for a very long time."

One of them – I think it was the one named Gus who Flynn fought at the pub – snorted. "That's unlikely, witch." He pointed to a figure standing beside the door. I recognised the female officer who'd spoken to us at the church, the one who lost her colleague to the fae. She caught me watching her and made a slicing motion across her throat.

My body jerked as the panic crashed over me. My ears rang. Heat surged through my body, followed by a sharp, stinging pain along my right arm, so intense that tears sprung in my eyes and I looked down to make sure the limb was still there, still attached to my body. It felt like someone had hacked it off. The pain seared down my leg, carrying with it a paralysing fear that everyone and everything I loved was about to be murdered in front of me.

My weight slumped against my captor. He yelled at me to move, but my body wouldn't obey. Two other men ran over and they dragged me out the side gate and into the meadow, where an even bigger crowd waited. Torches flickered over the faces, so many faces I recognised from the village. So many people who wanted me dead. They must be right about something.

It looked like the movie set of some hillbilly horror film, only it was sickeningly real.

"I had to knock this one out." someone called. They dragged Arthur's body beside mine. Blood pissed from a cut on his head. As they threw him down beside me I noticed his stomach rising and falling. He was breathing. But for how much longer?

"No!" Maeve reached for Arthur, but her captors tore her

away. I lurched toward her, but rough hands pulled me back. Someone threw a black hood over my head and tripped me so I slammed into the earth. The pain from the fall became one with the pain in my arm and leg, surging through my body and driving my panic to the brink. My whole body spasmed. I lost control of my motor function. I was a trembling, sobbing ball of uselessness.

Corbin...

The thought pricked through my ruined mind. *Where's Corbin?*

"Did you get the fire out?" Blake called to Flynn.

"Aye...but they started another one and I—" Flynn's voice dissolved into a scream that curdled what was left of my mind.

They're going to kill us all. They're going to torture Maeve, Corbin, and the others in front of you, and it's all your fault.

The fear completely paralysed me. Wild, wretched noises fell on my ears, and it took me several moments to realise I was the one making those horrid, inhuman sounds.

Something hard hit my cheek. I turned my head toward the blow and copped an apple in the eye.

Sweet juice exploded over the front of my hood. The villagers jeered as they pounded us with stones, fruit, even the butts of their wooden torches. I jammed my face into the ground in a vague attempt to protect myself. Hard objects battered my body, followed by the blows of fists and feet.

"Witch!" "Sorcerers!" "You killed my sister!" "You cursed me with cancer!" "Die, you evil creatures!"

"I can't use my magic!" Blake yelled.

"Me neither," Flynn called back.

I couldn't use my magic even if I'd tried, but now I knew it was no use. My mind drew back to a night outside the squat, where a guy had paid for a half hour with me. I'd taken him around the side of the building, to an area we usually used for customers. We had an old rotting couch there, and some supplies for shooting heroin in a tin behind the rubbish bins. As I went around the corner, two other guys came out of the shadows, their teeth glinting, their eyes hungry for violence.

I'd curled up into a ball then. I went to a different place. Their blows slammed into me, their hands tugged down my pants, but I didn't feel any of it. I was somewhere else. I'd moved into this weird dream world beyond fear.

I went to that same place now. Objects thudded against my skin, knocking my brain around my skull. My friends screamed. But I wasn't there any more. I was a ghost, floating above my broken body, watching the horror with detached interest.

Sometime later, it might have been minutes or hours, rough hands grabbed my body and hoisted me to my feet. I slumped against them. My legs didn't support my weight any more. Maybe they were broken. My hood was ripped off.

My ears buzzed. Dried blood glued my eyelids together. I managed to throw one open, but the sight that greeted me made me wish for the darkness again.

At the front of the crowd stood Daigh, his arms held above his head like Christ at the crucifixion, a look of utter triumph on his face. Beside him, fae stood in neat rows, bows drawn and pointed directly at us. At *me.*

"Hello, daughter," he addressed Maeve.

"I knew you were behind this," she growled from somewhere on my left. "You lied to me again."

He shrugged. "I'm not the only one who lies. You told a lie to your friends tonight, didn't you, daughter? You didn't think to tell them it was *you* who broke the magic of the protective charms and let the humans into the castle."

His words made no sense. He might as well have declared Queen Elizabeth was a teapot. No way would Maeve have done this. That's not possible. Even if she'd wanted to, she never would have even had the chance...

I waited for Maeve to deny it, but she didn't. "Why did you do this?" she cried, her voice high, wavering.

My heart ripped into pieces as the truth of her lack of denial slammed into me. *Maeve did this? But why? She loves us. She loves me.*

But no, of course, she didn't. She *couldn't.* Because no one could love me. I wasn't worthy of love, I'd been shown that time and time again, but still, I refused to let go of my hope. Maeve had let us *all* believe, when really...she'd been under Daigh's spell the whole time...

"I did it all for the dream," Daigh said. "Because I finally understood how to get what I want."

He lifted one arm above his head. The fae behind him parted, revealing a structure that turned my blood to ice.

An open bonfire burned bright, in fragrant disregard for the summer fire ban. The swaying grasses of the meadow had been stomped flat and covered with dirt and splatters of quick-dry concrete that held in place triangular wooden scaffolds. From each scaffold protruded a long, pointed stake.

Six stakes.

My eyes darted between the towering horrors, noting every detail true to the vision in Maeve's dream. All except one thing. A figure slumped at the base of the last stake, tied from head to toe in thick rope. Blonde hair matted with blood plastered against her listless face.

Kelly.

Beside me, Maeve howled. It was a sound of such raw terror that it broke what little composure remained inside me. My muscles gave way, and I collapsed forward again. My captors let me fall, and my body slammed into the ground.

The vicar walked out to stand beside Daigh, and raised his

own hand to the heavens. In his fingers he clutched a battered bible. "Tonight, we punish those who've brought Satan within our midst. We cleanse the village of Crookshollow and restore righteous justice to our land."

"No, no, no, no," Flynn kept saying. Arthur bellowed. I guess he'd come to again. Maeve begged Daigh to spare our lives, to spare Kelly's life.

But Corbin...where's Corbin?

"I told you I would never burn my only child at the stake," Daigh grinned. "Throw that one in first. He's already gone."

The men moved around me, trudging across the meadow toward the stakes, carrying a heavy shape between them. They dumped it down on the ground in front of one of the stakes, dragging it up so the moonlight caught a cold, pale face.

Corbin.

No.

Glassy eyes stared back at me, unseeing. His body hung limp, not responding to their cruel movements. Blood pooled around a knife sticking out of his abdomen.

Corbin was dead.

TO BE CONTINUED

Need to know what happens next? Find out in the next book, *The Castle of Spirit and Sorrow.*

Read it now: https://books2read.com/spiritandsorrow

Can't get enough of Maeve and her boys? Get *The Summer Court* – a Briarwood short story – for free in *Cabinet of Curiosities*, a Steffanie Holmes compendium of short stories and bonus scenes. To get this collection, all you need to do is sign up for updates with the Steffanie Holmes newsletter.

http://www.steffanieholmes.com/newsletter

Start the Grimdale Graveyard Mysteries series and dive into a new adventure in the same world as Nevermore Bookshop: http://books2read.com/grimdale1

"Go on, dearie. Let me have a little sniff of that salty goodness."

"No," I snap under my breath as I snatch the pretzels from the tray table and stuff them in my pocket.

For your information, I'm not hanging out in the world's grossest sex club. (That was two years ago in Amsterdam. My shoes stuck to the floor.) I'm sitting in my seat on a flight somewhere over the United Arab Emirates, minding my own business and trying to ignore the ghost of a blue-haired old biddy who is annoyingly fascinated by my airline snacks.

"Pleeeeease? Just hold the bag out so I can have a whiff."

I glare at her before turning my body toward the window. Outside, the world is dark – the kind of deep, unsettling darkness that makes you remember you're hurtling through space at a gazillion miles an hour with only a computer, a hopefully not-drunk pilot, and the laws of physics standing between you and a fiery, dramatic death. We're somewhere over the Middle East, but the cloud cover is so thick that it looks like we're flying into a black hole.

Most people in the cabin are settling down to sleep, but I won't get any peace as long as Chatty Cathy insists on a running commentary of my snacks.

"I know you can see me, dearie," she sighs. I watch out of the corner of my eye as she hovers over the empty seat beside me. "My good friend the headless pilot told me all about you. Well, he didn't tell me so much as gesticulated. He said your thighs were much bigger. You should eat more, put some meat on those bones – starting with those pretzels in your pocket."

I groan. Stupid ghosts. They have no right to be gesticulating about the size of my thighs, which are perfectly fine as they are, thank you very much.

It figures that airplane ghosts talk to each other. There aren't that many of them compared to, say, hospitals, old asylums, and Starbucks stores. They generally stick to the plane where they died but they can hop off at airports and float around in the terminals like some kind of spectral hen party, swapping gossip about their flights. The Headless Pilot and I had a run-in on my flight from Bali last year, and it was not a pleasant experience. I was on the loo, reading a smutty romance novel on my phone and enjoying hour three of *absolutely no dead people* when he stuck his torso through the bathroom door and shook his neck stub at me. I screamed bloody murder because that's what you do when you have a see-through neck stub in your face, and the stewardess had to break down the door because she thought I was having some kind of fit. They didn't believe my story about seeing a spider, and I've been banned from that airline for life.

Ghosts are nothing but trouble.

Usually, airplanes are one of the few places in the world where I'm blissfully free of ghosts for a while. Statistically, not that many people die on planes. It's one of the reasons I decided to leave my small British village of Grimdale the moment I got my GCSE and embark on a backpacking trip around the world. It wasn't the most pressing motivation, but it definitely factored high on my 'reasons to get as far from Grimdale as possible' list.

And now, after all this time, I'm heading *back* to Grimdale, a place I very much do not want to be, because of the terrible thing...

No. I squeeze my eyes shut. *I don't want to think about that. If I burst into tears on this plane, Chatty Cathy will never let me hear the end of it.*

"Excuse me, ma'am?"

I open my eyes and see the reflection of a man in a business suit in the window. Ghosts don't have reflections, so it's a real live person talking to me. That doesn't happen often – my resting bitchface is so legendary that sonnets have been composed in its honor.

I spin around. Businessman McArmaniPants flashes me an apologetic smile. He leans forward and puts his arm on the back of the seat, right through the old lady's spectral head.

"Argh, watch where you're putting those skinbags, you rotten oaf!" She jerks away, holding her head as she hops angrily down the aisle. She looks like a chicken with her bony elbows jerking wildly. I cough into my hand to cover my smirk.

Businessman McArmaniPants flashes me a megawatt smile. "I didn't mean to startle you. I noticed that this seat is empty. I wondered if I could sit next to you – I'm near the back and a kid spilled his orange juice and now everything is sticky—"

"Sure." I pat the seat, grateful for his presence. He'll act as a buffer between me and the old lady ghost. "Please, make your-self at home. Stay as long as you like."

"Do not make yourself at home!" Chatty Cathy huffs, glaring at the man as he lowers himself into her seat. "This is my chair. I claimed it first. Get your own snacks to sniff."

"Do you want some pretzels?" I crack open the bag and offer it to my new seatmate, knowing that the ghost won't want to risk getting close enough to sniff them now.

"Sure." He takes a handful. "Hey, why are you poking out your tongue?"

"Oh." A blush creeps across my cheeks as the old biddy huffs away. "No reason."

Are you ready for a little ghost lore? I'm on the second leg of my thirty-two hours of flying from New Zealand to London, so I have time to kill.

Time to kill. Ha ha. I'm a comedian.

Here's the skinny on the spirits of the dead, aka, Bree's Ghost Rules:

1. Not everyone who dies becomes a ghost. You have to have unfinished business. Often, you don't remember what that business is, which I'm sure must be annoying.

2. Ghosts hang around the location where they died. There's an invisible force I call ghost mojo (it's a highly technical term I came up with when I was eight, shut up) that acts like a rubber band that pulls them back to the location of their death. They

can wander away from their death location, but the ghost mojo gets worse the further they go until it becomes painful for them to remain away and they get sucked back to their death place again.

3. Some ghosts, like my childhood friend Ambrose, aren't tied to a death location but instead, a place that's important to them. I don't know how it works, so I blame it on ghost mojo.

4. Ghost mojo is also why ghosts can fly through airplane bathroom doors but don't fall through the floor and out into space. Ghost mojo keeps spirits standing on the ground the way they did when they were alive.

5. Only very powerful or very angry ghosts can interact with the human world by moving things or flickering lights or writing on mirrors. Mostly they just waft around being annoying.

6. Despite not having noses, they can still sense strong smells, so they're forever lingering around when people are eating and begging to sniff my salty nuts.

7. Ghosts hate it when humans walk through them. *Hate. It.* Sometimes I do it just because I know it pisses them off so much.

How do I know so much about ghosts?

Because I'm the only person who can see them.

I had an accident when I was five years old – I fell off my bike and cracked my head on a rock – and ever since I've been able to see the dead. See them and talk to them and be infinitely harassed by them—

"Go on, dearie," the old lady pokes her head out of the luggage rack. "Just a little sniff."

I'm Bree Mortimer. And it's going to be a long flight.

TO BE CONTINUED

Start reading the Grimdale Graveyard Mysteries series now:
http://books2read.com/grimdale1

OTHER BOOKS BY STEFFANIE HOLMES

Nevermore Bookshop Mysteries

A Dead and Stormy Night

Of Mice and Murder

Pride and Premeditation

How Heathcliff Stole Christmas

Memoirs of a Garroter

Prose and Cons

A Novel Way to Die

Much Ado About Murder

Crime and Publishing

Plot and Bothered

Nevermore Murder Club and Smutty Book Coven

Fangs for Nothing

A Grave Mistake

Grimdale Graveyard Mysteries

You're So Dead To Me

If You've Got It, Haunt It

Ghoul as a Cucumber

Not a Mourning Person

Kings of Miskatonic Prep

Shunned

Initiated

Possessed

Ignited

Stonehurst Prep

My Stolen Life

My Secret Heart

My Broken Crown

My Savage Kingdom

Stonehurst Prep Elite

Poison Ivy

Poison Flower

Poison Kiss

Dark Academia

Pretty Girls Make Graves

Brutal Boys Cry Blood

Manderley Academy

Ghosted

Haunted

Spirited

Briarwood Witches

Earth and Embers

Fire and Fable

Water and Woe

Wind and Whispers

Spirit and Sorrow

Crookshollow Gothic Romance

Art of Cunning (Alex & Ryan)

Art of the Hunt (Alex & Ryan)

Art of Temptation (Alex & Ryan)

The Man in Black (Elinor & Eric)

Watcher (Belinda & Cole)

Reaper (Belinda & Cole)

Wolves of Crookshollow

Digging the Wolf (Anna & Luke)

Writing the Wolf (Rosa & Caleb)

Inking the Wolf (Bianca & Robbie)

Wedding the Wolf (Willow & Irvine)

Want to be informed when the next Steffanie Holmes paranormal romance story goes live? Sign up for the newsletter at www.steffanieholmes.com/ newsletter to get the scoop, and score a free collection of bonus scenes and stories to enjoy!

ABOUT THE AUTHOR

Steffanie Holmes is the *USA Today* bestselling author of kooky, spooky paranormal, cozy fantasy, and gothic romance. Her books feature clever, witty heroines, secret societies, quirky villages where nothing is as it seems, creepy old mansions, and alpha males who *always* get what they want.

Legally-blind since birth, Steffanie received the 2017 Attitude Award for Artistic Achievement. She was also a finalist for a 2018 Women of Influence award.

Steffanie lives in New Zealand with her husband, a horde of cantankerous cats, and their medieval sword collection.

STEFFANIE HOLMES NEWSLETTER

Grab a free copy of the *Cabinet of Curiosities* – a Steffanie Holmes compendium of short stories and bonus scenes – when you sign up for updates with the Steffanie Holmes newsletter.

http://www.steffanieholmes.com/newsletter

Come hang with Steffanie
www.steffanieholmes.com
hello@steffanieholmes.com